To Sandie,

Best wishes, hope you
enjoy the read.

THE
RECTIFIRES

S. Gardner.

xx.

THE
RECTIFIRES

SAM GARDNER

Illustrations by
Steven Burnside

First published in the United Kingdom in 2009 by Author's Voice Publishing

text © Sam Gardner, 2009
illustrations ©Steven Burnside, 2009

The Rectifires is a work of fiction. The characters, organisations and events it portrays are fictitious. Any apparent similarities are purely coincidental.

British Library Cataloguing in Publication Data
A catalogue record for this book is available from the British Library

ISBN 9781904408635

Typesetting and origination by BHB Studio
Printed by JEM Digital Print

Author's Voice is an imprint of
Bank House Media Limited
PO Box 3
NEW ROMNEY
TN29 9WJ UK

To Marg and Eddie, my mum and dad, for all
their love, patience and support.

FOREWORD
ALASTAIR CAMPBELL

When I first met Sam Gardner he was gingerly nursing a bruised and bloody nose. The scene was the crowded, run-down dressing room of Keighley Cougars rugby league club, on which I was doing an article for the *Times* magazine.

They had just beaten Oldham, and Sam explained the blood by saying that sometimes the best way to break a tackle was to crash head first into the ground, then wriggle free of the tacklers and get the ball back immediately to set up the next attack before the defence could organise themselves. Rugby league is a hard sport, and this was a dressing room full of hard men.

But in the bar afterwards I saw a very different side to Sam. After talking about his work as a teacher, and how he combined it with training and matchdays with the Cougars, he delved into a plastic bag by his feet. He pulled out a folder. Inside was a neatly typed manuscript. 'I've written a novel,' he said. 'I know you've done one, so I was wondering if you fancied reading it.' My own debut novel, *All In The Mind*, had been published a few months earlier, and he said he was looking for an outside eye to take a look, and give a bit of advice about where to send it.

I read it a few days later, and enjoyed it. I am thrilled for Sam that it is being published.

With uncertainty about what the post-credit crunch economy and society will look like, and with reality TV a prominent and fairly recent addition to our popular culture, *The Rectifires* brings together those two strands in a way that is as timely as it is, at times, chilling.

Sam clearly knows well the tough urban setting of Bradford and Keighley, my home town, and while there are elements of fantasy involved in the story of a video-obsessed entrepreneur filming his own band of costumed vigilantes chasing down criminals, it is never anything other than a convincing and compelling read.

Now that he has retired from professional rugby league, I hope Sam writes more novels. I would certainly read them.

Alastair Campbell

PROLOGUE

LORD
VENGEANCE

2024
THE SUNDAY NIGHT TROUSERS

Percy flicked the switch on the kettle. He tapped his foot on the clammy lino and hummed a nondescript tune to himself. He could just about make out his wife calling his name in a low throaty monotone from the sitting room. The noise from the kettle was almost loud enough to drown out her voice, but just to make it clear he hadn't heard her he began to hum the tune a little louder, and paced up and down the kitchen banging drawers. Then Percy stopped humming and began to talk under his breath. On his face there was a fixed smile. That same fixed smile he always had. The smile he wore when he cooked her meals three times a day. The smile he wore when he brought her a cup of tea in bed every morning. The smile he wore when he wheeled her round the park on a Sunday afternoon, only to be laughed at and insulted by gangs of teenagers who liked to sit on benches and spit on the floor.

Percy gritted his teeth.

–What do you want me to do now? Why can't you just leave me alone for five minutes?

In the sitting room Gladys was getting more and more frustrated. The multiple sclerosis that had blighted her later years seemed more determined than ever to rob her of her simplest pleasures and dignities.

All she wanted was to be together with her husband with a nice cup of tea when their favourite programme came on. The remote control that Percival had placed on the arm of her chair lay upside down on the carpet. Gladys despairingly poked her foot at it and managed to change channel. But now where the newsreader had been there was a big angry black man singing, no, shouting at her. He had an American accent and his words were accompanied by drums and scratching and wailing. Around his neck he wore a ridiculously large gold chain, which danced around his number 52. He seemed to be shouting about bitches over and over again, but the pretty girls who were writhing around behind him didn't seem to mind; in fact it made them seem to like him more.

But Gladys didn't like him. Gladys didn't like him one bit. His big black face seemed to be taunting her because she couldn't even have *Heartbeat* ready when her husband came back with their tea. Gladys loved watching *Heartbeat* on TV Gold. Set in a time not long after she was born, it was nostalgia and escapism rolled into one.

Yet Percival might not get back in time. She might miss the opening theme tune, and that was the best bit. The best bit because everything was still to come. The tea would be hot, the biscuits unopened, and she would listen to that music knowing it could be the best episode ever.

Back in the kitchen Percy had managed to calm down; he was no longer grinding his teeth, he had taken some deep breaths and focused on what he was going to do after *Heartbeat*. The programme he loathed. Percy caught sight of his reflection in the glass oven door. He could see he was smiling now. Smiling with his eyes and his face lit up.

He steadied himself and breezed into the sitting room, fixed smile in position. He answered his own question about what the matter was with Gladys when he saw the gangsta rapper and the remote control on the carpet. He flicked over to *Heartbeat* and replaced the remote on the arm of her chair. Not that she would want to change channel from the only thing she had looked forward to all week. Not that she would be able to lift, press and point the remote accurately enough to use it.

Percy slurped his tea loudly. Gladys rolled her eyes disapprovingly; turning her head was too painful now. But he had positioned himself out of range of his wife's disapproving look. He was feeling particularly rebellious tonight and allowed himself a little smirk. Had he not shown exceptional self-control, the smirk might have grown into a full-blown grin. Lesser men might have chuckled. But not old Percy. Far too sharp to be caught out. Far too disciplined.

As a little reward, Percy allowed his mind to wander away. No one could ever have known: he looked as if he was simply settling down to an evening with his wife. But Percy wasn't watching *Heartbeat*: he was staring straight through it. He could hear the sounds but they were not registering in his brain. He was too pre-occupied with his other Sunday night thoughts. His private Sunday night thoughts. The Sunday night thoughts that no one would ever guess.

Percy felt the Sunday night thoughts taking control of his body. His heart started to beat faster. He felt the pulse throbbing violently on the side of his neck; he was sure it must be audible. For a minute he thought his wife was going to say something. Percy made sure things didn't get out hand by focusing on Claude Greengrass trying to sell a cuckoo clock. He was immediately back in control again. It takes someone very special to do that.

Heartbeat came to a satisfactory conclusion. The theme tune started to play. It was over, for another week at least. Gladys tried desperately not to get sentimental. Percy showed his superb discipline by not jumping up as soon as the music started; it was at least half-way through before he even started to stir. He got up and switched over to BBC. There were the last fifteen minutes of a Jane Austen costume drama, and then a programme called *Rectifires Live*. But she could always use the remote control if it wasn't to her liking.

Percy sighed, and announced it was time for his Sunday night shop. It was a well-thought-out routine. It suited the pair of them really well. *Really well*. Percy had followed it for the last three months.

Straight after *Heartbeat*.

Like clockwork.

On Wednesday afternoons they drove out to Asda to do the bulk of their shopping for the week. It was a bit of a social event. Sometimes a familiar face said hello and asked how they were coping. Sometimes they stopped at the café for a pot of tea and a scone. Sometimes the fat, smiley checkout girl remembered Percy's name and used it as she counted his change.

The Sunday night shop was different altogether. This was when Percy went on his own for vital bits and pieces. The mini-market was just right for a quick Sunday night shop. It didn't matter that they had spare milk in the freezer. It didn't matter that there were usually road-works that held him up. It didn't matter that he could just as easily have done it on Monday when he took his wife to the clinic to see the nurse. The important thing was that the Sunday night shop was a good idea, and a system that worked exceptionally well.

Percy collected the teacups, washed and dried them, and put them back in their correct place. No corners cut. No hurry. Just the usual Sunday night routine. To the letter.

Percy could easily have climbed the stairs two at a time. But he didn't. Same routine. Same procedure. Sunday night shop. He went into his bedroom and opened his wardrobe. He took off his trousers and hung them neatly on the hanger, then put on his special Sunday night trousers. They were almost identical to those he had just taken off.

Almost.

The Sunday night shop was well thought out and well planned. It suited everybody. Most weeks, like this one, Percy was so thorough that he had done the Sunday night shop before Sunday night. Milk, bread, biscuits and other essentials were already in the boot of his car.

As Percy left the house his wife stared blankly at the TV screen – Jane Austen replaced by the doom-laden music of *Rectifires Live*, the fiery logo's unsubtle flames of retribution burning into the nation's subconscious. Percy reversed out of the drive and headed down the road. He drove carefully down the street towards Roberts Park, negotiating a series of mini-roundabouts before turning left, then second right into the overflow car park at the back of the running track. Percy was a careful driver and he checked his mirror occasionally, just as he checked side streets and slowed down as he drove past parked cars. But the way he checked his mirror was very much like he watched *Heartbeat*. Habit. Going through the motions. Because if he had looked in his mirror the way his wife watched *Heartbeat*, intently, analytically, purposefully, he couldn't have failed to notice the black van that was following him. The black van that had followed him from his home. The black van that had been waiting across the street since five that afternoon. The black van containing the people who had been watching Percy for three months. Watching him and getting to know all about his Sunday night routine.

Percy switched his headlights off and waited. To survey the scene. He knew he had picked a prime location, because he had used it a couple of times before. The path through the park was a well-known shortcut between the Old Tramshed and Fanny's Ale House, two popular drinking venues that always seemed to have drinks promotions or karaoke competitions on a Sunday evening to attract the last of the weekend's revellers.

Percy looked through his binoculars at the entrance to Fanny's. He could make out a young couple arguing over something on the steps. That'll do me, he thought. Argue with your boyfriend. Storm off through the park to the Tramshed. Come to Uncle Percy. Job's a good 'un.

He breathed a little faster and his breath steamed up the windscreen. He reached for his hanky and wiped it clear. By now the girl had crossed the road on her own and was heading for the park. She had her arms folded defensively and was close enough for Percy to see how pretty she was. She had long straight auburn hair. She was wearing a pair of fitted black shorts and long leather boots. Her red top, which Percy thought was unsuitable for a cold autumn night, barely covered the upper half of her body. Just before she reached the path through the park she turned round to remonstrate one final time with her man. Through his binoculars Percy could make out a spiky black tattoo horizontally across the base of her spine. In a short and surreal moment he vividly pictured his own wife with a similar tattoo on her own back. He shuddered, not liking it one bit. He liked the look of this girl, though.

Just then the man she had been arguing with came running across the road. They continued arguing, but the man's stance seemed less aggressive. He began gently kicking the ground, one foot after the other, then looked down with his hands in the back pockets of his jeans. When he stopped kicking he looked straight at the girl and spoke. She walked towards him, stopping with her hands on her hips close enough for him to reach for her hand with both of his. The man gently pulled her close and they kissed passionately for what Percy thought was an unnecessarily long time. Then they walked hand in hand across the road and back into Fanny's.

Percy took a deep breath and drummed his fingers on the dashboard of his car. The clock told him he would have to make his move soon. He didn't want Gladys asking any questions about why the Sunday night shop always seemed to take so long.

A slight commotion grabbed his attention. He looked through his binoculars over his right shoulder and saw a group of five women. They were older than the auburn-haired girl and a little fuller figured. As they stumbled down the steps of the Tramshed they laughed and screeched. One of them, with short blonde hair and a neck like a turkey, insisted in kissing the doorman on both cheeks before she left. The bald hard man carried on chewing his gum and apart from a brief nod kept the same expression on his face, to make it clear he had seen everything before and wasn't impressed. Secretly, though, the smell of liberally applied perfume and leather from her jacket aroused him.

Percy weighed up his options. He was well aware of the risks that this kind of target posed. There were five of them, and although they were fat and drunk there might be a have-a-go hero among them. He had experienced this before and not liked it. Not one bit. What Percy wanted was a nice clean getaway. No fuss. Back to Gladys, with the Sunday night shopping safely delivered.

However, with time running out and his confidence high, Percy decided to act. He climbed out of his car, leaving it unlocked, and began to walk along the path that would take him to the far side of the park. From there he could head towards them and towards his car at the same time. He could be back behind the running track and into the car park before they knew what had happened.

A group of women was stuttering and stumbling along the path. They were about twenty yards inside the park when Percy noticed that there was a straggler: the youngest and slimmest was still floundering at the entrance. This would make his task much simpler. He could stride past the main group and target the one at the back, leaving only one witness.

Percy noticed that the girl had stopped altogether: she was sitting on the grass and had taken her high heels off. She rubbed her feet and complained to the others.

Percy spoke quietly to himself.

--Keep walking, the rest of you. Just leave her by herself. She'll be fine.

But to his dismay, after gesturing and encouraging her to join them, they went back. She managed to regain her feet, but only just and in the manner of a newly born foal.

Percy was sure she was exaggerating and making an unnecessary fuss. And he knew there was no way they were going to carry on walking in his direction.

His worst fears were confirmed when they linked arms in a long line, with the new-born foal in the middle. They began to stagger out of the park and away from the dispirited Percy. When they reached the side of the road they began waving at passing cars. It wasn't long before a black cab pulled over. They clambered in, and made the short journey round the block to their next drinking destination.

Percy frowned, and looked up at the sky as if appealing for divine intervention. Through the trees he could see that the moon was almost full, with dark clouds intermittently drifting across its face in an unsuccessful attempt to hide its nakedness. Percy took a few moments to breathe deeply. Even before he looked down he felt more positive. He felt that his renewed sense of optimism was entirely justified by the good fortune he had enjoyed in recent weeks. As he brought his eyes down to the horizon again he immediately saw that his faith had been rewarded. It was a measure of the success of recent Sunday nights that he wasn't entirely surprised by what he saw.

Standing before him was exactly what he had been waiting for. Not more than a stone's throw away was the type of creature that had been conveniently appearing for the last few weeks, in six different locations. For the past six weeks Percy had not had to contend with unsuitable targets. With women appearing in crowds, or with their partners. With women who laughed at him or attacked him. With women who gave an uncomfortably accurate description of him to the police and the newspapers. And his recent exceptionally good fortune was about to continue. Because standing in front of him was an angel.

She was standing at the side of the path. Had Percy stopped to consider, he might have wondered what she was doing there. Why was this stunningly beautiful girl in her mid-twenties standing so still in the park? She was dressed very smartly but also very sexily, in a jacket and matching skirt. Had she been wearing a blouse, and had her skirt been six inches longer and her high heels not quite so high, she might have passed as being on her way to a job interview. Her jacket was buttoned tightly at her tiny waist. Her large, rounded breasts pressed firmly on the grey material, as though determined to force their way out. Her plump red lips contrasted starkly with her pale skin and long black hair. Percy fancied that she looked a little like a secretary in a porn film. But an extremely high-class porn film, he reassured himself.

But he did not stop to ask himself anything. He just took it for granted that somebody or something would continue to provide him with such sumptuous offerings. Like the delicious young nurse in Merton Park a week ago. And the orange and blonde dance teacher at the back of the high street the week before that.

The angel stood there. Percy could tell that she had noticed him but wasn't looking directly at him. She looked slightly nervous but not afraid as he strode towards her.

He stopped when he was no more than six feet away.

~Excuse me, miss.

She didn't look at him.

~Excuse me, miss.

Percy always preferred them to look him in the eye, and today he was going to wait for his moment. In the bushes something rustled, but he was oblivious. Things had gone too far. He was in the zone. Totally focused.

The angel was looking up in the air, perhaps noticing

the same inspiring vision that had given Percy strength just a few moments before.

~MISS!

Percy was almost shouting now, and this time it did the trick.

The angel looked down and met Percy's stare square in the face.

He did not waste another second. He whipped his knee-length overcoat open wide, like a condor gloating over its impressive wingspan. Percy held the pose proudly, as the special Sunday night trousers did the job they were made for. What made them special was that the crotch area had been completely cut away, allowing Percy to swing free in the cool autumn breeze.

The angel put her hands over her eyes and, as though reading from a script, wailed loudly.

~Oh my goodness! There's a pervert in the park! Somebody help me!

At that moment there was the most terrifying sound that Percy had ever heard: a powerful roar from behind the bushes. Before he had time even to close his overcoat a man with a television camera appeared from nowhere and stood beside the angel, recording Percy's every move. Percy spun round, hoping to flee in the other direction, only to see his path blocked by another film crew. Men carrying bright lights illuminated the bizarre scene. The angel continued to make sounds of distress but Percy, who remained silent, was the one in mortal danger. His pulse rate catapulted dangerously high for a man of his age. He felt his heart slamming into his rib cage. He gasped desperately for air, but his throat had tightened so much that he could only take small inadequate breaths.

Things were about to get even worse. Over his right shoulder the bushes began to move. Branches began to snap as something very big and very powerful advanced. The thing in the bushes let out another terrifying roar before making its announcement.

~Lord Vengeance at your service, Ma'am!

Stepping out of the undergrowth appeared a big and angry-looking man. He stood at least six feet five, almost a foot taller than Percy, but it wasn't his height that Percy found most terrifying. Lord Vengeance was almost as wide as he was tall, and his huge muscles burst from his black skin. He was almost completely naked, bar his dark trunks and darker sunglasses. A jet-black cape fluttered behind him as he strode purposefully towards the terrified old man.

Lord Vengeance grabbed Percy round the neck, making it nigh impossible for him to breathe. Percy sank pathetically to his knees. Lord Vengeance stared down into his eyes, and began to deliver a well-rehearsed monologue. He spoke loudly, gradually increasing the volume as he moved closer to Percy's face. His eyes bulged as he delivered a sermon about perverts who terrorised young women. His voice built in a crushing crescendo, and with one hand round Percy's throat he lifted him clean off the ground.

~Percy the Pervert! You have exposed yourself to the good women of Ravensbridge for the last time! Women will now be able to walk the streets without fear of meeting scum like you!

As Lord Vengeance held him, suspended and choking in mid-air, Percy's overcoat fell open. His shrivelled todger was exposed in public for one last time as it poked through the gaping hole in his Sunday night trousers. But what a way to go. Percy's final Sunday night shop was being beamed into the homes of millions. Lord Vengeance fans up and down the country were once again delighted with another superb result. And Percy the Pervert would stop living out his lurid urges. Forever.

PART ONE
SCHOOL DAYS

1994
KEY STAGE 1 ASSEMBLY

Edward looked along the row at the other children in his class. They sat in silence with their legs crossed and their backs as straight as ramrods. A few even had a single finger pressed vertically on their pursed lips as they hoped to win praise from their class teacher. Mrs Ibetson enthusiastically obliged, optimistically hoping that the one remaining member of 1Ib would follow their example.

Edward sat at an angle, his back hunched and his head in his hands, drumming his fingers on the sides of his temples. His eyes were closed and his curious mind rested as the middle-aged teacher huffed at the one person letting down her almost perfect class.

Even at this early age Edward knew he was different. He didn't care about getting a gold star on his chart for sitting smartly. He didn't crave the attention and approval of Mrs Ibetson as the others did. He craved answers.

Answers to questions about the strange world he had been born into six years before. He didn't dislike Mrs Ibetson or the other children, but they never gave him satisfactory answers to the probing questions in his head. Edward's language was not well developed enough to put his concerns into words. He knew he wasn't satisfied with what he was told. He couldn't accept and approve in the way the other kids could. And that is what so often led him into trouble.

Edward did not find it comfortable to sit up straight. So he did not. He did not like having his eyes open in assembly, because with his eyes closed he could take himself to a much more interesting place. So he closed them. He did not want to stop drumming his fingers on the sides of his temples. He liked making rhythms that only he could hear. So he carried on drumming. Edward saw no value in a gold star. You couldn't eat them. You couldn't swap them. You couldn't sell them. You couldn't even take them home. So he never tried to earn one.

After ten minutes of the droning assembly Edward had tired of thinking about giants and rainbows, so he opened his eyes and re-entered the real world. At the front of the hall there were three children, two dressed as pirates, reading from small cards. He couldn't hear what they were saying, so he focused his eyes on some shelves in the front corner of the hall. The top one was empty, mainly because at eight feet from the ground no teacher could comfortably reach it without the aid of a step.

Edward decided that he wanted to lie on it. This was a good idea because he liked to lie down: it was when he was at his most comfortable. He also liked corners. He was at his most comfortable when hidden in a small space. He would need to tuck himself right into the corner to make sure he didn't fall off. Lying there was also a good idea because things would look very different from that perspective. He loved to look at things from high-up places. No one would ever have looked at the hall from up there before. The assembly was bound to be much more interesting.

Edward could see there was a way to climb up. If he used the empty chair in front of the electric piano, and then the piano itself, he could reach the first shelf. From there he could haul himself further up. Then he could have a little sleep, a daydream or even watch the assembly.

Without further thought or hesitation Edward rose from his position at the end of the row and headed for the piano. It was only when he put his left foot on the chair that Mrs Ibetson began to react. She stood up, open-mouthed, as the strangest of her pupils proceeded to put his right foot on the electric piano. Pupils and staff alike began to murmur in astonishment as the small child balanced precariously between chair and keyboard. The loud discords created by Edward's plimsolled feet created mayhem, and music teacher Mrs Shoard rushed forward to defend her beloved Casio.

Mrs Ibetson assumed that Edward had decided to play the piano with his feet, but to her dismay he brought his other foot onto the piano and began to scale the shelves on the wall behind it. Mrs Ibetson accelerated forward and bumped into the retreating Mrs Shoard, who was always furious when musical instruments were manhandled.

Mrs Ibetson was reluctant to intercept Edward as he was now in a highly precarious position, balanced between keyboard and bookshelf. She began to try to coax him down, and as she did so a risk assessment of a year two assembly flashed though her mind. Could you really legislate for a year one child using a keyboard and chair as a stepladder to climb up onto a bookshelf? Ridiculously, and she knew it as soon as she said it, she offered Edward a gold star if he agreed to climb down at once. Unfortunately the offer seemed to have the opposite of the desired effect. He began hauling himself higher, using the wires attached to a corner speaker.

From Edward's point of view things were far from perfect. The commotion around the hall was not to his liking. He wanted to perch on the shelf and hide his face from it all.

Mrs Ibetson felt her heart stop as the speaker began to wobble dangerously above the bewildered children below. She had often worried about the speaker because of its size and its height, but had repeatedly reassured herself by confirming how firmly it was attached and how out of reach its wires were.

Suddenly the speaker began to fall. For one horrifying millisecond all Mrs Ibetson's worst nightmares seemed to be coming true: a serious or even fatal accident involving a child because of a risk she had overlooked. Luckily the wires were firmly attached, and the speaker was left d a n g l i n g   s i x   f e e t   i n   t h e   a i r . Mrs Ibetson turned her attention to dispersing the children, and for the first time, sensing her panic, two of them began to wail loudly, neither of them really knowing why.

Meanwhile, largely oblivious, Edward was still attempting to get himself comfortable. He was having a much more difficult job of it than he had envisaged. The shelf was narrower than it had seemed from below, and he wasn't able to lie on his side and tuck himself into the corner. The best he could do was perch on one knee and one foot and hold onto a cable on the wall to stop himself falling off.

All of a sudden he didn't want to be there.

Two teachers were urging him to come down, one forcefully, trying to assert authority, the other attempting to coax him. Edward's problem was that he *couldn't* get down. He wanted to, as he was feeling scared and flustered, and his knee was hurting from being bent double and taking nearly all his weight. He was sure the drop would kill him, even if he could free his legs to land on his feet.

Edward looked down briefly and saw that the keyboard was still in place, positioned in a way that might just break his fall. His knee was really hurting, and pins and needles were beginning to set in. He took a deep breath and let himself go.

1998
KEY STAGE TWO ASSEMBLY

Cockshott banging on about roller skates. Grey suit to match his grey hair. Short and squat with a little gold tooth. Since Cocky had taken over the headship he had set about banning things. Climbing frame. Playing behind the bunker. Marbles. Football stickers. All the things the kids lived for were being slowly dismantled.

After the climbing incident Edward had had to attend a special school. Combined with a string of other documented evidence, this had deemed him as unsuitable for a mainstream school – not caring for his own safety and unaware of the danger he was causing others. He was dispatched to an institution where he would have the correct supervision.

Edward hated it. Missing his friends, he struggled to build relationships. He got on with one boy, Max, but Max couldn't speak properly or even add up small numbers. Most frustratingly of all he often went to sleep in the afternoon, when Edward wanted to play. Some of the other children drooled uncontrollably. One made high-pitched screaming sounds incessantly and could hardly walk.

Every week Edward asked his parents when he could go back to the other school, and their determined expressions assured him that they were doing everything in their power for their son.

When Edward returned he eventually took nothing but joy from the unfettered fun he and his friends engineered in the classroom and playgrounds. But it wasn't always like that; he had to work hard at being 'normal' at first. Comments and whispers from pupils and teachers were a daily occurrence, gradually becoming less and less frequent.

On his first day back, when Edward walked into the assembly hall he felt his face burning. Kids pointing and sniggering. His sister crying. Teachers rolling their eyes and shaking their heads. As the school settled down to silence the words 'nut' and 'case' were muttered at various volumes in the rows behind him.

Some years earlier Edward's mother had had a frank discussion with her young son about upsetting people. He only understood that people were upset if they were crying, but his mum explained about people 'crying inside', which was much worse as it meant they took all the hurt around with them. For the first time Edward knew exactly what she had meant. His eyes were glazed, staring, in his own world yet acutely aware of the attention he was creating. There was a gap of about a foot either side of him, as his peers made it clear they would not sit next to him. Edward remembered how the children in his class used to do this to Bradley, who dirtied his pants. But now Bradley had a clean face and spiky hair, and was smugly and snugly sitting with a friend on either side.

Edward hated Bradley the most now. Hated him with a burning passion. More than the kids who made comments. More than the teachers who spoke up against his return to mainstream school. Because Edward remembered the smell of shit. When he used to sit next to Bradley when no one else would and stuck up for him. Because even at that early age he knew something was not quite right with Bradley. Edward's dad had explained the difficult circumstances of Bradley's family life, so Edward sat with him. Until he was almost physically sick.

Now, since Bradley had gone to live with his new parents, he was much more like the others. Freshly laundered, with all the right logos. And highly delighted that a different freak had come to take his place.

What made things worse was that Edward had actually been looking forward to this day. He had envisaged a triumphant return, his old pals ready to greet him. He thought they would be sure he was 'normal'. They would know he didn't belong in a special school. But time had done funny things. A year and two months was such a long time in the mind of a seven-year-old child. The memory of him was sullied by teachers' comments or parents' assumptions as they remembered his wild antics.

Looking back and reflecting on that day in the assembly hall, Edward put it down as one of his first rock-bottom moments. But, as he always told himself, rock was a very solid foundation to build on, and build on it he did.

Edward knuckled down. Something inside told him that for a while he had to be as normal as possible. He listened, worked hard and generally toed the line. His wild instincts for innovation and adventure were put on the back-burner.

For the first couple of weeks no one talked to him. After that he began to make up the numbers during games of football at breaktime. His skill and dexterity meant that he later became first pick, and eventually a team captain. During group work in class his ideas and invention gradually caught the imagination of the other children.

After eight months came a watershed. Edward was handed a piece of paper that meant he was invited to Daniel Abraham's birthday party. Time after time he had felt the indignity of being left out as invitations were handed out around him. He showed it to his mum with excitement and happiness.

He couldn't understand it when she wept. She bent down and held him tight, her tears streaming as she kissed him. He hugged her back, but this was too much for him. He cried because she cried, and once he started he couldn't stop. He wanted to be happy, but had to go to bed to hide so he wasn't embarrassed in front of his dad and sister.

After the party things ran smoothly. Edward's popularity grew, his time in special school a distant memory. He became part of the class again. And he gradually became a little more daring. The old demons started to reawaken. His ideas were always shared with Tony. Bright, athletic and popular, Tony was a main player in bringing Edward back to the mainstream. He openly encouraged and complimented Edward's plans, but none of them were actually carried out.

Edward was desperate for some action. He felt he had served his time by being normal and fitting in. He knew he was meant to be ashamed of the time he went climbing during assembly, but in secret moments he relished the excitement and daring.

Mr Cockshott was blathering on about this being

removed, that being banned. And Eddie knew he was going to make a stand. Of course there had been lots of talk, but so far it was all fantasy. When Eddie left that assembly hall he knew the time for action had arrived.

2000
RSPB

~NO STUFFED BIRDS!
~NO STUFFED BIRDS!
~NO STUFFED BIRDS!
No football. No skipping or handclaps.

Year six had organised a protest. Or at least Eddie had organised a protest. And now everyone was joining in. Marching and chanting under the RSPB banner. Made in the library, covertly.

And others were joining in. They didn't know what they were chanting. They didn't know why. But it seemed like fun.

The commotion was easily heard from the staff room. The dinner ladies seemed powerless against the mob.

~NO STUFFED BIRDS!
~NO STUFFED BIRDS!
Cockshott had recently taken a delivery in wooden

cases. Various species. A fine visual resource. To help children learn about habitats and food chains.

~Staff room. STAFF ROOM!

Eddie was half-crouching, directing operations from the rear.

The mob headed up to the staff room window. The chants were all the louder. Feet were stamping. The children's revolt. Too much had been banned. Now it was their turn.

Eddie was not holding the banner. He was not even chanting that much. He didn't want to be picked out as the ringleader. His time was to come.

~NO STUFFED BIRDS!

~NO STUFFED BIRDS!

Dinner ladies panicked. They tried to usher the children away, but their ineffective actions emboldened the mob.

Beautiful.

Some of the mob began banging on the staff room window.

~NO STUFFED BIRDS!

~NO STUFFED BIRDS!

All of a sudden Cockshott was on the playground with a piece of paper in his hand.

~I AM GOING TO WRITE DOWN THE NAME OF ANY PERSON WHO IS NOT LINING UP IN FIVE SECONDS FLAT! AND I WILL PHONE THEIR PARENTS!

The cries of the mob began to die down. Those holding the banners were hauled inside, along with a couple of the dopier bystanders. For Eddie it was just the beginning.

~I AM GOING TO DEAL WITH THESE IDIOTS FOR STARTERS, BUT EVERY SINGLE ONE OF YOU

WILL BE DEALT WITH! I'LL GET TO THE BOTTOM
OF THIS OUTRAGE ONE WAY OR ANOTHER! AND
I'LL MAKE YOU WISH YOU'D NEVER GOT OUT OF
BED THIS MORNING!

Cockshott jabbed his finger menacingly, small flecks
of spit flying from his mouth. Eddie had never seen his
face so contorted and angry. Everything about his
demeanour suggested he was serious.

This was perfect.

Shouts of rebellion gave way to mutterings of
discontent and eventually to silence as the hordes began to
drift back into line. Eddie and Tony made their way
submissively to where the rest of their class was standing
in single file.

Cockshott headed back inside. The rest of the school
stood muted, waiting for their teachers to collect them.
Dinner ladies walked up and down, control restored. One
hundred and twenty children stood waiting, still and
silent, with nothing to look at but the school building in
front of them.

The audience was ready.

Then two children from year six broke ranks and
made their way to the front entrance.

From the outset Eddie had planned that Tony should
be first up, with him following behind. But somehow in all
the excitement Eddie was the one who was shinning up the
drainpipe and pulling out a banner from beneath his jumper.

The crowd began to mutter and point.

~NO STUFFED BIRDS!

~NO STUFFED BIRDS!

Eddie struck up the war cry once again.

His long-awaited moment of glory was about to arrive.
But for that he needed the whole school behind him,
chanting with him.

He waved the flag from the roof.

There was laughter, cheering and commotion. A few joined in, but they were not in unison.

They were holding back.

Eddie quickly realised what they were waiting for. What was needed.

The dinner ladies began flapping once again.

~Get down . . .

~Right now. Mr Cockshott is just back inside. You're going to hurt yourself . . .

They were closing in on the base of the drainpipe where Tony stood.

The mob were waiting for Tony.

Waiting for Tony and Eddie to lead the chant.

Eddie knew that he needed Tony, and then everyone would join in.

And Eddie would be a hero.

There was still the possibility that he was just a lunatic.

Eddie was waiting for Tony.

~Come on, Tone! Quick! Gerrup here!

Tony suddenly seemed undecided.

~Tone! QUICK! DO IT! COME ON! DO IT FOR ME!

There was desperation in Eddie's voice now, and in his heart. The dinner ladies were almost within grabbing distance of Tony. He had to make his move.

All the discussions they had had. The planning. The bonding. Eddie's journey back into the mainstream. Never a doubt that he would bottle. Together all the way.

But he needed his friend to make his move.

As he promised he would.

Urgently.

And then he did.

The dinner ladies were with Tony now. Eddie was not saying anything any more, just staring intently at his friend. His eyes were pleading, but deep down he knew his cause was lost.

Tony's expression had changed. He made a gesture, which Eddie had to replay in his mind to comprehend.

Tony was beckoning Eddie to come down. The chameleon had changed his colour. His face had a sensible look. The look that the teachers loved. The look that told adults he could be trusted and was telling the truth. Not the look that he had when he was laughing and plotting and scheming and swearing.

Eddie once again experienced a sad, sinking feeling in his stomach. He tried to fight it off by marching up and down defiantly.

Alone.

~NO STUFFED BIRDS!

~NO STUFFED BIRDS!

But his voice was higher pitched and showing signs of panic. He tried to hold up the flag, but it was too wide and part of it hung limply: it was designed to be held by two people.

No one was joining in now, but there were comments and laughter. Cockshott had re-emerged. Eddie knew the game was up. He looked down at the expression on Tony's face. It registered the same disapproval as the headteacher and dinner ladies around him.

Tony was never to be forgiven.

2013
POKER

OK, I'll deal. Seeing as though I'm out.

Isn't it great that we're still all mates. Some of us still from primary school. All these years later.

And this poker lark, for a fiver a time it's a good value night out.

See we'd probably never all meet up if it wasn't for the game.

Good excuse to have a good yarn.

Old Tony over there.

Always seems to be at his house.

Such a good host.

His missus knows the score. Makes us a few nibbles, says hello.

Then fucks off.

Perfect.

Always been there or thereabouts has Tone.

Never been really close mates, mind.

Suppose because he's got so many.
But good value.
Good laugh.
Always up for a bit of banter.
Like we're having now.
Wonder what I'll deal up here.
Hope someone goes all in.
Want to get back in the game.
Long way to deal these cards.
Down the other end of the table.
Slide well, though.
Nicely varnished.
Like everything in Tone's house.
Not flash but well looked after.
And there's a big bottle of red just to my left.
Almost full.
Here's an opportunity.
One for you, you still in?
Not got three cards, have you?
No?
Another one over there . . .
FUCK!
Oh shit!
Oh my God!
Sorry!
Red wine all over.
Carpets.
Curtains.
Wall.
Photographs.
Hope it stains.
Take that.
Cunt.

2003
GOLF BALL CHALLENGE

~Edd·ie
~Edd·ie
~Edd·ie
~Edd·ie

The chant in the classroom had reached an unprecedented volume. Kids from 8 Postgate and 8 More had come to join the commotion, and watch Eddie Shearer as he rose to the challenge of his latest stunt. A simple but brilliant idea that Eddie had dreamed up on the bus home the evening before.

That night he had put homework on one side to prepare for this moment, although he had not anticipated things would come this far. He had hoped he would have won the challenge and be basking in glory by now.

Eddie stared at the fire alarm five yards away from him. He squinted slightly to try and focus on the small lettering: 'smash glass to sound alarm'. He would have to be deadly accurate to force Horner into an impossible situation.

Around the fire alarm was a large black piece of card which had been stuck to the wall. On the card were white chalk marks where the golf ball had struck progressively closer to the thin glass cover.

The rules were simple. Each mark had to be closer to the fire alarm than the last one until someone bottled. Then a winner could be declared.

Eddie figured that if he aimed right at the centre of the fire alarm, *right at the very centre,* he might be able to pull it off. He reckoned that his aim was good, but not good enough to hit such a small target. The inch he would miss by would make a mark a little closer than Horner's last shot.

Horner must have been in one of his eccentric moods. Some days he wouldn't begin to get involved in these daft schemes, but every now and again he really surprised Eddie. Like today, when he had nonchalantly stood up and hurled the golf ball to within a thumb's length of the fire alarm, without building tension or lapping up the atmosphere of the baying crowd.

Eddie could never do that. For him that was what it was all about. That is what had him hooked. Addicted. Addicted to that unique cocktail of fear, adrenalin and attention. And that is why he would always take that final shot.

Always.

Eddie allowed the crowd to crescendo until they couldn't shout his name any louder. He had to let them believe that he might just back down, so they needed no encouragement to shout his name. They knew that a decent chanting session would guarantee another shot from Eddie.

~EDD-IE

~EDD-IE

The noise was deafening. Some of the lads started to drum-roll their hands on the tables. Eddie knew that sooner or later a teacher would be alerted to the furore in 8 Huxley 's form room. So he would have to act.

Now.

Eddie raised his arms and gestured for calm and quiet, as though the success of the shot depended on it. Almost instantly the crowd fell silent. The only noise was a gentle scratching sound as Eddie applied chalk to the golf ball.

He took a deep breath and let it go.

The silence that fell on the room in the split second when Eddie threw the ball was broken by the tinkling of glass. For one second no one said anything, stunned by the inevitable.

Then came the noise. A loud shrill wailing noise, echoed in buildings all around the school. The alarm was much louder than any fire alarm Eddie remembered. He looked at the source of the noise in disdain, as though accusing it of over-reacting to his innocent little prank.

This was not the result he had envisaged or wished for, but Eddie had considered it as a possible outcome. Therefore he had mentally prepared himself for it. He thought quite a lot about the consequences of his actions, so if the worst happened he had strategies to cope.

In this case Eddie was going to own up as soon as possible. Admit the prank and offer to pay for the repair to the fire alarm. There was no way he could stomach a cover-up. They would know whose form room it was immediately, which would make him number one suspect anyway. If there was an investigation someone would squeal on him. Especially if it helped them get out of trouble. In Eddie's mind, though, he had always pictured some other half-wit smashing the fire alarm – at which point he would have stepped forward and chivalrously revealed that it was his idea. By taking the heat off someone else he would gain credibility from his classmates, and ease his conscience.

The Horner situation was different. To involve anyone else he would have to split on Horner, which was a non-starter. So he had to take all the heat himself.

Eddie sat quietly in the form room, pondering his next move while the rest of the class charged out of the door, shouting at the top of the voices and piling dangerously down the stairs. As Eddie finally trotted down the stairs a few moments behind them, he noticed a small, retarded-looking girl with both hands on the outer window sill. She seemed to be trying to make her way back inside the building. He couldn't believe she didn't realise there was a fire alarm, what with all the noise and pandemonium. Had it been a real fire, Eddie told himself, he would have helped her out, but in the circumstances there didn't seem much point. He felt a slight pang of guilt as he walked away, but this soon disappeared as he entered the playground. Other pupils smiled at him with knowing looks, word of his stunt having spread fast. He liked the attention; it restarted the adrenalin that had died ever so slightly in the last few moments. Although he still wished someone else had smashed the glass.

Eddie walked over to the rest of his form. Miss Peacock was standing at the front with her register. He could tell by the way she was looking that she knew it was him. He didn't hesitate. He went straight to the front of the line to hold his hands up.

WRINGING WET RACHEL

Rachel Cassells made her way tentatively along the covered walkway that led to her form room. Four dim lights covered with a dirty plastic coating gave inadequate illumination for students and teachers with perfect eyesight. For Rachel, a child with a serious visual impairment, it was a major ordeal. At primary school Rachel had spent years learning the layout of the building, just as the staff and children had become familiar to her. She had moved around confidently and had been respected by peers and teachers. She was well above the expected level for her age despite her disability, and by the time she left year six her impairment went largely unnoticed by those around her.

Sadly, things had become much more difficult when Rachel started year seven at the comprehensive. No longer were people kind and familiar. Hordes of adolescents with sports bags barged and bustled her, not always deliberately but with a cruel impatience that made her feel like a disabled child again. In her world of blurred shapes, being hit on the head even lightly was unsettling at best, terrifying at worst.

Rachel was gradually learning the school's layout. She was becoming much more organised, and on this particular morning had thought ahead. She was going to the toilets well before the end of break, so as to avoid the crowds of year eight students heading for their next lesson.

As Rachel neared the end of the walkway the light became stronger. Her strides became longer and were almost of normal length as she reached the open air. She even let go of the wall that she had been trailing her fingers along. She smiled as she counted the seventeen steps that she knew she had to take before she turned left.

This isn't so bad after all, she thought to herself. She told herself that in a few weeks she would be moving even more confidently than she had done in primary school. On her eighteenth step she reached out for the silver shape that she knew was the door handle to the Allingham building. She opened it confidently, and after a slight pause to check that no one was coming through she strode inside and headed for the stairs to the toilets.

She put her right foot on the bottom step, and her left hand on the banister rail. The fact that she was on the left should have given her safe passage up any flight of stairs in school, as this was the rule on all staircases – to allow children to move freely without too many collisions. It did not always work in practice, as there always seemed to be an impatient group of boys who overtook everyone by running up the middle. These were the main source of the knocks and jolts that Rachel routinely received.

Rachel was about to take her second step when she heard a penetrating, high-pitched sound, so loud that it was painful. But it was not the pain that caused her heart to sink to the pit of her stomach. It was the knowledge of what that sound was about to bring.

She had witnessed a fire alarm at the school once before, during her first week, when a teaching assistant had guided her round. She observed with some bewilderment how frantic and highly charged it was. At primary school fire drills had been nothing more than an inconvenient pause in her lessons. Classes simply filed down the stairs and out of the building, and lined up to be registered. Here the alarm seemed to signal a simultaneous outpouring of panic and aggression.

Matters were made worse because it was break time: there were no teachers in form rooms to direct the mayhem into a semblance of organised evacuation. Almost immediately a swarm of year eight students came pouring down the stair towards Rachel, yelling at the tops of their voices like Red Indians riding into battle. Their excitement was fuelled by adrenalin after they had witnessed the latest stunt in their form room. There was no way they were going to notice a small year seven girl with thick-lensed glasses standing awkwardly on the bottom step.

And they didn't notice her. Rachel was caught up in the mayhem. Surrounded by a swathe of bodies and noise, she was dragged and jostled out of the door she had just come through. Relieved that she hadn't been knocked to the floor, she grasped a windowsill and tried to regain some composure, straightening her glasses and attempting to slow her breathing to its normal rate.

It was at this moment that Rachel realised just how badly she needed to go to the toilet. Before the fire alarm had gone off she had been calm, in control and had a strategy. In a matter of seconds all this had gone. She was more flustered now than she had been for years. She couldn't think clearly, which was unusual for her. At primary school this would never have happened. Never. Someone would have noticed her. Someone would have protected her or looked out for her. A teacher, a cleaner, even one of the boys who thought they were tough.

But not here.

Rachel knew what her immediate needs were. She would have to make her way back inside, fire alarm or no fire alarm.

She had just started to make her way towards the door when she felt a hand on her shoulder. She couldn't clearly make out a face and when she heard him speak she didn't recognise the voice. Rachel had become something of an expert in judging people by their voices, and she could tell that he thought of himself as important and influential.

~Come along, young lady. We need to get everyone lined up as soon as. This isn't a drill as far as I know. Lives could be at risk.

~Yes sir, I just need to . . .

~No buts, girl, this is an emergency! Now come along at once.

Rachel felt a pang of anger. She hadn't even used the word 'but', and nothing riled her more than not being listened to.

~Please sir, I won't be long. I just have to . . .

Rachel was cut off in mid-sentence. The blurred face was speaking loudly about safety measures and routines and no exceptions.

The more he talked the more desperate Rachel became. The thought entered her head that she might not actually be able to hold on. The more she thought about this the more panic-stricken she became. And the more she needed to go.

Then something happened that made Rachel feel even worse. The blurred figure began to lead her. She felt a strong grip on her wrist as he continued talking and preaching in an authoritative manner, which reached a volume entirely inappropriate to a conversation between two people. Rachel hated to be dragged in this way. When the teaching assistants led her at primary school they allowed her to walk at her own pace, and only intervened where necessary.

The blurred figure was walking her much too quickly and was clearly not listening. Rachel knew she had only one option left. An option she didn't want to take. It was an option that demeaned her. It took her back to her days at nursery, before she had learned and studied.

~But I need the toilet. Now!

It had the desired effect. The blurred figure stopped walking and stopped talking. Had Rachel had normal vision, she would have realised that there was hardly anyone about to hear her. But she couldn't see that there was no one there, and imagined there were at least a dozen others pointing and laughing.

The blurred figure was taken aback, but he soon composed himself.

~This is a fire alarm. There's no way I can allow you back inside the building. I'm sure you can hold on for five minutes. As soon as your form tutor's registered you and given the all clear you'll be able to go.

Rachel knew her situation was grave. Her panic and desperation suddenly intensified. She wanted to cry, but was so short of breath that she couldn't even do that properly. The blurred figure was leading her past lines and lines of chattering schoolchildren. Rachel could tell by the size of the black shapes that these were some of the older ones. Soon she would be at the end of the playground with the rest of her year group.

It was when she realised this that she made a decision. If her brain were a debating chamber it wouldn't have been unanimous, but it was enough to send the signal to her bladder to relax and relieve herself. It was as though her brain had made the decision on the basis of damage limitation. In a few years the children at the higher end of school would have left; and there was a chance the children in her own year at the far side of the playground might not find out. Of course Rachel knew this was a very small chance indeed. But it was a chance.

In truth, considering there were more than five hundred schoolchildren on that playground, not many people actually noticed. There were a lot of other distractions, and most children were engaged in their own conversations. Only a handful pointed and laughed or made cruel comments. Most who saw only went as far as alerting the person next to them. A few felt sorry for Rachel and said nothing. One girl from year ten directed the attention of her classmates away from what she saw, to spare Rachel their sneers. But Rachel couldn't see what was happening, and her logical conclusion was that everyone saw her. And everyone was laughing.

It was the most humiliating moment of her life.

2005
T BOMBERS

They all liked this idea. It had the ingredients that made them tick. But what made it made it so popular was the knowledge that they could talk their way out of trouble if they did actually hit a teacher. You were allowed to play with small footballs on the top yard, so as long as everyone stuck to the story and no one squealed a direct hit could be passed off as an accident. They just had to make sure that the people taking pictures on their phones were discreet.

By now 10 Huxley had developed a code of honour, where people didn't grass so much. In year eight most of the form wouldn't have thought twice about shopping one of their classmates. Things had moved on: all of the boys in the class could now participate with relative confidence.

To a casual observer of the upper playground, the year ten boys appeared to be having a kick around with a football. But if someone had been analysing them more closely they would have noticed that there was no point to their game. There were no goals, no teams, no one they were trying to keep the ball from. Nobody put a tackle on anyone or seemed to care if they lost the ball.

At the far side of the playground two of their comrades, armed with mobile phones, lay in wait. These carefully chosen and expensive phones were capable of producing fairly acceptable stills and even rudimentary video. Most weeks went by without a single teacher getting hit, but even the near misses made good footage if the teachers in question had no idea how close they were to being taken out. And afterwards there was no case to answer, no need to apologise profusely, no need to explain to the teacher how strong the wind was, or how it was unusual for the goalkeeper to kick the ball that far.

Horner was always first on the scene, lying through his teeth, if there was contact. Looking at the teacher squarely in the face, with genuine sorrow in his voice, he always ensured there were no comebacks. There was one time when Horner really had to show his mettle. Mr Bryson, the history teacher, had been hit on the back of the shoulder by a good accurate punt from Horner. There shouldn't have been a problem, but Donovan and remedial Dylan burst out laughing. Horner had to work overtime with his remorse, only breaking off to reprimand them. Mr Bryson wasn't convinced. He knew deep down he had been set up, but he didn't have the energy to launch an investigation. He accepted the apology, warned the lads to be more careful in future and went to the staff room for a cup of tea and a sandwich, looking forward to the end of the day – another step closer to his pension.

Donovan came in for abuse for putting the operation at risk, and copped a few slaps around the head for having such a high voice. He fully deserved it, of course. There was plenty of time to laugh later. Remedial Dylan's outburst was overlooked: he didn't know any better.

By far the best result to date was Eddie's long shot on Mr Waddell. At the time it hadn't seemed that spectacular. The ball had only really skimmed the top of Waddell's head, and the fat bespectacled teacher hadn't made that much of a fuss. But when the phone footage was analysed you could see clearly just how close the ball had come to hitting him square in the face. Mr Waddell's delayed reaction was very funny. With precision timing, camera phone two captured the image: Mr Waddell ducking down with a bewildered expression on his face, almost half a second after the ball had whizzed past, and his thinning ginger comb-over momentarily standing on end to expose his bald head. Beautiful.

Camera phone one, operated by Donovan, provided some excellent rolling footage, although Donovan never really got the credit he deserved. He managed to capture Mr Waddell ducking, and also followed him as he continued his walk towards the staff room, showing his angry and suspicious glances in their direction. The camera continued to roll as they kept silent and disciplined until he was completely out of sight, and then recorded their jubilant scenes of laughter and relief. It was a dynamite package. Donovan's hand had been steady throughout, and he had continued to record when others might have joined in the celebrations. But this had more to do with his isolation from the rest of the group than his talent as a cameraman.

As the days went by the game remained popular, and occupied the boys most lunchtimes, but to Eddie things were starting to get a little stale. It had been a good idea but they were now in their comfort zone, which is where he never wanted to be. No adrenalin, no point. But he felt the project deserved one final push. A spectacular moment that couldn't be bettered. Then they could celebrate and move on. He had been racking his brains, but couldn't come up with a feasible plan, so he waited, hoping that sooner or later the ideal opportunity would present itself. And on one fresh October lunchtime it did.

The 10 Huxley boys were kicking the ball around aimlessly as usual. There had been a couple of attempts on female teachers, but they were yards wide of the mark and didn't even cause them to break their stride. It seemed that fewer teachers were venturing across the playground now, choosing instead to take the covered walkway.

Eddie picked up the ball and bounced it a few times. He strained his eyes to scan the far side of the playground. It was full of year eight and nine kids chasing a ball around as if their lives depended on it. Just behind them, in the courtyard at the back of the playground, groups of girls and soft lads stood talking in groups near to the tuck shop. Then the door leading from the Allingham building to the courtyard slowly opened and Mr Smith walked out into the courtyard. The strap of a laptop computer case was over one shoulder, and he carried a cup of tea.

Eddie alerted the others.

~Get in. Time for action everybody. ACTION!

Eddie was the only one who had spotted the teacher so far, and he followed him intently with his eyes. After a few steps Mr Smith paused. This was a critical moment: the point at which teachers decided if they were going to walk the long way to the staff room under the covered walkway, or cut across the playground and risk dealing with an incident. At first Mr Smith headed towards the covered walkway, then checked himself, turned and opted for the short cut.

Eddie let out a huge sigh of relief. When he breathed in again his heart was beating faster and his palms were sweating, but his eyes were smiling.

By the time Mr Smith had walked down the dozen or so steps to the playground the Huxley boys were in position. Dylan was on camera one, Donovan on camera two, and the rest of them were acting as though they were waiting for a pass. But there was only one person who was going to take this shot.

Eddie continued to bounce the ball, steadily and with both hands. He breathed in deeply through his nose and his eyes never left the target. Mr Smith was a good thirty yards away when Eddie bounced the ball one last time and let it go.

It felt like a good shot as soon as the ball left his laces. Eddie had put a bit extra into it to give it plenty of height. It seemed to hang in the air ominously before making its descent. It was a surreal moment, with most of the hundred or so kids in the playground totally unaware of what was happening, while eight lads from 10 Huxley watched intently, about to burst with excitement. As the ball came down everything seemed right about the shot. Then Mr Smith stopped, to speak briefly to a girl in year eight. The football landed harmlessly about three feet away. Mr Smith gave a smile at his good fortune and continued his journey.

Eddie was fuming. He was livid. This didn't even constitute a near miss: the ball and Mr Smith probably wouldn't be in the same shot, and he hadn't stopped to tell the boys to be careful or make sure the ball stayed at the top end of the playground.

~Quick! Dildo! Get me that ball back!

Eddie gestured furiously to Dylan to retrieve the ball. He knew he had about ten seconds before Mr Smith made it off the playground.

Obediently Dylan scampered towards the still-bouncing football and firmly rolled it back. Eddie moved forward to save time, and by the time he picked the ball up he was much closer. No further than fifteen yards from the teacher. He didn't have time to set up another high looping shot. He was too close to be accurate, and by the time it came down there was every chance that Mr Smith would be out of the playground.

So Eddie swiftly bounced the ball once on the floor and drilled it hard towards his victim. He struck it so firmly that there was no need to take into account Mr Smith's momentum, nor was there any chance of the ball being caught by the wind. It went straight and hard and at a cruel speed.

Only a super-slow-motion replay would have been able to do justice to the perfection of this shot. Eddie had kicked the ball drop-kick style, striking it just after it hit the surface of the playground so it was travelling upwards from the ground. The first thing it hit was Mr Smith's cup of tea, which he was carrying just below chest height. Most of the contents of the cup found their way onto the teacher's shirt and trousers. The ball was then deflected upwards, where it hit him in the side of the neck, knocking him off balance. What happened next was even more extraordinary. Mr Smith completely lost it. Somehow the cup had fallen off the saucer but remained, on its side, wedged between the saucer and his shirt. But he was so angry that he picked up the cup and smashed it on the floor, swearing loudly.

--Bastards!

By now this was not just a 10 Huxley incident; it involved the whole playground, all attention drawn by the commotion. Mr Smith stood there ranting and raving, his shirt drenched and his cup in pieces on the ground.

Suddenly he seemed to realise the predicament he was in and how the incident might escalate out of control. He gritted his teeth, scooped up as much of his cup as could and headed hurriedly towards the staff room. For the rest of the afternoon he wore a PE-style polo shirt, and news spread quickly of the story behind it.

MR SMITH'S STRUGGLE

Gary Smith wondered why he had done it. Why had he accepted Miss Sanders' offer of a cup of tea? He was due back in the staff room for a meeting in ten minutes. By the time she had gone to the kitchenette in the home economics room and brought it over he would only have a minute or so before he had to set off again.

It only took a moment before he discovered the answer: because there was something slightly sexual about having a cup of tea made for him by a woman. He half-imagined he was drinking it in bed first thing in the morning. He imagined rolling over and making love to her after he had finished the last mouthful, with that extra little bit of sugar. He loved it when she checked if it was two sugars.

~Come now, Miss Sanders! You must know my routine by now.

Or,

--Make it two and a half – I'm feeling a little naughty today!

As Miss Sanders left the room Gary allowed himself a good look at her bottom. He loved those smart pinstriped trousers that made everything tight and curvy and begging to be stroked. He thought she should wear those trousers every day, hating the sack of a dress she wore on Wednesdays. Sometimes he even turned down a drink as a silent protest.

Gary had often thought about asking her round for dinner. He had even thought of a good line, and practised it in front of the mirror.

--Goodness me, Miss Sanders! How many cups of tea must I owe you now? I've lost count. I think it must add up to a three-course meal. You must call round some time and allow me to cook for you.

But he didn't want to mess things up. He considered her slightly out of his league.

Gary had struggled hard to get where he was. To some it might not sound much, a chemistry teacher in a secondary school, but he considered it a massive achievement. He was by no means a naturally gifted scientist, but all through school he had persevered and had gradually made sense of what he was studying. He was a natural communicator, though, and because he had struggled himself he was expert at explaining things in terms his students could understand.

Gary was in his third year at the comp; his first year had been as a graduate trainee. He was thrust straight in to school life, not really knowing what to expect, but survived and became fully qualified. In his second year, as a fully fledged teacher, he battled against unruly classes that other teachers had given up on. By the end of the second year he felt he was slowly but surely winning the respect of the students. Their behaviour was still poor sometimes, but he felt as if he had at least half of the class on side and willing to learn. His goal in his third year was to establish himself as a teacher whom you didn't take liberties with. Gary always tried to present himself as thorough and professional, and hoped this would rub off on the students so he could concentrate on education – where his pleasant nature allowed him to get the best out of them.

In his first year some students had tried to test him and openly poked fun, but this was happening less and less now and his career was gathering momentum.

As Miss Sanders picked up the kettle she wondered how many cups of tea she would have to make before he asked her out. She returned to the classroom, where he was still marking books, and delivered his tea with a smile.

Gary didn't bother making any quips. He had exhausted most of his lines, and besides his mind was on the meeting he had with Mr Duffy in two minutes' time. He tried to take a big sip from his drink, but it was hot and he scalded his lip: there was no way he was going to be able to finish it before he set off. Not wanting to risk leaving it, and Miss Sanders finding it, he decided to take it with him. Walking round school with a hot drink was an obvious health and safety hazard, but he had seen more senior members of staff doing it – so Gary slung his laptop over his shoulder, picked up his tea and set off for the staff room.

He strode confidently down the stairs and headed for the covered walkway, the long way round. He made a quick calculation of how long it would take to reach the staff room and realised there was a good chance he might be a few seconds late. To avoid a raised eyebrow from Mr Duffy he checked himself, turned and headed towards the playground.

Immediately Gary could see it was a good decision. The playground looked fairly calm and there were only a couple of balls being knocked around. At the near end there were a few year sevens having a game of football, and at the far end a few year tens knocking a ball around. Both games seemed tame and unlikely to explode into violence.

He was about three-quarters of the way across the playground when he heard a familiar voice call his name. Abigail Summers, a year eight girl, broke away from the game of football with the boys. She was not really interested in the game but it gave her an opportunity to flirt with the lads and get into the odd play-fight.

~Yes, Abigail? What can I do for you?

~My mum saw you in Matalan last night. She fancies you. Will you go out with her?

Gary stopped walking and turned to look at the giggling freckled face standing before him. As he did so a ball flew past at head height only a yard or so away. He briefly glanced across the playground, but it wasn't obvious where it had come from so he carried on talking.

~All I can say is that your mother has very good taste.

~Will you go out with her?

~Abigail! I have enough of you with two hours a week of science. I don't want to be your stepdad as well!

And with that he continued across the playground. Both man and girl had a smile on their face after the friendly exchange. Gary just about felt comfortable with this level of banter: he felt he had built up enough respect that it wouldn't undermine his authority in the classroom.

His smile did not last long.

From nowhere.

Without warning.

Gary felt a brutal impact on the left-hand side of his jaw. Almost instantaneously he felt a scalding pain on his chest and ribs. He felt his shirt sticking to his skin, intensifying the pain, and for a few moments he was too stunned to do anything. When he regained his senses after a couple of seconds he began frantically to pull the shirt away from his chest. When the searing pain began to fade he started to realise what had happened.

There was a football still in motion a few feet away. Gary realised he had been set up. No one in the playground was taking responsibility. He had no way of telling who had done it. On the spur of the moment he blamed everyone, including Abigail Summers. For a split second he lost control. Not quite enough to lash out and hit a child, but enough to slam the tea cup into the ground.

He yelled at the top of his voice.

--Bastards!

The whole playground went silent. Everyone was looking in his direction. It was the silence that brought him round. Gary took a couple of deep breaths with his hands on his knees and began the damage limitation. Without looking up he collected together as many broken pieces of tea cup as he could and, still fuming, stormed out of the playground and into the main building, in no fit state for a meeting.

What hurt Gary most that day was not the sharp blow to his chin. It was not the scalding hot tea on his chest. It was not even the humiliation he felt when he had to explain to Mr Duffy why he had missed the meeting, or when he had to ask around the staff room for a spare shirt.

What hurt him most was the backward step he took with his students. The story swiftly went around school and was exaggerated, not that it needed exaggerating. There was someone in each class who was best at imitating

the Mr Smith paddy. In his lessons Gary heard the word
bastards muttered gradually louder and louder when his
back was turned. If he ever challenged this the answer was
always the same.

~But it's all right for you to say it, sir!

And he never accepted a cup of tea from Miss Sanders
again.

After two weeks she stopped asking.

2006
YEAR 11: BLACK SHEEP

The Huxley boys sat in the best corner of the common room, having commandeered the juke box. They had politely bullied the fat geek girls into ejecting their Simply Red CD and were now playing aggressive techno at just the right volume. Loud enough to annoy and distract, but not loud enough so they couldn't continue their conversation.

About drinking.

Drinking bitter was very important. Some lads in their year drunk lager, some even out of bottles. But they were just gay homosexual bastards.

They talked about pubs where you could get a decent ale. Where landlords were experienced and could pull a proper pint, but not experienced enough to recognise that they were all under age. They feigned knowledge of the process that ensured a full body and a creamy head. Not like the stupid slags who wouldn't overflow it and left the head frothy.

Eddie had been deeply embarrassed to the point of humiliation when he had been sent back to the bar at Otley Rugby Club. He had waited to be served by Vicky Mega-Breasts so he could have a quick chat and give himself a little stiffy. He stood there transfixed while she slopped out the bubble-bath Watleys. He knew he had asked for Black Sheep and was about to tell her, but the sight of her heaving cleavage left him dumbstruck. The heads on the pints were a good two inches. He knew he was in for some grief when he got back to the table, so he topped up their pints with his own and hoped they would think he had had a couple of cheeky gulps at the bar.

~What the fuck's that?

The lads stared suspiciously at their pints, holding them up to the light. Taking a sip. Analysing the flavour. Prodding at the head.

~This is fuckin' Watleys!

~Is it fuck. Get it down yer.

~It fuckin' is! It's a different colour! I'm not drinking this shite!

~I asked for Black Sheep. There's no fuckin' difference anyway. Just fuckin' drink it.

They all looked at him as if he had told them he wanted to kill their families.

~How fuckin' stupid can you be? That Watleys tastes like fuckin' cat piss! Why would you go to the bar and get Watleys when there's Black Sheep on draught? I bet you even got that Vicky Mega-Breasts to pull it!

Eddie's doleful expression let him down.

~He fuckin' did an' all! The cunt!

~Get back to that fuckin' bar and get that Peter to pull us a pint of fuckin' Black Sheep. That Peter knows how to pull a decent fuckin' pint. This cunt goes and gets Vicky Mega-Breasts to pull his pints. I tell yer what, she might have nice bangers but she can't pull a fuckin' pint. Look at the fuckin' state of that!

There was no way back. The group had built up too much momentum. Spurred on by the effect of their first three 'proper' pints, they were united in their disgust at the breaking of this most sacred of taboos. It was a damage limitation job. Eddie considered handing the drinks back and demanding they were swapped. The lads assured him that this was right and proper, if it was true he had asked for Black Sheep.

But he didn't have the front to go through with it. The reasons flashed through his brain like bullets from a gun.

Under age.

Should have said sooner.

Too cheeky.

Scupper chance with Vicky Mega.

Waste of beer.

Embarrassing.

He got round to the side bar, which was deserted save for two old boys who were standing sipping whisky, glad to be away from the noise of youngsters and loud music.

The barman was stacking some soft drinks bottles, and Eddie used his name to catch his attention.

--Four Black Sheeps, please, Peter, when you've got a minute.

Eddie felt in his pocket. His paper round money, topped up with the four pounds he had stolen from his mother's tin, was running low. Enough to buy this round and then he was struggling. He didn't need this. He could forget going into Leeds later. His anger began to seethe.

Peter set to work expertly pulling the four, creamy, tight-headed pints. As he stood them on the bar one by one, tall, proud and golden, their heads formed with regimented accuracy, Eddie could see the error of his ways. It was almost offensive that Watleys should be standing on a tray on the same bar.

But they couldn't be wasted.

Eddie took a deep breath. He picked up his own three-quarter pint of Watleys and slammed it down his neck with six wide-mouthed aggressive gulps. He burped silently but felt good, knowing that the extra alcohol would soon be in his system. He eyed up the next pint and attacked it with gusto. The extra volume proved more of a challenge. He got just past half-way before he pulled away gasping. One of the old boys gave him a quick glance before continuing a conversation about old-fashioned forwards.

With bulging eyes Eddie continued, determined to re-coup some of his investment. By the time his watering eyes sighted the bottom of the empty glass his stomach was feeling dangerously full.

He stood upright and sucked in the air, his throat desperately grateful to take in something that wasn't Watleys. He focused on a picture on the wall and swallowed repeatedly to keep the contents of his gut in place. But he had only put away half of what he had paid for.

Momentum. He had to keep going.

Eddie picked up the third pint and started to take smaller mouthfuls, much more hesitantly.

At the half-way point he knew he had gone.

He stood bolt upright and focused on the picture once again. He swallowed hard over and over. The two old boys gave him their full attention, bemused at the gasping young man. His stomach began to gurgle and he started to retch. Then he ran.

Eddie almost made it. Only about half a pint of puke hit the floor and caught the corner of his jeans. The rest cascaded outwards, splattering the toilet pan and seat. It was relatively painless but he was taken aback by the sheer volume of liquid produced from the depths of his guts.

He didn't hang around. With a handful of toilet roll he wiped his mouth and jeans, before courteously paying attention to the toilet seat. He rinsed his mouth with water and was soon back in the bar, where the two old boys acknowledged his arrival with knowing looks.

Spotting the remaining two pints of Watleys, still standing in shame on the bar, Eddie picked them up to move them to a back table, but their faint smell churned his innards once more. He was sick again, but this offering was no more than a mouthful. And that is where he held it. Swirling around his teeth, the beer vomit swelled his cheeks.

He scanned the bar, looking for an outlet. Then he spotted it. Four pints of Black Sheep, ready to be delivered to their eager owners. As soon as the idea registered in his brain his phone was out, and into video mode.

Eddie held the phone in front of his face and deposited a small offering in three of the four pints. Stirring them quickly with his finger, the liquids combined. He went down on one knee as though tying his shoelace and spat the excess into the carpet. He smiled into his phone camera, addressing it directly.

~Now let's see if you boys can recognise Watleys *second* time round.

As Eddie returned with the pints the others complained about having to wait. A lot of their jibes were repetitive, but it wasn't often they got him on the receiving end and they were on a roll.

Eddie looked submissive. Defeated. Head down, he sipped his own drink, playing with his phone with the other hand. He flipped it round, in record mode.

His three friends took hearty gulps of Black Sheep.
~Now that's a proper fuckin' pint.
~Just slips straight down.
~That Watleys has got that aftertaste.
~Full of chemicals.
~Gives you a bad hangover an' all.
~Can't beat that Black Sheep.
~Superb.
~Hand pulled makes such a difference.
~Like mothers' milk.

2007
YEAR 12: EIGHTY-ONE DAYS

By now the Huxley boys didn't always talk about beer. Sometimes they talked about birds.

Eddie had copped off with Jenny Partridge from the year below at an eighteenth birthday party. She was certainly not considered well fit by the learned majority as she came to school looking respectable, as though her mother had dressed her. Quite naturally anyone who went there was liable for a ribbing. Eddie was surprised how much she improved when she was out of uniform and in her going-out gear, but that was never going to carry any weight with the lads. He got the grief he deserved.

In the years to come Jenny learnt to manipulate her school uniform like the others. One day a long fitted skirt with a big slit. Another day shorter: not quite a mini but getting there. Subtle touches of make-up moved her slowly but surely into the in-crowd. The fitted short-sleeve blouse that hugged her midriff eventually clinched her promotion to the premier league.

But by then it was all too late for Eddie. He had well and truly fucked up. And the seeds of the fuck-up were well and truly sown in the conversations of the Huxley boys, now joined by Si Reynolds, who had dropped down a year after failing all his A levels. He pulled no punches, and was apparently more experienced in important matters.

~You coming down the Station for a few tonight, Ed?

Eddie squirmed.

~Nah. Can't tonight.

~He's off to the cinema.

~He's taking that Jenny bird.

~What, Partridge in a pear shape?

There was laughter round the table.

~You still seeing her, Eddie?

~Fuck me. It's getting serious! You getting much action out of her?

~Nah, not really. Not really had many opportunities.

~What! You're not gettin' your oats and yer still hangin' around with that?

More laughter.

Eddie was hurt. But he battled to front up.

He would remember that line for the rest of his life; it was one he often replayed. He could see where everyone was sitting. He could picture the expressions on their faces, knowing he had been challenged and waiting for his comeback. He wished he had responded differently. He wondered what would have happened if he had defended her honour and confirmed that he was serious about her. He could have had another eighty-one days. And then some.

But it didn't happen. It wasn't in the script.

Eddie did have a come-back. And considering how hurt and flustered he was, he was surprised at how well it went.

~Simon, Simon, Simon. You really are a slow learner aren't you? You really think I'm in it for the romance? It's not like you and that jinner bird you fell in love with, you bushy eared old cunt. Fuck me. You're gonna be thirty-five before you get outa this school.

~Chill out! Looks like I really hit a raw nerve there. So, c'mon then. What you got in mind?

Eddie took his mobile phone out of his pocket and lobbed it in the air, catching it with the same hand.

~Got some footage planned.

~What, with a bird?

~Just you be in that corner. Monday morning break. I'll have it ready.

~Tell us what is. Eh, lads, I reckon he's gonna propose!

Eddie didn't dignify Si's last comment with a response.

The rest of the lads pestered him for clues, but Eddie wouldn't reveal anything. Mainly because he didn't have a plan.

But he would get one.

He always did.

CERTAINTIES

Eddie lay back on his bed and stared into space.

Still no plan. Nothing feasible anyway.

Thinkthinkthinkthinkthinkthink.

He tapped his head gently with his mobile phone, hoping that his faithful tool would change from servant to source of ideas.

He preferred ideas to evolve naturally, never being totally comfortable when under pressure. But every now and again, he told himself, it was necessary. And now was one of those occasions.

He thought of his mates. He thought of the jokes they told. And the scenarios. Jokes about scenarios. Over and over. They never came true, but what if they did?

He could make them happen. He could set it up.

An idea began to grow in his mind. It was as though it had been there all along. Just waiting to be discovered. It was perfect.

A trip to the cinema. Urban legend. Joke scenario.

Lads' humour.

And into the bargain he could get rid of the monkey on his back that was Jenny Partridge, and end the looks, sneers and comments.

Because it would look as if he had been building up to this moment. This was the right way to go. The perfect thing to do. Just how it should be; how it needed to be. Inevitable, really.

At least, that is what he told himself.

Inside, deep inside, he was having doubts. Niggling doubts, suggesting that he cared for this girl. And she was beautiful. Fucking beautiful. Why couldn't they see it? Would they ever see it?

A distant feeling told him he would regret this in the future. But it was soon washed away in a tidal wave of adrenalin as he pictured the triumphant scene in his mind, showing the lads his latest footage. Them sitting round, pissing themselves laughing while he remained composed. As though it was easy. As though it was natural. Like a striker scoring from twenty-five yards and showing no emotion. That's what he wanted. And it far outweighed any lingering doubts he had about some silly bird.

ACCOMPLICE

Now the idea was well and truly formed in his mind Eddie knew he needed someone to shoot the footage. He wondered whether it was time to raise his game a little. Would mobile phone pictures be enough to do it justice?

He knew he would only get one shot. There would be no chance to re-set. One take only. Lighting was a problem.

He scrolled down the address book in his phone. Each name was unsuitable. Most would refuse. Some she would know. Others he couldn't trust to hold their bottle.

Then his heart raced momentarily.

Stuart.

Perfect.

An old name from the past. He had left the comp at the end of year seven. Jenny would never have known him. He was a crazy kid, and he and Eddie had bonded instantly. Stuart had come down from a well-heeled school in Scotland, and when his parents decided that one year in a comprehensive was more than enough they moved him to Leeds Grammar.

Eddie had kept in touch intermittently for years.

Considering the wealth of Stuart's parents, he felt reasonably confident that Stuart might be able to supply the equipment. Something small, easily concealed but high-spec enough to get around the lighting issue.

And Stuart was just the man to front it.

Excitedly, Eddie pressed the dial button.

On no counts did Stuart let him down.

POPCORN

For most of the evening he had almost forgotten. He had enjoyed her company. The fact that her casual clothes had changed her so much excited him. He was sure she looked better than just OK. He was certain she looked quite fit. With none of his mates around to tell him otherwise he was sure.

Eddie glanced at some of the other couples and was positive that Jenny measured up well. Standing close, he smelt her perfume and clean shimmering hair. She was understated in her fitted jeans and black top, but he was sure she looked sexy. He imagined what she would look like if she was *really* done up. But there was more to it than that. They had started to really get on. To understand each other. She mentioned his mates, and how he was often stand-offish when he was with them.

~It's not because they all think I'm a little geek from the year below, is it?

It was not what she said but the way she said it. There

was no self-pity in her accusation: she spoke with humour and a knowing sideways smile. Like a headmistress who had caught a small child doing something naughty. Eddie laughed it off and poked fun at the behaviour of his peers. They laughed together as he played down his role in their pranks. As though he was above it and only joining in to humour them.

The laughter broke down any lingering tensions. Their gazes met and they shared smiles for longer and longer. They became closer as they queued for tickets. By the time Eddie had paid their fingers were locked together, and he felt butterflies take flight as never before.

He sat in the cinema, three rows from the back and right in the corner, a large tub of popcorn at his feet. She had bought it, which in years to come led him to bang his head against the wall. Gently at first, but then harder and harder. It was the fact that he had decided to abort mission that got to him the most.

If only she hadn't . . .

Minstrels or ice cream . . .

Eighty-one days . . .

But a share-size popcorn tub had fucked it.

~If you've bought the tickets, at least let me buy the popcorn.

She smiled before resting her head on his shoulder.

He responded by putting his arm around her. She traced patterns with a finger on his leg, just above his knee. He closed his eyes. He loved that. And for a few moments he was perfectly happy.

Then Stuart entered. Innocuous, with a small duffel bag over his shoulder, he climbed towards the back row. He glanced once in Eddie's direction but for no longer than he glanced anywhere else. Their eyes met for a split second only. What a pro.

Relaxed and looking forward to the film, Jenny closed her eyes with her head on Eddie's shoulder. She opened them briefly to reach down for a small handful of popcorn. She loved the warm, salty taste, and knew that once she started she might not be able to stop – happy, cosy and in her own world. So much so that she hardly noticed that the unassuming young man had selected a seat directly behind them, even though half the cinema was empty. But he did not knock their seats or rustle sweet wrappers. He never made a sound. And for the best part of two hours she completely forgot he was there.

For most of the film Eddie's mind was locked in a battle for the correct course of action. For the first half-hour he allowed himself to wallow in the pleasant warmth that seemed to be radiating from his stomach. For years afterwards he returned to this and wondered how best to describe the feeling. He could never quite find a name for it, but he knew he had never again felt anything close.

After thirty minutes Eddie felt a gentle flick on his ear and a couple of taps on his head, which brought him back to himself, reminding him why he was there. He remembered his mates back in the common room. He thought about going back to them on Monday morning and telling them that he and Partridge in a pear shape were an item. A proper couple. He pictured their faces and their comments. And that helped to bring him round. He sat upright, swallowed hard and breathed deeply. He knew what he was doing. He knew who he was. He had to arouse himself.

Jenny watched as the credits began to roll, feeling slightly sleepy in the dark. Her head was still resting on his shoulder as the lights gradually came on. She was almost full of popcorn, but was sure she could manage another mouthful. She reached over to the tub, now resting on

Eddie's lap. Unusually he didn't tilt it towards her: she had to reach right over and drop her hand in at ninety degrees. Jenny blindly reached inside until she reached the level of the popcorn. As she did so she was shocked to feel an alien sensation.

Something hard and meaty rubbed against her wrist and fingers. She was about to withdraw her hand when she saw Eddie nodding encouragingly, as though willing her to look inside. She moved her head to see.

At first she couldn't see anything clearly, her eyes still adjusting to the dim lighting. Then she gasped in horror. Eddie's erect todger was proudly poking through the salty kernels. At the moment she realised what her hand had been rubbing against she noticed the anonymous figure behind them holding a small camcorder, a thin shaft of light shining in her face.

Jenny felt breathless, sick and faint. She wanted to cry or scream, but she couldn't. Her chest felt tight and she covered her mouth with her hand, overwhelmed by so many horrible truths hitting her at once. She looked into his eyes with a hurt expression that haunted him for the rest of his life.

The footage showed Eddie giving a thumbs up and a nod of the head.

~Job done. Nuff said.

But inside he was crying.

Eighty-one days.

Eighty-one bastard days.

2008
YEAR 12

Eddie sat on the grass bank with a handful of the lads from 12 Huxley . It was late April and the early signs of a scorching summer were beginning to show. The girls were taking advantage of this, wearing clothing appropriate for the temperature.

This gave the Huxley boys the chance to sit about and ogle and talk. It was a period of inactivity that ate away at Eddie for the rest of his life. The other Huxley boys either never thought about it again or looked back through rose-tinted glasses. Eddie looked back through shit-coloured glasses.

There they were sitting on the grass talking about crap. Going over former glories. Talking about scams in year nine. Talking about which girls were fit. Talking about which girls were mingers. Talking about what they would like to do to the fit ones. Talking about how much money they would need to do anything with the mingers.

Talking. Always talking.

In his mind's eye Eddie could hardly see any mingers. It was before the girls were old enough to let themselves go. When they were slim and pert with fresh shiny skin. Before they had the chance to go to university and drink dangerously four times a week and eat kebabs. Before they had children that their bodies never recovered from. Before they smoked themselves sour. And the boys in Huxley just let them go. Sitting there talking, while pretty girls sat or danced or walked all around them. Girls in year eleven. Girls in year twelve. Girls in year thirteen.

When Eddie was middle-aged he often returned to this scene in his mind's eye. He would stand up, wander away from the Huxley boys and chat to one or two of the girls. Nothing special. Nothing flash. Just a polite enquiry. What are you studying? How's the course going? What are you up to this weekend? No need for the killer line. No need to make yourself look great in one sentence. No need for the stand-up. Just a polite enquiry and a way in for later. What a waste. What a terrible waste.

Their inactivity was compounded by the fact that the Huxley boys were into nothing new. No new ideas, no new scams. Some of the teachers believed they had grown up a little bit. Some of the parents thought that it was because many of the bad influences had left school. But that wasn't it. The scams had stopped because the brain behind them wasn't functioning normally any more. The brain behind the scams wasn't working out how to give the boys their next adrenalin hit. The brain was thinking about *her*.

Because Jenny Partridge was now premier league. How short memories were. Had she really changed that much? Eddie had known she was stunning, but now he couldn't have her. And she was capturing the eyes of the other lads as she sauntered round school.

The lack of ideas had left a vacuum. A vacuum that would have to be filled by others. And that it was happened this particular morning.

Horner approached the group on the grass, followed by Tony and Steve who were laughing excitedly.

~Hey, Eddie! Have a listen to this. You're gonna love this. Tony's thought of this great idea.

Tony had come up with the plan to ski and sled down the bank, using a Kwik Save sign as a dry ski slope. This sign had been stolen by the Huxley boys some months earlier as part of a craze for pinching signs and flags to display in their common room. The Kwik Save sign was ridiculously large, designed to cover the front of the whole store. Even the floor space in the common room was too small to accommodate it, so it was folded away in Dildo's garden shed.

Tony wanted to borrow the sign and was happy for Eddie to be in on the plan. He used Horner as the go-between.

Horner was beaming.

~It'll be awesome. I'll bring some skis. Steve's bringing a sledge. It's gonna be a right laugh.

Eddie frowned non-committally. There was a major problem with the plan: it wasn't his. He would have to be a tag-along like the rest of them. He gave the nod for them to borrow the sign, but said he didn't really fancy joining in, intending to watch from a distance and hoping it wasn't too successful.

The next day, during first break, Eddie noticed Dildo unrolling the huge plastic sheet down the bank. Walking across the football pitch were Horner, Steve and Tony, all dressed in daft woolly hats, scarves and gloves under the April sunshine. Horner was wearing ski goggles and carrying skis over his shoulder. Steve was carrying an old wooden sledge. Tony had his arms free, which allowed him to swagger – making it clear he was the leader and instigator.

Other students stared in bemusement and anticipation. While Horner fiddled with his ski boots Steve and Tony took their positions astride the sledge at the top of the slope. It looked quite funny, and Eddie reluctantly laughed along with the others.

Steve and Tony attempted to push themselves away, but without success. The plastic was warm and tacky, which created too much friction. There were sighs of disappointment as they struggled and scraped at the top of the slope, looking ridiculous in their winter get-up.

Eddie breathed a sigh of relief, but this was short lived. All of a sudden Horner spoke.

~Water! We need water!

He scurried over to some year nines.

~Lads, can I borrow your water?

Without hesitation a water bottle was offered, then another, and another. Horner poured the water onto the top of the banner. The sledge moved a small but significant distance.

~More! We need more!

What happened next was amazing. People who had been watching in bewilderment a few moments earlier sprang into action. They began to rush around, filling water bottles and tipping them onto the banner. The quantity wasn't enough to lubricate the whole slide, but this didn't deter the scores of helpers. Tough lads were helping. Geeks were helping. Little kids from year seven were helping. Pretty girls from year eleven were helping – to Eddie's dismay. Each one was greeted with a smile and a handshake from Tony, who was lapping it all up. As if he was the king of the world.

Eddie took some solace in the fact that *she* wasn't helping. But she was sitting and watching and seemed to be amused. He had heard a rumour that she liked Tony, which made him throw up. But nothing had happened to prove this.

The flurry of water bottles gathered momentum. The school had not seen community spirit like this for years. Eddie was clutching at straws now, but he hoped they wouldn't be able to get enough water down for the sledge to slide quickly. Just then he noticed a commotion. Some year eleven lads who had got hold of cleaners' buckets and had filled them with soapy water were heading towards the top of the slide.

Why the bloody hell are they helping out? Eddie thought. The year eleven lads, who always got their football kicked away and had their prettiest girls cherry-picked. It didn't occur to Eddie until later that Tony was neither a ball-kicker or cherry-picker. He was just a nice guy who had time for everyone, and was now reaping the rewards.

The buckets of water were tipped down. They made a huge difference. Through his laughter, Tony was directing operations.

—Just a bit more! There's a little dry bit in front of that runner.

—Quick! Quick!

It was then that she got up. She sprang to her feet, clutching her own water bottle. Mineral water, Eddie noted, from the petrol station.

—I'm not that thirsty anyway.

She laughed as she ran over to the top of the slide.

—Where shall I pour it?

She splashed the remainder of her drink where she was instructed.

~Now give us a push!

She needed no second invitation to place her hands on Tony's shoulders. The force she provided was all that they needed to slide down at speed. Everyone was laughing, no one more so than Tony, who engineered a comedy fall at the bottom. He and Steve, still wearing hats and scarves, were tangled up and in hysterics.

What happened next turned Eddie's stomach.

She skipped down to the bottom of the slope to help Tony up. Eddie noted that Steve was in greater need, as he was sprawling in a ditch lower down, but it was Tony she went for. She held his hand and pulled him towards her as he clambered to his feet.

They continued to hold hands for a few seconds when Tony stood up. That was enough for Eddie. He was up and off.

Less than a minute later Eddie was locked in a sixth form toilet cubicle, throwing up his breakfast. His insides contracted, forcing out multitudes of potent vomit. He puked again and again until his stomach was empty. But he couldn't stop his gut wrenching and twisting as he failed to expel the image of Jenny and Tony holding hands.

Somehow, though, despite the acute pain in his stomach, despite the vile acidic taste in the back of his throat, Eddie began to feel he was being cleansed. It was as though his mental pain was physically manifesting itself and violently leaving him. Eventually he spat the last traces of bile from his mouth, and knelt there gasping for air where so many others had crapped that morning.

Eddie wiped his mouth on some toilet roll. He put the lid down and sat on the pot with his head in his hands, trying to pull himself together. His eyes were watering, his stomach ached and his mouth felt as if he had eaten a dead rat. He knew now he would be badly dehydrated. He was at absolute rock bottom.

Outside the sound of laughter was replayed again and again as others waited for a turn on the sledge or the skis. Even passing teachers laughed as they shook their heads. The only hint of a reprimand was from Mr Peters, who reminded them to have everything packed away when the bell went.

As scams go it had almost everything. It was funny, original and it captured the imagination of the whole school. There was no adrenalin rush, but the laughter and community spirit were unsurpassed. Barring perhaps the manager of Kwik Save, no one had suffered.

Then *she* made Eddie sick.

Eddie decided there and then that he needed something to come back with. Nothing had happened since her. At home in the evening all he did was lie on his bed and think about her. Replaying the events in his head.

Eighty-one days.

Eighty-one days.

How he could have done things differently. If only he hadn't . . .

What else could he do to impress her?

Eddie was hardly bothering with school work and his grades were beginning to suffer. He hadn't had a decent idea for ages, simply because there wasn't room for anything else in his mind. She was draining him. She was killing him. Perhaps he should kill her first.

Sitting on the toilet Eddie took three deep breaths and started to concentrate harder than he had ever done before. He pressed the heels of his hands hard into his eye-sockets until only darkness prevailed, trying desperately to force her out. Just for a few moments, so he could remember what it was like not to have her in his head. For a few seconds, somehow, he managed it.

When Eddie left the cubicle three minutes later he was driven. He knew whom he had to speak to and what he had to say. He could get anything out of Horner.

Eddie sat in the passenger seat of Horner's car, encouraging him through the gap in the hedge, reassuring him that there was plenty of room and telling him to put his foot down. Horner did so, and was rewarded with scratches from branches on both sides, immediately disproving Eddie's claim. But this didn't really matter. Eddie had the car where he wanted.

Behind them trailed the banner-cum-ski slope, attached to the car's tow-bar with skipping ropes. Horner drove to the far penalty area and revved the engine a couple of times as he stopped. Eddie jumped out.

~Right! Let's go grass surfing!

Eddie stood on the banner with his left foot forward and arms apart, ready to balance. The car pulled away slowly and Eddie found himself sliding, his feet only separated from the grass by a thin plastic sheet.

Those looking out of the sixth form block window were treated to a rare sight. School maverick Eddie Shearer, who had been strangely reserved in recent months, was back, and back with a vengeance. He skilfully stayed on his feet behind the small green hatchback despite Horner making a number of arcing turns across the football pitch.

Eddie yelled out as he struggled to keep his balance.

~More gas! More gas!

Horner increased his speed as instructed, and began to make a left-hand turn to avoid the goalposts. Eddie stayed upright for a remarkably long time, but the centrifugal force threw him sideways into a tumbling fall that looked as painful as it was. Naturally he bounced back up, forced himself to laugh and jogged back onto the banner.

~Same speed on the straights, but slow down a bit on the corners. Try a figure of eight, then finish off straight through the goalposts.

Horner did as he was told, and more and more people came outside to watch the second bizarre occurrence of the day. Eddie felt he was a natural, and doubted very much if anyone else would be able to stay on their feet as long as he did. He hoped the onlookers would appreciate this too.

As he successfully made his way round the first bend Eddie noticed that *she* had stopped to see what was going on, but after only a few seconds she continued on her way. He was seething. He didn't fall off once in the next figure of eight, but it meant nothing to him without her there to see it. Why wasn't she impressed? It was miles better than some muppet on a sledge. In his anger he yelled at Horner.

~Faster! Foot down! Top speed through the goalposts!

Horner obliged, and Eddie wondered if she was looking out of a window. As they travelled at speed through the goalposts he jumped up and grabbed the crossbar, his momentum helping to swing his legs high into the air. When he released his grip his landing was far from perfect, but he stayed on his feet. It was an impressive trick, especially with no practice.

A sizeable crowd had gathered. There were a few handclaps and some laughter, but nowhere near as much as Eddie had hoped for. Despite his best efforts it came nowhere near Tony's makeshift ski slope. People had been part of that: they had all been welcome to have a turn. They all helped to make it work. They all risked getting into trouble. They were entertained and involved. And

Tony was such a nice guy that nobody wanted to deny him his moment of glory. With Eddie they just felt they were being shown off to.

Eddie didn't see this, of course. He decided the luke-warm reception was because they didn't appreciate how difficult it was to stand up on a plastic sheet at forty miles per hour. He needed to show them. He needed someone else to have a go.

~Right, Horner. Your turn!

~I'm not sure . . . I . . .

~Come off it. You'll love it. It's awesome.

Eddie looked Horner in the eye.

~You'll never get another chance to do this again. You'll be a fucking legend.

~But you're not insured for my car.

~What are you talking about? We're on a private field.

Eddie knew he was pushing things, but hoped Horner was just thick enough to believe that this comment was relevant.

~Peters is coming. We're in deep shit.

A look of concern and resignation crossed Horner's face. But things had gone too far for Eddie. He stepped forward and grabbed his friend, both hands on his shoulders.

~We're in deep shit anyway, mate. You probably more, with you driving. You might as well take the glory too. Do it for the boys!

And with that Eddie more or less frogmarched Horner onto the banner, after easing the car keys from his hand.

Eddie realised Peters was watching them and knew he had to move fast. He hadn't passed his driving test, and badly over-revved the engine as the car lurched away.

Horner went down immediately, and there was a ripple of laughter from the onlookers. Eddie began to feel better. In the rear view mirror he saw the nervous and rueful look on Horner's face.

This time Eddie's take-off was much smoother and Horner managed to stay on his feet for forty yards or so. That's far enough, thought Eddie to himself, and he made a sharp left turn. Horner went down heavily as soon as they changed direction, but he didn't bounce up as Eddie had. As Eddie looked over towards the school buildings he saw Mr Peters, arms folded, waiting for them to come back. This surprised Eddie, who had half-expected to see him running over to flag them down.

—Come on! Get up! We'd better go and see Peters. Just one more quick spin on the way back. Do that trick like I did between the posts. The birds'll love it.

—My knee's killing me.

—Come on, mate. Let's finish this in style. We always see things through to the end, you and me. Let me help you up.

Horner found Eddie's hysterical laughter quite disturbing. Even so, the weak-willed young man allowed himself to be dragged back onto the banner.

—I'll take it steady. You don't want to be walking all the way over there with your dodgy knee.

—OK then, but don't go through the goalposts.

Eddie put his thumb up and nodded his head, so technically he didn't lie. But it was very important to show how difficult it was to grab a crossbar at high speed. He skipped round to the driver's seat and pulled away slowly: he didn't want Horner to fall down so soon. When he saw that Horner had a firm footing he changed into second gear and put his foot on the gas. They were on the half-way line, but Eddie needed more speed to make sure

Horner didn't nail the stunt. This meant going for third, something he had only just mastered in his driving instructor's car.

The gearstick didn't slot into place as he was used to, so Eddie looked down momentarily to guide it home. By the time he looked up he had drifted some way to the left of his target. He was approaching the edge of the penalty area at thirty-five miles per hour, with the hapless Horner somehow still upright.

Horner had quite naturally believed his friend, assuming that in gradually turning left Eddie was doing as they had agreed and was avoiding the goal mouth. But in a desperate attempt to rescue his plan, Eddie pulled hard right on the wheel. As he neared the penalty spot he panicked that he might scratch the car as he was very close to the left goalpost. He breathed a sigh of relief as he passed by without touching it, but a noise from behind changed his mood.

It was a combination of a dull thud and a high-pitched ping, like a rope on a flagpole. For a moment Eddie comforted himself that it couldn't be Horner hitting the goalpost because there wasn't any screaming or swearing. But there were sounds from the onlookers. First there was laughter, but it was stifled and short-lived. The sort of laughter that stops suddenly when you realise you shouldn't be laughing at all. Then there were gasps. Horrified gasps. And swearing. Eddie braced himself. He had feared the worst for a dreadful few seconds, so he was pleased to see that Horner's head was still attached to his body. Somehow his brain gradually filtered in the vision that sprawled before him.

Horner's arms and legs appeared normal. There were no obvious signs of damage around the torso. Despite Horner's twitching, semi-conscious face being very pale, his eyes, ears and lips were pretty much intact. What Eddie saw last of all was more difficult to stomach. He had never seen a nose like this before. It looked as if it had been turned inside out and upside down. Most of it was spread flat against the left cheek. Less than a third remained near where it should have been.

Eddie considered squeezing the two parts back together, but quickly ruled this out when the blood came. Eddie had never seen blood flow like this before, not even on TV comedy sketches or on *Casualty*. The head of sixth form began to stride forward, feeling a bubbling concoction of anger, horror and contempt. Mr Peters fixed his glare on Eddie, partly because looking at Horner made him feel nauseous. For a good few seconds he was completely lost for words. But there was no need to speak because his look said it all.

2014
CATAMARAN EXCURSION

Matt Horner

This is the life!
Holiday time!
Sunshine, music, birds.
It's worth all the money and hassle when you get moments
like this.
Those birds are definitely looking over.
Saw them in the club last night.
They look tidy.
Nice bodies.
Got to go over and do some groundwork.
Bound to pay off later.
Hot as hell here, though.
Relaxing for a while.
Just starting to fry a little now.
Could go for a dip off the side of the boat.

Lads say that the snorkelling is awesome.
Say it's like another world down there.
Would love to give it a go.
If only . . .
Well it's been a while . . .
Maybe . . .
Might be OK . . .
But not worth . . .
Those birds.
But it's hot.
Starting to sweat.
Fuck it.
Gonna give it a try.
Mask fits well.
Might just give it a whirl.
What's the worst that can . . .
Cold!
Not even that bad.
Refreshing.
Fine once you get moving.
And so clear. Can see so much. So peaceful.
Relaxing.
Just floating along.
Don't feel hung over.
And out again tonight.
The birds on the boat.
Awesome.
Get a closer look at those fishes.
Just steady.
Still got it.
Strong swimmer.
Not far down.
Diving . . .
No probs.

FUCK!
PLEASE NO.
Fucking felt that pop.
Heard it too.
At least there's no . . .
But there fucking is now.
And tons of it.
Blood all over.
Water turning red.
Clamber on boat.
Centre of attention.
People looking.
Repulsed.
Those birds.
Nose streaming.
Eyes watering.
Can't see at all now.
That fucking rep.
Just leave me.
Where's my towel.
Fucking Kwik Save.
Bastard sign.
Bastards.
Shearer.
Eddie Shearer.

CHRISTMAS 2008
YEAR 13: TIGGER

School Christmas party.
Terminal One, Shipley.
Can't arrive sober.
Get loosened up with a few at Horner's.
I love this shit.
It's good round here an' all.

Horner's old man is a right laugh. Doesn't mind us getting pissed an' that. Was a bit funny with me for a bit after the nose incident an' that. Seems to have come round a bit now. But we were both equally at fault. Big payer to school funds, though. Probably what saved us from both being kicked out. Silly old cunt. This is always the best bit. Looking forward. 'Cos owt could happen. Anticipation.

Partridge bound to be there. But no biggie. Just as long as she doesn't cop off with Tony, I'll be fine.

Yes, this is the best bit. All lads together. Not too pissed yet, but getting there. Having debates. Like our own House of Commons. And recalling. Memories. All the way back through school. The times. The laughs.

Tony's like me in that way. Can remember everything. The detail. What people said. The looks on people's faces when summat happened. And your own imagination can help fill in the gaps.

And everyone loves Horner's dog. Little cairn terrier pup with bags of personality. Loves to chase the ball. We all had a laugh with the little fella when we first came in.

But now the little fucker's making a right racket.

Just as I'm telling a story. And everyone was listening.

Shut the . . .

Someone throw a ball for the little bastard.

Yap yap yap. Fuck me dead.

Hello, who's this?

Dildo and Steve are here.

And now Tigger's really going berserk. Jumping around. Wish I could get that excited.

And what's this he's sniffing?

Bloody hell, they've only gone an' brought McDonald's!

Fair go, lads, eating's cheating. But I reckon they need to line their stomachs.

So what's with the chocolate shake? Actually, bloody nice those thick shakes.

Go on then, gi's a bit.

What, finish it? Had enough?

Nah. Only want a bit. Tastes nice but doesn't go down well with the beer.

No one else?

What about Tigger? You want a try?

Want some Tigger?

Yes . . . good lad!

Bloody hell, he loves that!

Lapping it up.

Go on, lad!

OK, *have some more. Look at 'im. He's still licking my finger now!*

There's none on there any more. An' he's still licking away. Mad little fucker!

Here have some more.

But will he lick my finger now it's sticking through my flies? No problem!

He dun't give a fuck! Look at 'im go! Waaheey! Look at this, lads.

I thought I might get some action from a dog tonight . . .

Fuckin' everyone's really laughing now.

Top quality!

Fuckin' hysterical.

I can top it, though.

Eddie can top it!

Get my plums out.

Give 'em a quick tug through my flies. Leave 'em there sagging down for a bit like we do in the pub.

Pink, wrinkly, hairy.

But Tigger don't care!

Get a bit o' chocolate shake on 'em!

Feels cold.

Shit. Bit on me jeans.

Get it off, Tigger! Get it off!

Go for it! An' he's up on his hind legs. Lapping it up!

Bloody hell, that tickles. Well gentle, though. That's enough, boy, that's enough!

You'll have to get down.

He's not happy. Wants some more. Wants to suck on Eddie's chocolate sack!

Horner not looking happy either. Lighten up, bro. It's not cruel. It's Tigger's tasty treat time!

Yeah, let's crank this up. Come on. This'll be an all-time great. These are the best ideas. Spontaneous. Phones out. Get recording. Come on! On yer feet. In a line with yer plums out. Come on, get up. And you, Horner, soft cunt. Looks like you've been the one training him. Either you or your old man. Come on, Steve's done it. Good lad, Dildo. Come on quick, before your old man comes back in. Fuckin' get up here an' get some milkshake on yer nads.

Right, we'll all line up with plums out an' get Tigger to go down the line. One by one. Play some Christmas music on the stereo. All wear those stupid Christmas hats. And smile. I'll pan down.

You go first, Steve. That's it. In line. I'll film. Got longest record time on my phone.

Course I'll do it.

You know I'll fuckin' do it!

Have I ever let you down?

Have I ever fuckin' bottled out?

I'm the only one you can fuckin' trust. That's why I should go fuckin' last.

OK!

We're rolling.

Good lad, Steve. Tigger knows what to do! Tickles, dunnit?

He's loving it. Chocolate or no. The little fucker sure as hell wants to make sure he an't missed a single drop.

Come on, Tigger, time moving on. Need to get all the boys in.

Leave 'im alone.

LEAVE 'IM ALONE, BOY!

Come on.

He's not having it. He wants Steve's knackers!

Look, even when I pull on his collar.

He's straining and growling. Come on, boy, there's more next door!

Fuck me, he's a feisty fucker! Yanked him really hard that time. Still back in there.

He needs a smack on the nose. Try not to catch you, Steve.
Wooow!
He looks angry now. He's well pissed.
Snarling like a bugger. Better keep hold of his collar . . .
Shit, slippy fingers.
Fuck me.
He's back onto Steve's bollocks.
Dopey cunt just stood there.
But he's not licking now.
Sharp little teeth, angry growl. Steve making a strange noise.
Loud and high-pitched.
I'm pulling hard on the dog.
He won't let go.
Biting and snarling.
What's that spurting?
Blood?
Spurting all over.
Oh my God.
Lads not laughing now. Apart from Dildo. But not really
laughing. Sort of hysterical scream.
And they're shouting at me now.
But I'm trying to pull the dog off.
I'm pulling as hard as I can.
But his scrotum seems to be stretching. Teeth locked right
into the skin. And I'm pulling and pulling. Got hold of the dog
like a rugby ball.
That must hurt.
Skin round his bollocks stretching.
Not any more.
They've split open.
Let go, Tigger!
I'm working on the little fucker's jaws now.
Fuckin' bit my finger! Sharp as fuck!
Must be hurting Steve's bollocks.

His face is turning white. He looks faint.

I can't carry on tugging. I'm gonna rip his testicles right off. I can see them! The tubes! The dog's got one in its mouth.

Need to think! THINK!

Quick as anything I drop the dog.

Steve's still standing up somehow. Tigger's suspended in the air hanging from Steve's shredded scrotum.

Others just standing there gawping.

But I'm onto it.

Grab the vase of flowers and wang the water over the dog. Proper soak the little fucker.

But it's let go at last.

It still looks nippy, but not for long after I twat it hard with the vase on the head.

Now Steve's collapsed.

Some cunt call 999.

Take it easy, Steve. You'll be fine.

What's that?

On the floor?

Get it away from the dog in case it wakes up.

Is that his bollock?

IS THAT HIS BOLLOCK?

Put it somewhere.

I don't know.

Fuckin' pick it up.

It's your mate's bollock!

Ice. Put it in some ice.

Steve, you'll be fine.

Ambulance on its way.

There's only one of your nads fallen out. Your other one's fine. I think.

Hospital will get that straight back in. No problem.

We got it in ice.

You got in ice, right?

In there, Horner?
You dick!
Not that ice! That's half-full of whiskey!
You'll pickle his bollock!
You daft cunt!

SUMMER 2009
PREGNANT

Laura bent double, panting and gasping for air. The man she loved spoke firmly but with encouragement.

~Breathe deeply, but try and bring it back to normal.

Stan came up behind her and rubbed her back.

~Try and stand up straight and keep walking. You've got forty seconds before you go again. You can do this. The next one's always the hardest. You're doing so well.

Laura did as her boyfriend suggested. She walked along the track with her hands behind her head, her breathing gradually slowing as she gathered her composure.

~This is a massive effort. Keep it going on these last two. Use your arms more in the last hundred when your legs get tired.

Laura nodded and spat on the floor, too exhausted to waste any effort speaking. As she walked she scanned the four hundred metre track. The old-fashioned cinders crunched under her feet as she prepared herself for the final two laps. The steep grass banking around the perimeter was deserted, apart from a father and son fiddling with a large model aeroplane in the top corner near the back straight.

~Ten seconds . . . five, four, three, two, one.

Right on cue Laura set off on her ninth four hundred metre lap: Stan was only allowing her sixty seconds between each one. As she set off round the first bend he looked at her in admiration. West Yorkshire Police had given her very favourable feedback in her application, the only stumbling block being the agility course, which involved turning and running against the clock. She had narrowly exceeded the maximum time allowed, and it was proving difficult to gain the extra speed and spring to achieve the target. Nevertheless the police recruitment officer agreed to approve her application on the proviso that she met the required standards, and she was due to start her basic training in less than seven days.

Stan researched training methods for speed endurance and put her through her paces. She took to it without question. When she finished this next lap he decided he would call her Laura Lionheart. She deserved it. He was pleased.

As Laura headed down the back straight Stan saw that the father and son he had noticed earlier were still tooling around with a model aeroplane. There were vast unoccupied areas to the sides of the running track and he wondered why they didn't take it there. The clumsy-looking plane floundered just a few feet into the air before crashing nose first into the grass bank.

As Laura battled her way over the finishing line for the ninth time, Stan jogged with her. He checked his stopwatch and saw that she was only running a second or two slower than her first effort, confirming what he suspected: that she was running just as hard on the last laps as she had on the first.

—Keep going, Laura Lionheart. You can do this. One more and we're done. I'm so proud of you. Those pigs had better let you in after this.

He lovingly wiped her running nose and held her water bottle to her lips. She took a small sip. She was breathing at an alarming rate. Wheezing a little.

Stan was a little concerned. She had worked tremendously hard, but he didn't want to overwork her and make her ill. But at the same time he didn't want her to feel they had pulled up short of the target.

He whispered in her ear.

—Take your time on this one. Just get round. I won't start the stopwatch this time. One more and we're done. I'll give you a rub-down and make tea.

As she set off on her final lap he clicked the stopwatch to start.

Father and son were beginning to have a little more success.

Plane climbing.

Girl running.

After a record flight time of around ten seconds, the plane actually cleared the banking and made it onto the outside lane of the running track. The buzz of its sputtering engine came to an abrupt halt.

Stan glanced at his stopwatch and noted that Laura was again keeping pace with her earlier times. After a hundred and fifty metres she was still striding. Still battling. Stan felt a lump in his throat.

From his position on the finishing line, Stan saw the small child scamper down the banking to pick up his model plane. Its wingspan was wider than he was tall, but he struggled back to his dad.

Dad fiddled with the propeller and the engine span back into life once again.

Child eagerly waiting.

Dad keen to build on success.

~Don't fucking launch it now, you dick.

Laura struggling fifty metres away from the final corner.

Child excited.

Dad pleased to be making progress. Being a good dad. Doing things with his kid.

Stan watching.

Laura approaching the final corner.

Dad standing, arm cocked.

Child wide eyed.

Stan biting his lip.

Stan knew Laura was working so hard that she would be focused on getting round the last two bends. Concentrating on getting one foot in front of the other.

Heart pounding.

Lungs heaving.

Legs screaming.

Throat burning.

Then Dad launched it.

~Fuck me dead.

The plane sailed into the air. Engine buzzing proudly on its best ever take-off.

The excited child clapped his hands.

Dad was even more excited, but managed to stay quiet.

The plane was easily going to be in the air for longer than ten seconds.

The plane was still in the air when it cleared the banking.

The plane was still in the air when it flew over lane one and two.

The plane was still in the air when it hit Laura.

But she had managed to take evasive action, and it only hit her on the shin.

And she swore.

In front of the child.

—Language!

He gestured towards his son.

Laura bravely stumbled on.

Then Dad said something else. Not as loud.

Stan couldn't hear exactly, but one word might have been 'fat'. And one word might have been 'bum'.

Whatever it was, the child laughed.

Stan thinking.

Laughed.

Stan running.

Laughed at Laura Lionheart on her final lap. Of ten. With only one minute's rest between each one.

Because she wanted to get into the police. To make a difference.

And she would be great, because she was brainy and kind. Determined and tough and well organised. And beautiful.

And someone flew a plane at her.

Stan thinking and running.

Why couldn't they wait?

Stan could be quite placid. He didn't look for conflict; it sometimes came looking for him.

There was a small child present. It was an accident. No major harm was done.

But the cunt could have taken the plane anywhere else. Acres of open space. No one else around. Four football pitches to the side of the track. But this was where the banking was at its highest. Best place to launch a plane.

But the cunt could have waited.

Waited till Laura had finished her last lap.

Or at least until she had gone round the corner.

Stan thinking and running and shouting.

He was excited. His child had been disappointed when the plane didn't fly. But now it was improving. Dad was getting the hang of it. He wanted to build on his momentum. There was a gust of wind rushing up the banking. He was a good dad, and they were there first.

But the cunt shouldn't have made a comment. It could have been more serious. It could have hit her head or her knee. Anyone would swear. Even in front of a small child.

He couldn't be seen to condone that sort of language. And he didn't want his son to think it was his fault.

A line had been crossed.

He insulted Laura. Maybe. The kid laughed.

He should be sorry.

He would be sorry.

Cheeky little bastard.

Stan thinking and no longer running.

Stan stamping and plane cracking.

Wings snapping.

Body bending.

Nose crunching.

Kid wailing.

Dad charged aggressively down the banking full of bravado, hoping Stan would run away or at least stop. But Stan didn't move as he reduced the plane to splinters.

--I hope you're gonna pay for that, pal!

Dad looked a bit pathetic as he failed to follow through his initial charge.

--Of all the places you could have gone! Of all the times you could have set it off! You set it off while she was running round the corner! You dick! Am I shite gonna pay for it!

Laura stepped between the two men.

--Look, you nearly knocked my head off, mate. You really should have thought about where you were going to fly it. It was going to get damaged anyway slamming onto the running track like that.

Laura's tone was calmer, and Stan stopped wrecking the plane.

Dad started to salvage what pieces he could. He was defeated, but he had to have one last side-swipe.

--Don't know why you're running. Not doing you much good.

Laura had had a lifetime of comments like this, since she had been bullied at school for being fat. They were less frequent now. She knew she wasn't slim but she had a healthy shape. The scales told her. The mirror told her. Her running times told her. Her friends and family told her. The lustful eyes of men in the pub told her. Her self-esteem restored, occasional comments no longer bothered her. She put them down to jealousy or to men scratching around for an insult because they had been rejected.

It was different for Stan.

His line had been crossed.

Again.

Soon he had Dad by the throat, driving him backwards so he stumbled and fell onto the banking.

Dad's face began to turn red as Stan tightened his grip, shouting at him to take his words back as his head banged repeatedly on the grass.

Dad was fighting for air to breathe, never mind apologise.

Laura surveyed the scene and knew it was wrong. Criminal damage and assault. And in front of a distressed young child who was being made to witness his father being throttled.

But as she watched she loved Stan more than ever. Loved him because he was standing up for her. After years of torment on school buses and wishing someone would give her a break. Waiting for someone to fight her corner. Wanting someone to admit he was her friend in front of the old kids or the cool kids. Now there was someone. Someone who would help her. Train with her. Stand up for her. Fight for her.

Love her.

She knew it was wrong but she burned with love for him. So she didn't stop him.

That was left to the kid.

The boy watched in horror as his father's face turned a shade of red he had never seen before. Then he rushed down, crying and shouting, and hugged his dad's leg.

The sight of the stricken child brought Stan to his senses, and he let go. The tears of father and son made him a little guilty.

Stan felt Laura tugging his arm.

~Come on.

They made their exit towards the car park.

Laura held his hand tightly and rubbed his back, as his breathing began to slow down in the same way her own had minutes earlier.

~Thanks for that. That idiot needed teaching a lesson.

Laura's hand strayed from his back to his buttocks.

Stan felt better. The early signs of guilt were washed away as she gave her approval.

He smiled back, looking into her blue eyes.

--I love you.

She was speechless for a moment, but held him even tighter as if to say that the feeling was mutual.

Laura, not for the first time that evening, began to breathe a little deeper, but this time it was because of the sexual energy building up inside her.

Stan felt her circling his buttocks softly with her hand. As they crossed the car park she slowly but firmly moved her index finger towards his scrotum.

They drove home in silence, with Laura gently rubbing his crotch and feeling his hardness swelling. By the time they were inside the flat he was on her. They embraced passionately, gasping for air and tearing at one another's clothes. There was a possibility that Laura's flatmate might return home at any time, but they ignored this.

Firmly, almost violently, Stan pushed Laura against the dining room wall. He caressed her breasts and hips as she let out little gasps and moans while pulling him towards her, spurring him on, inviting him in.

In a flash he spun her round and forced her backwards onto the dining table.

She perched on the edge of the table, moist and breathless, her eyes blazing with lust and passion. In one swift movement he yanked down her cycling shorts and knickers. She leaned backwards, sending place mats and sauce bottles crashing to the floor.

She opened her legs, revealing the hidden fruits of her neatly trimmed bush.

Not caring.

Yearning.

Burning with love for him.

Desperate to be penetrated.

As Stan's own tracksuit bottoms and pants hit the floor, his half-nazi sprang into full salute.

In a moment of learned routine and responsibility, he paused the surging sexual tidal wave and began to fumble around on the floor.

Where were they?

Floor?

Wallet?

In the car?

Full salute waning.

Laura impatient.

~Just fucking take me!

I want you inside me!

Now!

Fuck me!

Hard!

COPPERS

Eddie, Steve and Horner sat on a bench in Leeds town centre carefully watching the two female police officers. Horner's nose was almost back to normal thanks to some skilful surgery. Steve's scrotum was an ugly mess, but the doctors had managed to salvage the testicle that was still attached and said it should be able to do its job. With persistent persuasion, Eddie had managed to convince everyone that everything was back to normal, and outwardly at least that is how they behaved.

The policewomen were about fifteen yards away from them in the crowded square. They were bending over a down and out who was sitting on the floor with his head bent to his knees. Eddie couldn't decide if he was a drunk, a beggar, a criminal or a combination of all three. Whichever, the two officers seemed to be giving him an extremely hard time.

Eddie caught a glimpse of the man's eyes as they rolled around his head. It seemed to pain him to be awake, and he was incapable of focusing on anything for more than a second or two. One of the policewomen had wandered a few paces away from the stricken man to speak into her radio. The other was giving the tramp a stern lecture, accompanied by a vigorous round of finger-wagging and pointing. Eddie thought that she looked extremely self-righteous, and began to feel good about what he was about to do. Not that he'd ever felt too bad about doing it.

~Right. Let's do this thing. For fuck's sake don't hang about once you've got the footage. Get away sharpish in different directions. And if you get caught don't say you know the other two. Just say you were filming the bum.

~We know what we're doing. It's not like we've never done this before.

~OK. But remember where we meet. Fifteen minutes. No sooner. Right. Pass me the merchandise.

Steve looked both ways before sliding the 'merchandise' along the bench. Eddie scooped it up and held it one hand while the phone cameramen took to their positions.

Eddie did not decide which of the two he was going to target before making his move. It would be whoever was in the most convenient position. As it happened, the one with the radio blocked the path between Eddie and the finger-wagger, so she was the one who copped it.

Eddie pressed the 'custard pie' firmly into her face, and turned and fled before she realised what was happening. The custard pie was simply half a can of squirty cream on a paper plate, but it had the desired effect: to make a mess of her face and uniform.

What happened next rather surprised Eddie. By now he had a wealth of experience of this sort of situation, and he knew that most people remained frozen to the spot.

But she wiped her face as best she could in a single gesture and gave chase for all she was worth. The finger-wagger had stopped talking, but she remained with the tramp and watched open-mouthed.

Eddie could tell from the noises the policewoman was making that she was running at maximum effort. He was on his toes, and even though he hadn't yet reached three-quarter pace he was still able to stay comfortably ahead. He expected her to give up when she realised the cause was hopeless, but she stayed with him for a good hundred yards, sidestepping pedestrians and negotiating kerbs. As Eddie rounded a corner he almost twisted his ankle avoiding a bike that had been chained to a lamppost. He decided it was time to put her out of her misery and make a clean escape before something went wrong. He relaxed his fingers and jaw and began to pump his arms as he accelerated to full speed.

The wind rushed past his ears as he picked his knees up high. He knew after a few seconds she would have to give up the ghost, and after about ten he allowed himself to glance behind him. He was relieved to see that he was correct: she was floundering along some distance behind, apparently bent double in exhaustion. Eddie headed for the meeting point, excitedly anticipating the latest footage.

2009

JUSTICE

As Laura strode along the Headrow in Leeds town centre she felt a strong sense of pride that she had to fight not to show. She was proud of her success in the lengthy recruitment process. She was determined not to look like another arrogant copper, and was genuinely pleased to be serving the public. It was her very first time on the beat. She hoped that somewhere along the line she would make a real difference.

Laura was fully aware of the hostile attitude that large parts of the community had towards the police, but her faith in human nature made her believe that she could go a small way towards changing it, if she treated people with respect and decency. Of course many more experienced officers believed her to be incredibly green and naïve. She knew that. She even accepted that after a few years on the job she would probably change her attitudes herself. But at the moment she was doing what she had always done, which was follow her gut instinct.

For these reasons Laura was happy as she patrolled Leeds town centre. Even her experienced mentor, Emma Butcher, couldn't spoil anything.

PC Butcher was ferociously ambitious and determined to carve out a reputation as a hard woman. She didn't want anyone thinking that because she was female she would be soft on the low-lifes she encountered daily. Considerate and caring never gets anyone promoted, she told herself, and no one who met her would have put her in that category.

When she first heard she was to partner Laura she wasn't too dismayed. She feared Laura might be a bit of a drip at first, but such was her confidence in her own ability that she felt she could easily whip her into shape.

The two policewomen had a relatively quiet morning. As they rounded a corner that took them onto a busy pedestrianised street Laura quickly scanned the area, as she had been taught to do. Her attention was drawn to a man in his late thirties who was moving differently from everyone else. Apart from those who had stopped to sit and chat, most people were moving in straight lines from shop to shop. This individual was moving in circles, from person to person, walking with them and talking to them, although hardly any of them looked at him. PC Butcher had spotted him too.

The man became more and more frantic in his movements. After being ignored by one couple he let out an incoherent cry of frustration, staggered back to an empty bench and slumped on it, beating his fist on the woodwork. The two policewomen were looking at the same man, but each saw a different person.

PC Butcher saw a blight on the town centre. She saw somebody who wanted to take from others without being prepared to work. Somebody who made the streets ugly and unpleasant. The sort of person who would harm the town's economy if allowed to operate unchallenged. She saw the person who lied to passers-by and harassed them into handing over their money. She knew any money he had would be spent on heroin or crack cocaine. If he overdosed, it would be the hard-working police, doctors or nurses who would have to sort him out, when they could be looking after more deserving people. Most of all she saw him as a waster who would now waste her time. She wanted to investigate terrorism and organised crime, and he was someone who represented everything she wanted to get away from.

PC Laura Brock saw someone in desperate need. She wondered how the man's self-esteem had been so damaged that he had to beg for money. She wanted to know what talents and abilities he had, and how they could be harnessed for the better. More importantly, as he began to roll around on the bench and slump onto the pavement, she wondered if he was in need of medical attention.

Not surprisingly, the policewomen's approaches differed starkly. PC Butcher was the first to speak to the man. She lectured him on his behaviour and spelt out the risk to his liberty if it continued. She stood upright, and occasionally he rolled his head round to look at her, slowly opening and closing his eyes but not showing any signs that he understood.

Careful not to interrupt her colleague, Laura waited for a pause before kneeling down to speak to the man. She tried to coax his name out of him, but unless he was christened 'fuck off bitch' she was not successful.

Laura noticed open sores on his face and neck, and

heard that he was wheezing badly with quick and shallow breaths; each was more grating than the last. She hesitated no longer, stepping away from the man to radio for medical assistance.

As she began to speak she was suddenly aware of someone swiftly approaching her. She turned to look, and the sensations of pain and wetness hit the side of her head. For a few seconds she staggered, dazed. Her instincts told her she had been assaulted, but it took her a few moments to piece together the details. Her face, hair and top of her uniform were covered in cream or foam, and a plastic paper plate dropped forlornly to the ground. The pain was short-lived, little more than a gentle slap.

Some passers-by shrieked and gasped; others laughed. The homeless man continued to struggle and wheeze, oblivious.

Laura's assailant turned on his heels and strode away.

The second she regained her composure, confusion was replaced by rage. Laura cleared her face and eyes and was running for all she was worth. For a short time she was convinced that she was catching up, and she began to think about what she would do when she ran him down. But when he glanced over his shoulder and saw she was giving chase he seemed to move up a gear. His long, loping action seemed to take him another twenty yards clear.

Laura gritted her teeth. Determined not to give up.

He swerved athletically round a corner, not seeming to slow down. Laura attempted to do the same, and was slightly off balance as she avoided a bike and tried to straighten up. She saw the bollards in front of her in time to side-step them, but her feet were a split second behind her brain. Her ankle gave way and she felt herself plummeting downwards. She didn't reach the pavement as her fall was broken by the bollard.

It thudded into her abdomen.

Laura lay stricken on the ground. Fight as she may, she could not draw air into her lungs. She wanted to cry but all she could manage were faint high-pitched gasps. Eventually she managed to draw in enough air to stop herself passing out. Even though she wished she could. She felt a sharp, intense pain in her stomach alongside dizziness and nausea. As each took hold she longed for another. Seven pedestrians passed by before an elderly lady tried to make her more comfortable. She held her hand and stroked her face to take her hair away from her mouth.

In foetal position, curled on the pavement, Laura could not express her gratitude. But at least she didn't feel alone, and she squeezed the old lady's hand as tightly as her broken spirit would allow.

A short while later Laura became aware of her colleague. The kindly and maternal voice and touch that had comforted her were replaced by an impatient, authoritative monologue. She heard her name spoken sharply amid a barrage of commands and instructions. PC Butcher urged her to respond.

But she wasn't OK. She couldn't breathe properly.

Although she couldn't quite embrace unconsciousness, Laura closed her eyes tightly and tried to shut out the noise of the city.

She lost track of time, but was vaguely aware of medical staff and a mask over her face. The next few hours passed in a haze of lights, doctors, curtains and trolleys. Then she was spoken to.

The sedation was wearing off, and the procedures and probing had ended some time before. Although the pain still throbbed inside, its cutting edge was dulled. For the first time since the incident Laura felt almost ready to rejoin the real world.

None of what she heard surprised her.

Nasty blow to the abdomen.

Internal bleeding.

Bruising.

Lengthy rest and recuperation.

Drugs to prevent infection.

One cracked rib.

Very painful, but should make a full recovery.

Then the tone of the doctor changed.

Unfortunately . . .

Unable to . . .

Inevitable that a trauma like this would cause . . .

Hopeful that future fertility won't be affected . . .

But on this occasion we were unable to save the pregnancy.

We're sorry, Ms Brock, but we must inform you that you've suffered a miscarriage.

It didn't register at first. Laura couldn't take it in. She repeated the words over and over before they had any impact. And then it was a second body blow.

Had she known?

Had she suspected?

How could she?

Just ignore . . . ?

They all hit her at once.

Realisation.

Pain.

Confirmation.

Loss.

Anger.

Hatred.

Guilt.

Panic.

And other emotions that there simply weren't words to describe.

She didn't take the news well. She began to writhe and weep. She clawed at her hair and dug the heels of her thumbs hard into her eyes.

This made her insides hurt even more, but even this didn't still her. She had never fully understood the self-harmers she had come across.

Now she did.

Even in that darkest moment she knew she would heal. That time and hard work and experience would bring her through. In the same way that she had come through all the other trials and tribulations of her life.

And compared with the next person to hear the news she coped rather well.

PART TWO
THE UNIVERSITY YEARS

FRESHERS' MONTH

I can sort of understand Freshers' Week.
Everybody dressed up and pissed and fucking about and that.
Breaks the ice.
Gets people involved.
Meet new people.
Too many new people.

Some of these cunts act like they're best mates already. Only known each other five minutes.

That's why I need some time alone. Just me, the Yorkshire Post and a pint of bitter. Just helps me take it all in. Get it straight in my own mind.

And this fancy dress shite is getting right out of hand. It's virtually every day.

Take these dickheads for instance.

It's 2.30 on a Wednesday afternoon in the Skyrac, and there's a set of twenty-odd of 'em dressed as golfers, doing some sort of pub golf bollocks.

Some look half-pissed already. A mixture of lads and birds.

Some tidy birds as well. They're mouthing off about hockey and rugby. Some rugby club cunt probably organised a joint do with the hockey birds. Hoping to get a shag out of it.

There's that ginger bird Kim from my politics module. Seemed a good sort in the seminars.

Friendly.

Not chatting now, though.

Sort of half-acknowledges me, then carries on laughing at some Cockney twat banging on about how hammered he and his mates were last night.

Yeah, fucking hilarious. Never heard anything like that before.

I realise I'm looking at the cunt and he clocks me.

Only for a moment.

He carries on talking shite and fit Kim carries on laughing and tossing her hair.

Why are fit birds such shite judges of character?

The Cockney cunt is wearing a Pringle tank top, checked trousers and a golf cap.

But there's nothing under his top so he can show off his muscles.

Weasel.

'Cos you see plenty of golfers dressed like that.

He looks over again.

I forget I've been staring at him.

He clocks me again and looks a little agitated.

He carries on working Kim, but his hand is tapping the table where he talks.

He stands up.

Confident.

Shouts over to the rest of the dickhead pub golfers.

Starts organising some 'court session' or some such bollocks.

Pints are lined up.

Tables are dragged around, getting right up my earhole.

Seems as though he's appointed himself high court judge.

Now he's coming over.

He's polite but he asks me to move.

Explains how he needs the bench I'm sitting on for the court case.

It's the best spot for the judge to address everybody from.

It seems like a reasonable request to all the other dickheads.

But me and the cunt know what it's about.

He thinks I was eyeballing him, so he had to get one over.

'Cos he thinks I'm an easy target.

Some loser reading his paper, when he's got his gang and all these birds.

I could move quite easily.

No big deal.

No one would think any the less.

But I hate cunts like this, so I stand my ground.

Big mistake.

The cunt carries on with his court case, sitting right next to me.

Talking shite about misdemeanours and heinous crimes like being sick and getting knobs out on the dance floor.

And everyone is laughing and sucking up to the cunt.

Worse still, he keeps trying to involve me.

I start to feel like a dick, just sitting there pretending to read my paper.

And the cunt calls me the 'clerk of the court' and 'my learned friend'.

And all the golf cunts are laughing along.

Laughing at me.

Even that Kim.

No one stands up to him.

They're all happy to kiss his arse, pleased it's me and not them.

I try to think of some comment that'll put the cunt down.

But my mind is blank.

And there are at least twenty of them who'll laugh at anything he says.

I consider just walking away, but worry I'll look like even more of a tool.

So I sit there.

Detached.

Taking it all.

But storing it.

Because I'll use it.

His time will come.

And so will theirs.

Then I think I'm not gonna be able to take any more.

I'll be forced to beat a retreat.

But suddenly the Cockney twat is up and flapping about.

Telling every cunt to drink up. There's one little fattish lad just got a fresh pint. The Cockney twat's making him down it in one. You can tell the lad don't want to.

But Cockney twat has got everyone chanting.

Chug. Chug. Chug.

The fat lad does his best, but he looks like he's gonna fall short.

So Cockney twat makes out he's helping him.

Tips the bottom of the glass higher.

But the lad can't take it. Spills the pint down his stupid yellow golf top. Then the Cockney's making him turn the pint upside down. So the last bit of pissy Stella is dribbling through his hair. And that's what the Cockney wanted. Someone else fat, wet and stinking of stale booze.

And I hate him even more. Treating his mates like that.

All of sudden he's all over him. Telling him he loves him, giving high fives, telling him he's a fucking legend an' all that shite.

Then he's back over to me. He's saying he's sorry for disturbing me and knows every man should be able to enjoy a quiet pint, saying he likes to do the same. He's straightening the tables and wiping up odd bits of spilled beer. He offers me his hand. There's no one really taking any notice now.

I've softened up a bit. In a moment of weakness I take it. He shakes it normally.

Says no hard feelings. Loud and clear.

Then he squeezes it.

Harder.

His hand slips down so he's got my middle knuckles.

Now he's crushing my fingers.

He leans in and whispers, sneering.

Tells me I'm one weird fuck.

I feel something surging through my body.

Whatever it is, I'm high on it.

I'm like a volcano.

But I don't erupt like some do.

I've never lost it and lashed out like some do.

But the pressure this time is immense.

I can feel it wanting to burst out behind my eyes.

He makes the same mistake so many others have when I feel like this.

Thinks I'm almost crying.

And he tells the fat kid so I can hear.

And when he's gone one tear does escape.

But that's all that's gone.

One fucking tear.

The rest is stored inside.

Bubbling.

And it will be unleashed.

Make no fucking mistake.

BRAVEHEART

Ben had been looking forward to the Braveheart night for weeks. He had planned for it meticulously. The first fifteen had Lincoln Uni at home, and they were shite. The girls' hockey were at home too, and he arranged it so they started early and could watch the lads' rugby. There was a very good chance he would score a couple of tries, which would help the girls get moistened up and ready for the pub crawl.

Things were going better than planned.

The Leeds Met forwards had ground down their opponents in the first half, but were only leading by one score. The hockey girls had arrived for the second half, wild hair and make-up, with tartan mini-skirts. Ben had been keeping himself nice and fresh, just leaning on in rucks and mauls and hardly bothering to scrummage. With the girls there he was ready to take centre stage. He began to make devastating surges through the fragile Lincoln defence, crashing over for two tries in quick succession.

~GO BENNY!
~GO BENNY!

The girls chanted and pranced around, trying to keep warm as they sipped bottles of cider. Ben pretended to be indifferent, focusing on the match, but the next scrum he found himself packing down with a semi on.

Before he knew it they were in the SU bar.

He had been working extra hard in the gym lately, ready for a night like this. He wore a kilt and sandals and a raggy black singlet, with plenty of holes to show his pecs and abs. He wore small touches of blue make-up, but had arranged for one of the girls from beauty therapy to do it properly so he didn't look like an idiot, like some of the others. He had borrowed a large theatrical silver sword so everyone knew he was William Wallace. The drinking games and forfeits were ready. All he had to do was lap it up and enjoy. They ordered taxis to take them to Arcadia, the bar that started their Wednesday evening Braveheart pub crawl. Ben was in the highest of high spirits.

An hour or so later Ben emerged from Arcadia, flanked on either side by a tartan-clad hockey girl. In the build-up to Christmas Otley Road was awash with students, most of them in fancy dress. Ben wanted to make sure his posse caught the most attention, and he had acquired a small loudhailer.

~Onward my brothers and sisters! Follow William Wallace to the Skyrac. We must repel the English. Twenty-four pints in the Skyrac will defeat their armies!

He charged up the road, sword pointing ahead, with his followers in tow. Some girls at the back struggled to keep up.

~Dig deep, sisters! We must run between each

hostelry to evade the marauding English cavalry!

He jabbed them up the backside with his sword as they yelped and giggled, gradually breaking into a run.

With about a hundred yards to go to the doors of the Skyrac all eyes were upon them. Superheroes, people tied together, toga parties and a couple of smurfs all turned to look at the noisy highlanders of Leeds Met rugby and hockey teams.

Not many people had noticed the battered old pick-up truck with four masked men crouched in the back, waiting at the traffic lights.

They soon would.

There was a faint red reflection from the barrels of their guns. It changed to amber, then to green.

MASSACRE

OK, this is it, boys. Lock and fucking load. Remember, avoid civilians. But any fancy dress cunt is a legitimate target. According to intelligence reports our primary targets are wearing Highland-style Scottish shite or some bollocks like that. If we see them they get it big time. Good luck!

The lights change and then we're into it.

At first I think I'm going to bottle it.

Then the others start firing and I've got no choice.

These two smurfs are at a cashpoint.

My first couple of shots hit the screen where he's just put his card.

He turns to face me, so I give him a burst in his stupid blue chest.

Glad I'm wearing this balaclava.

He goes down and his mate tries to run away.

I turn my attention to him but my shots are arcing wide.

The lucky bastard manages to escape round the corner.

The first smurf is on his knees now, calling me a fucking wanker.

I give him five more shots, two of them in the neck, and he soon shuts up.

I look to the other side of Otley Road, where the others have been giving it to these dickheads in pyjamas. They've got their legs tied together like a three legged race.

The bastards have no chance of escape, so I take pity on them – only firing a couple of volleys at two saps waving their arms about.

A bit further down the road these super-hero knobs have clocked us and worked out what's happening.

Fucking cowards.

They're under benches and behind bins, but we're soon on them.

As we drive past the cunt dressed as Batman climbs on the bench.

He's suddenly grown some bollocks when he thinks we've gone.

He's beating his chest and banging on about his costume getting ruined and how much it cost.

I give my orders for a U-turn.

I'm not taking shite like that.

Fucking zero tolerance.

This is my time. Batman or no.

He shuts up sharp enough, with four automatic weapons trained on him.

He stands there on the bench, palms up.

Apologetic.

Defensive.

Trying to reason.

So we give him it.

All of us.

Forty or fifty shots at least, till he's back under the bench and looking a right mess.

I look down Otley Road again.

Then I clock them.

Primary target.

I shout and point.

The pick-up begins to move forward, but I bang on the roof for it to stop.

We all jump out.

Begin to walk.

Slowly.

This has to be savoured.

The Cockney cunt stands out a mile.

He's still playing the big man, even now.

Got this big sword and holding it like he's some sort of ninja.

Still trying to front it up.

So I shoot him in the face point blank.

I know we talked about avoiding eyes, but this guy pushed it too far.

It caught him in the lip and nose, and blood streams from his nostril, mixing with the turquoise.

He looks well shocked but he's still eyeballing me.

A quick burst to the legs and he's back on the deck, where he belongs.

Next thing I know fit Kim comes storming over, looking well stressed out.

Her tartan kilt can't be more than seven inches long.

Reckon she thinks she's safe just 'cos she looks sexy.

Looks like she's gonna come and try and slap me.

Can't stand birds who think they can do what they want just 'cos they're fit.

Fit Kim gets one in each tit for her troubles.

She screams like fuck.

I know these paintballs hurt but she starts to sound a bit psycho.

Hysterical like.

Probably 'cos her top's ruined.

One or two others are screaming an' all.

My instinct tells me it could be time to leave.

So I give the signal and we're back in the pick-up, speeding away.

We jump the lights and get lucky as we bezz it round the corner.

There's a group of nuns walking onto Otley Road.

I fire my last remaining ammo into the middle of them.

It occurs to me that there's actually a convent somewhere round here.

I didn't see them clearly, but at this time of night they'd have to be pissed-up fancy dress student cunts.

Surely to God.

2010
BELFAST

Eddie scanned the itinerary and was excited in a way he hadn't been for a long time. He was genuinely interested. He looked forward to questioning and talking to real people who had been involved in the peace process in Northern Ireland. The Orangemen, Sinn Fein politicians, former members of the RUC, current members of the police service, the DUP, the PUP, the SDLP and the Ulster Unionists. They were all there. Some in organised forums at Belfast University, but others in their own back-yard. They would be going into the Orange Lodge in the morning, and the Shamrock Club on the Falls Road in the evening. Eddie reckoned there couldn't have been many people alive who had gone to both on the same day.

Eddie savoured the excitement, lying back on his bed and closing his eyes. Some on his course would regard this as a bit of an extra piss-up, no doubt, but he was determined to get much more out of it. For a few moments he felt as he did when he was a child and told he was going somewhere special or exciting, like Shibden Park in the snow. There was no need for an adrenalin hit. There was no need to create a scene or think up a new scam. The trip was complete as it was. There was even a mild love interest – that dark-haired Linda from the Isle of Man. It had everything, and for a few minutes Eddie tasted innocence once again.

But only for a few minutes.

Eddie was like an alcoholic admiring the different colas in the Co-op. It was only a matter of time before he rounded the corner and loaded his trolley with spirits.

Yes, the trip was a good one. Good enough to stand alone and be memorable. It was a once in a lifetime chance. It must have taken a hell of a lot of organising, what with travel, youth hostels and audiences with so many groups in such a short time. And it had all been offered to him on a plate for a measly £145.

The thing was, it was such a fertile environment for top-quality footage.

Eddie remembered the Bruce Willis film where he walks round Harlem with a sign that reads 'I HATE NIGGERS'. An idea had begun to grow in his mind. The adrenalin had started to flow, mildly tinged with guilt and fear of the consequences. Eddie was learning to deal with these as he began to accept the inevitability of his ideas. They came to him through no fault of his own and, addicted as he was, resistance was futile.

SHANKHILL

Eddie loved being in a car with his mates. When they were all together like this it usually meant they were on a lads' weekend away. Either ready to go or reminiscing about the previous night's frolics. Any gaps in conversation were filled with classic Arctic Monkeys or Kings of Leon tracks, the music that fuelled their adrenalin and celebrated their debauchery.

On this occasion things were slightly different. For a start they were in a Transit van. Secondly the tension was higher than it had ever been before. They all knew they weren't risking trouble with their parents or even the law. They weren't risking a bit of pain. They were risking a serious kicking. Or maybe worse.

Eddie lay in the back of the van going through his stretches. If nothing else he was ready to run. The pulse in his neck and the dancing in his stomach told him he could run like the wind if he had to. When they stopped at some traffic lights Eddie saw a huge mural on the side of an end terrace in which four masked men stood proudly with rifles at the ready. Above them a brightly painted Union Jack was emblazoned on the red brick, accompanied by thick black letters reading UVF. Eddie was sure the figure on the left was looking straight at him, Mona Lisa-style. He looked away, telling himself how ridiculous this was, but allowed himself a quick second glance.

The masked man was still observing him.

Eddie wondered how such a skilful artist had been recruited to paint such a mural, but this thought was overtaken by a longing to be back inside the van after the job was done, listening to the Kings again.

The van went through the traffic lights and turned left. After a minute or so it slowed, and came to a halt. Horner looked round from the driver's seat.

~OK, Eduardo. The time has come. The Shankhill Road.

~Right. Eddie's ready. And don't fuck about with the pick-up! Do what we fucking agreed.

~All right . . . It's your fucking idea. Don't do it if you're so bothered.

Eddie was a little put out and embarrassed. Not least because he was being caught on camera: Steve had started to film the build-up. Horner had started to become more assertive since his forced independence at university, and this sometimes caught Eddie by surprise.

~All right, all right. I trust you.

He reached forward to shake Horner's hand.

~It's just I'm a bit wound up by all this shit.

~Tell me about it! You've been shitting bricks all morning. I'll do it first if you want. I'm not bothered.

That would have been the ultimate climb-down. And Eddie wasn't even sure that Horner wasn't bluffing. With his new-found confidence he might well take up the mantle. And all the glory.

~Nah, fuck it. I'll be reet. See you in five.

And with that Eddie stepped out of the side door of the van, adorned in the Celtic shirt he had picked up on eBay. It had a small cigarette burn on the stomach and was slightly too tight, but it was capable of doing the job it had been bought for.

For the first hundred yards absolutely nothing happened. The intense adrenalin surge when he first stepped onto the street seemed to have been wasted. He was simply walking on his own along a Belfast pavement.

The first local to register his existence was a small child aged about three. His sisters, supposed to be looking after him, were practising a dance, leaving the infant as the only Loyalist to tackle the intruder.

~Fa bich!

~Fa bich!

Eddie knew he was being insulted; the child even gave his best attempt at a slap. This proved difficult as he was giving everything just to keep pace with Eddie's long nervous strides. Eddie wasn't sure if it was the Celtic shirt that had provoked this response, or whether it was the fact that he was a stranger. He reasoned that it was more than likely the child greeted everyone this way.

If nothing else the small boy drew more attention to Eddie. Curtains began to twitch as people began to wonder what the commotion was. Eddie suddenly focused that on the pavement he was very near to the houses' front doors, which would give him little opportunity to take evasive action if someone decided to burst out and have a pop at him. Eddie veered into the middle of the road and broke into a slow trot, which he calculated should be enough to see off his young tormenter.

Undeterred, the child began to run flat out, and also moved to step off the pavement. As he did so a car emerged around the corner fifty yards ahead. A sinister thought crossed Eddie's mind. Could it be thought he was deliberately leading young Protestants into the path of oncoming traffic?

He scarcely imagined the sort of punishment that would be meted out to someone who did that here. Especially someone dressed in a Celtic shirt. As the thought crossed his mind Eddie turned and scooped the child up, placing him safely back on the pavement.

The moment that Eddie touched him the child began to scream wildly, as though with some sharp pain. He began to hammer at Eddie with clenched fists, and between his sobs he screamed.

~FAT BICH! FABITCH!

A second thought occurred to Eddie. He had lured a child away from its sisters. He had been seen picking up a toddler. He had emerged from a van. He was wearing a Celtic shirt. He was more than likely suspected of being a Fenian child snatcher. The Transit sat waiting with engine running and door open. All he wanted now was a nice clean chase and some decent footage.

Suddenly the whole street seemed to burst into life. From the activity that erupted there must have been many watching ever since the van pulled into the street. The girls began screaming and running towards their brother. The driver of the vehicle ahead had stopped his car and was striding purposefully towards Eddie. Two youths emerged from a house and began swearing and shouting sectarian abuse. The noise crescendoed as more and more people added their voices to the threats. Eddie couldn't afford to hang about any longer. The chase was about to begin. He started to run.

His first obstacle was the man from the car. Having built up a head of steam, sidestepping him was relatively easy. It was not until he was really close that Eddie noticed the man was brandishing a heavy-looking spanner, with which he took a lusty swipe. It missed, but he felt it whirr past his face.

Eddie got right up on his toes and began to sprint for all he was worth. The near miss with the spanner focused his mind on survival. He knew it would take a top-class sprinter to catch him from behind, but was still wary because top-class sprinters have to live somewhere. In front of him people were emerging from houses and challenging him, causing him to step and swerve. Then objects began to rain down. At first it was small stones, then larger ones, then milk bottles. Eddie took a glancing blow from a stone to the head, and a heavier one to the ribs from a bottle, which smashed as it hit the ground. Eddie knew a full-blooded blow might bring him down, and he didn't want to think about the consequences. He had planned to milk the whole situation by playing the matador for the last bit of footage, but he wisely assessed the situation as too dangerous and headed straight for the Transit door.

As Eddie ran up, Horner jumped out to get a good shot of the mob and capture the dramatic picture of Eddie diving into the van from the outside. It was not until later that Eddie realised how daring this was, and how much more effective the pictures were. Horner was voluntarily putting himself in the firing line.

Had he actually flipped? This was a serious situation. There was no telling what the mob might have done had they got hold of him. But Horner went through with it. Eddie tried not to think about this too much as they headed back towards the city centre.

2012
CLEVELAND, OHIO

Eddie gazed out of the window of the office block where he worked. He could see the crowds building up and filing towards Jacob's Field, the huge baseball arena that was the home of the Cleveland Indians. He never imagined this would be his first job out of university, but the chance of a three-month work and travel adventure in the United States seemed too good to turn down.

Eddie shook his head as he considered the numbers. There would be another forty or fifty thousand of them in attendance for a midweek game. All paying twenty dollars plus for a ticket, and carrying a wad of cash to spend on overpriced junk food when they got inside. All this to witness the most boring game in the world.

In truth Eddie didn't really think baseball was that boring. He had been to a couple of games, and although he found them decidedly slow he admired the skill and accuracy of the fielders in particular. This was just one of his quiet mental rants, which was bound to manifest itself verbally in the future – when enough alcohol had been consumed. There was no point saying baseball was slightly boring or a bit dull: it had to take the world crown for being shite.

As Eddie observed the crowd he made a quick estimate of the ratio of white faces to black: around three to one in favour of whites. He knew from his own experience and from conversations that this was not typical throughout the city; indeed, when he caught the bus to work every morning he was usually the only white person on it. Around sixty per cent of Cleveland's population was black.

This was why Eddie could not believe what he was reading in the newspapers and hearing on the radio. The Ku Klux Klan had announced that it was planning to hold an outdoor public rally right in the centre of town. What's more, they had been given permission by the mayor (who himself was black), and could expect full protection from the city's police force.

Eddie couldn't for the life of him see how this was going to work. It just had to kick off. He understood that freedom of speech was a big thing in the States, but wondered what it took to get something banned on health and safety grounds. All he knew was that he had to be there.

Eddie sat on the crowded train and studied the simple line map that listed the stations for Cleveland's Central Square. He had been out drinking the night before but he felt no ill effects. He knew why. On days like this the adrenalin that built up washed away any symptoms of a hangover. He had the same feeling as he did on that morning in Northern Ireland. No headache, just thoughts buzzing around his head and energy coursing through his body.

When Eddie was in this frame of mind the only things that seemed to cause him discomfort were basic tasks, when his brain was working at a simple, functional level. To think like this he had to put the brakes on and slow everything down, which caused his head to ache.

After a few moments staring at the map, his head began to throb. Eddie allowed his mind to wander to the place where it was most comfortable: contemplating the excitement that was to come. He quickly felt calmer, and knew what the only answer was to his problem. He would have to apply his own logic to the map. More often than not this was flawed, and completely different from anyone else's. Written instructions, verbal directions, any kind of list: all were a nightmare for Eddie. As a child he had often marvelled at how his dad could stop and ask for directions and remember five or six separate instructions. He naturally assumed it was something he would learn to do when he got older, but he got even worse as he got older, having neglected the functional part of his brain and indulged its wild and creative element.

Eddie looked up and down at all the people crowded onto the train. He knew that not one of them would have any trouble reading the map. It made him angry. To make himself feel better he confirmed to himself that he could beat every single one of them in a race over two hundred metres. Or if they were to be judged on a five minute impromptu speech he would beat them at that too. But right now the important thing was reading a rail map effectively, and that test he failed miserably.

Settling on a mysterious logic that made sense only to him, Eddie left the train at the wrong station. It was blatantly obvious that he had made a mistake: the station was a single platform apparently in the middle of nowhere, and no one else left the train. It was a measure of Eddie's stubbornness that he stood on the platform and allowed the train to leave. He could easily have jumped back on, but he opted to avoid that slight embarrassment and hoped his logic had somehow served him well.

Eddie asked a maintenance man where they were, which confirmed that he had left the train one stop early. He wandered up and down the platform for a while wondering what to do. After a few minutes he saw another train approaching. This would have solved his problem right away, and he would no longer have had to worry about being late – if it hadn't sped past. As the train approached, showing no signs of slowing, Eddie stuck his arm out, as though catching a bus on Yeadon High Street. It was only when the train was disappearing into the distance that he thought to himself how ridiculous this had been.

The passing of the train confirmed one thing. He wasn't going to stand about waiting. He looked at the rail map on the platform. He looked at the train tracks disappearing round the corner a few hundred yards ahead. The distance on the map seemed like nothing at all, and when he was on the train the stops had come along every few minutes. Eddie took a deep breath and surveyed the tracks. He felt the energy inside him demanding to be released. He jumped off the platform and started to run.

As Eddie got into his stride he began to feel better. Even though he was pushing towards sprinting pace his breathing remained deep and steady. The sleepers seemed designed to fit his stride and his eyes smiled as he settled into a rhythm. He thought about the film *Stand by Me*, and how this was a perfectly reasonable way to get from one place to another.

It began to drizzle, but he maintained his pace, feeling no signs of fatigue. He never considered putting his umbrella up, but swung it back and forth as though it was a baton in a relay race, building momentum. He thought about his classmates back at the comp and laughed as he ran.

~I wonder what you're all doing right now.

He reckoned it was something predictable, like playing pool or watching television. With an air of superiority he upped the pace even more, briefly covering three sleepers at a time. No one would ever guess that he was in Cleveland, USA, late for a KKK rally, running through the rain along the city railway tracks.

After more than five minutes of very brisk running Eddie began to feel a little fatigued. His breathing had quickened considerably and his legs were starting to feel heavy. His pace slowed to a more comfortable speed, but he was still making solid progress. Calculating that he must have run almost a mile by now, and with six or seven more minutes of steady progress would be at his destination, Eddie began to wonder what would happen when he reached the central station. Would it be easy just to hop onto the platform, or would he be in some sort of trouble? Eddie was sure he could talk his way out of a situation as long as he could get the officials to understand his accent. His thoughts were interrupted by a shout.

~HEEEEY!

~OOOAAAAY!

~HEEEEEEEEAAAAAOOO!

Eddie looked to the top of the huge embankment that stretched up on his right. He saw a figure about a hundred and fifty yards away waving his arms. Eddie could see the man was black, but nothing more. His first instinct was to increase his speed and hope this person would leave him be. But the man was not to be deterred. As Eddie increased his speed so did he, and he came scrambling down the hill. The embankment consisted of loose soil and small shrubs, and when the man lost his footing he put a hand on the ground to maintain his balance. All the while he never stopped shouting and waving. There could be no doubt that his appeals were directed at Eddie.

By now the man was no more than seventy yards away, and for the first time Eddie could make sense of what he was saying.

~HEEEY!

YOU GOTTA GET OFFA THE TRACKS!

COME OFFA THE LINE!

Eddie looked up but didn't break his stride. He continued running, but realised it was the right time to leave the track. Trains had come past on other lines, with their drivers giving disbelieving looks of contempt – but as someone was actually bothering to scramble down the banking he decided to pay him the courtesy of finding out what he had to say.

Eddie maintained the same pace and the same stride length and, as though it was the most natural thing in the world, veered to his right and continued running, steeply up hill, across the loose soil and towards the man.

As Eddie neared his interceptor he knew exactly what his first words would be. He was pleased with himself because he knew they would be appropriate in the USA and back in England. In the USA they were a general greeting; in England they would mean 'What's the matter with you?' Eddie smiled, because he knew with two small words he could have the best of both worlds. To put the icing on the cake he decided to use a local Cleveland slang expression as well, one that was often used between friends in a macho sort of way.

--What's up, dawg?

He smiled. The man who had scrambled down the banking was speechless.

Eddie used the brief moment to survey the character standing in front of him. The man was dressed extremely scruffily. He was very thin and looked malnourished. He had several teeth missing and the ones he had were in pretty bad shape. Eddie placed him in his mid- to late thirties, but he wouldn't have been surprised if he was ten years out either side. He was wearing a red sweatshirt and grey corduroy trousers. They were small in size but still too big for his slim waist and exposed his underpants at the top of his trousers. Eddie quickly concluded that this was not a fashion statement. On his feet he wore battered white sneakers; the right shoe had a floppy sole.

Eddie immediately felt guilty. The last thing footwear in this kind of condition needed was a downhill run across gravelly soil. Some of the soil had clearly found its way inside them. He noticed the man's indifference to this, and quickly guessed that he was homeless. Suddenly the man found his tongue.

--You can't go running on the railroad, man. They'll have you arrested.

--Yeah, OK, sorry about that. It's just I got off at the wrong stop. I need to get to Central Square for the Ku Klux Klan rally. I'm going to be late. I thought if I ran along the track I'd make it.

--Hey, man. Where you from? You from Australia or something?

The embankment man looked more and more bewildered.

--I'm from London.

This was Eddie's standard answer. There was no point in trying to explain that he was from a once-proud textile city called Bradford, whose rugby team were world champions. It was completely lost on the Americans.

~You're from London? They run on the railroad in London?

The embankment man carried on asking questions, intrigued and apparently desperate to soak up as much information about London as he could.

Eddie took time to answer and the embankment man lapped everything up, as if he was speaking to a being from another planet.

~They run on the railroad in London?

~No, not really. I just got off at the wrong stop. I need to get to Central Square. Am I anywhere near?

The embankment man stood upright.

~I'll take you. I'll get you there.

With that they walked up the embankment. Eddie's suspicions that the man was homeless were confirmed when, on nearing the top, he darted under a bridge and began to tuck plastic carrier bags of clothes out of sight – clearly because he intended being away from them for a short while.

The homeless man wasn't aware of the KKK rally in the town centre, the only person in Cleveland Eddie had met who wasn't. For the last few weeks debate had raged in all the local newspapers, and it was the main topic on news channels and talk radio shows. You would have to live by yourself under a bridge not to realise what was going on.

When they reached the top of the embankment Eddie saw that they were on the city outskirts and guessed it wouldn't take long to reach their destination. He could probably have found his way on his own, but he decided to allow the homeless man to take him anyway. His companion moved briskly, like someone in a walking race trying to cheat, stopping every so often to pick up litter. On a couple of occasions they were almost run over as he darted into the middle of the road to grab a crisp packet or Coke bottle. Eddie followed him, thinking they were going to cross the street, but then had to put the brakes on, turn back and dodge the traffic again.

~I'm trying to clean up this town. And all they do is hate me for it.

Eddie said nothing. In different circumstances he might have allowed the homeless man to elaborate, but he needed to focus all his attention on staying alive.

They passed the station where he should have disembarked, and when the homeless man pointed to his destination Eddie shook his hand and thanked him sincerely.

As Eddie walked down the steps towards Central Square it became clear that something extraordinary was going on. There was a very high police presence and, bizarrely, six people dressed in furry cartoon animal costumes. Eddie found out later that they had been sent by the Cedar Point theme park to try and lighten up the situation. There were also people standing in pairs who were wearing luminous bibs, with the words 'Observers of the Peace' emblazoned upon them in black letters. One of each pair was carrying a clipboard. As he passed Eddie asked what they were doing.

~We're here to observe the peace.

Fascinated, Eddie quizzed them further.

~So what would be the best outcome for Cleveland?

~For as many people as possible to ignore the Klan, and for the day to pass without incident.

~And what are you going to do to make sure that happens?

Eddie was in Paxman mode.

The woman paused and looked bewildered.

--We're here as volunteers for the city to observe the peace.

Eddie could have continued, but he felt he had them worked out. They were people who felt they should do something but didn't really know what, so in the end they did something random, regardless of the fact that it had absolutely no impact on the situation at hand. It reminded him of the terrorist attacks on the 2012 Olympics. Shortly after the 29/7 atrocities he had gone to his local gym to discover that as a 'security measure' they had temporarily scrapped their computerised entry system, making everyone sign in manually. Eddie had pictured Osama bin Laden and his followers discussing potential targets:

Target 1: Olympic Park, London.

Target 2: Buckingham Palace, London.

Target 3: The Aquatics centre, during team USA training session.

Target 4: Hollings Hill Health Club, Bradford, England, during over-forties aqua-aerobics.

At least if the terrorists decided to fly a plane into the gym the manual sign-in would provide an excellent first line of defence.

Overhead a helicopter buzzed about. He couldn't see if it was police or the media. (It was actually the police *with* the media.) Eddie had been hearing speculation about how much the security operation was costing, and as he rounded the corner he knew it wasn't going to be cheap.

Signs had been put up to segregate supporters of the Klan from its opponents. They had to enter the block from different sides. Eddie headed for the entrance marked 'OPPONENTS OF THE KU KLUX KLAN'.

A wire mesh fence sealed the block off. About a thousand people milled around outside, and a queue of people waited to get in. Dispersed among the crowd were police officers whose job it was to repeat a simple message.

--You're allowed one key and one piece of ID. You won't be allowed in with anything more.

Eddie put both hands in his pockets. In the right he was carrying his wallet, which contained about two hundred dollars and all his cards. In the left he had a bunch of keys and a few dollars in loose coins. Everyone was searched before they went through, first with a hand-held detector, then physically by a police officer, and finally they had to take their shoes off. People were being turned away if they were carrying too much, so Eddie needed a plan.

He knew pretty much immediately what he was going to do; he just needed to decide where and how. Earlier he had noticed a small garden with a tall evergreen tree surrounded by small shrubs as its centrepiece. When he saw an empty McDonald's bag on the floor he scooped it up, in the style of the homeless man, then went to sit on the wall next to one of the shrubs. He wasn't sure if a key and a piece of ID were compulsory, but to be on the safe side he took his driving licence from his wallet and removed his house key from the ring. Everything else he rolled up inside the McDonald's bag. When he was sure no one was watching he stashed it under the shrub. He desperately hoped that a homeless person didn't come to 'clean up' this particular part of town.

With his key and ID, Eddie made his way back to the wire fence and joined the back of the line. Despite the large numbers milling around the queue was relatively short and the police were processing people very efficiently. About half of those searched were allowed through.

As Eddie got near the front of the line he took out his key and his driving licence. His pockets were completely empty. He was frisked quickly but thoroughly before being made to remove his shoes. He heard a commotion on the other side of the fence, and when he was finally allowed to move on the old adrenalin began to churn again. He didn't know what to expect, but he knew it was going to be big.

He found himself in an area about the size of three tennis courts. It was completely sealed off by metal wire fencing, which stood about ten feet high. Directly in front of the pen were some steps, leading to a platform from which the KKK were to deliver their message.

To the right, in a pen of their own, were the media, at least a hundred of them. Beyond the reporters was a pen for supporters of the KKK, but the media people had their equipment stacked so high that Eddie couldn't see who had turned up to support them.

The pen in which Eddie found himself contained people who appeared to be slightly hysterical. They were already chanting, shouting, weeping or praying. There was a large contingent present from the Nation of Islam, who stood out as they were all smartly dressed black men wearing suits, bow ties and hats and the most composed of all. Eddie spotted representatives from Jewish groups, Christian groups, lesbian groups and some who were just angry people. The one thing they had in common was that they were highly emotionally charged.

Eddie took the time to wander round and soak up one of the most intense atmospheres he had ever experienced.

After about five minutes he heard a familiar tune blasting out of the speakers at the side of the stage. It was a tune he had heard many times before at football games or boxing matches on the television. It signalled the moment when the KKK marched out of the government buildings behind them and took their position on the stage. There were twelve of them, all except two wearing long white robes and a pointed white hood. Their leader, the Reverend Nathan Forrest, wore the same style robes, but his were black in colour. His second in command had red robes.

As they took to the stage the crowd around Eddie surged forward, shouting and booing and banging on the fence. On the other side a solid line of police stood shoulder to shoulder, their faces expressionless. Behind this line stood a second line, just a few feet from the stage. The Reverend Nathan Forrest certainly couldn't have had any complaints about security.

Even though the reverend was shouting and had the benefit of a microphone, there was no chance that Eddie could hear what he was saying, such was the intensity of the noise around him.

One of the groups, with a large female contingent, managed to get a coherent chant started.

~Hey Hey! KKK! Go Home! No Way!

But on the whole the noise was mainly screamed abuse.

Eddie focused his attention on one particular youth. When the Klan had first appeared he had rushed forward manically.

~Fuck the Klan! Fuck the Klan!

He slammed the palms of his hand on the fence so hard that it made Eddie wince. After a minute or so the young man changed the focus of his anger.

~Fuck the police! Fuck the police! They're protecting them!

The police, obviously under instructions, didn't

change their stony expressions. They stood with their hands behind their backs and never said a word, neither to protesters nor to each other. Clearly frustrated, the young man turned ninety degrees and rushed to his right.

~Fuck the media! Fuck the media! They're in on it! Fuck the media!

Later, when Eddie retold the story, he described the young man as 'just one of those young lads who wants to fuck everything'. He considered this quite witty, but it never got the laughs he thought it deserved.

He surveyed the scene and was pleased he had made the effort to be there. But he wasn't fully satisfied. He needed to take things to the next level. In an instant he knew how.

At the very beginning, when the Klan had first marched out, the front of the pen nearest the fence had been jam-packed as everyone surged forward. After about ten minutes quite a few moved to sit on the steps at the rear of the pen. Others, perhaps suffering from feelings of claustrophobia, decided to observe from further back. Every so often there was a gap at the front of the fence, filled after a few moments by someone who had found a burst of energy or anger.

Eddie stood about fifteen yards from the fence. He took some deep breaths as he bounced up and down on the balls of his feet like a boxer; once again he felt the adrenalin building up, that wonderful feeling of anticipation in his stomach. A girl of about seventeen with a large afro hairstyle at the front of the pen suddenly screamed something incoherent, breaking down in tears. Two other girls, one who looked like her sister, came to console her. They remained in a group hug for a moment before moving to the back of the crowd.

This gave Eddie his chance. He got up on his toes and exploded into a run up before the gap closed, slamming his right take-off foot on the ground to give him the height and distance he required. The next thing he knew he had his arms and head above the top of the fence and was desperately scrabbling with his legs. The fence was clearly designed not to be scaled. He desperately wrestled with his own bodyweight, but got the feeling the struggle was in vain. He felt the power draining out of his arms as he doggedly tried to hang on.

In desperation he turned round to the startled crowd.

~Help me! Push my feet up! We can't let them get away with this! We need to storm the Klan! Push my feet up! Push my feet up!

In an instant half a dozen willing hands provided a platform for Eddie's feet, and he was propelled upwards. Soon he was able to swing one of his legs over. It was slightly uncomfortable, but ten feet up in the air, at the front of the pen, he had a fantastic view – right into the supporters' pen. There were no more than twenty of them, all looking at him. Eddie shook his fist and pointed. There was no way he was going to be heard, so he didn't worry about shouting anything meaningful. He concentrated on the visuals. He made his face look as angry as he knew how, and moved his lips as if giving an impassioned speech.

Eddie gained only a token reaction from the supporters' pen. He had them down as onlookers rather than supporters. So he turned his attention to the Reverend Nathan Forrest, who was clearly in no mood to take things lying down and was clearly put out that someone had taken the attention from him: most of the media cameras had turned to face Eddie. The reverend walked to the edge of the platform and directed his rant directly at him. Eddie could see his contorted face screwing up with rage as he stamped his feet and pointed.

Eddie thought he made out some of the words. He certainly heard the words 'nigger lover' and 'disgrace', but this confrontation had nothing to do with debate: it was all about posturing and gesture. Eddie pointed aggressively and made sure his lips never stopped moving. He was now miming the words to 'My grandfather's clock' to make sure he didn't appear lost for words. He slowed right down and just about heard himself.

~And it STOPPED . . . SHORT . . . NEVER TO GO AGAIN . . . WHEN THE OLD . . . MAN . . . DIEEEEEED!

It was time to survey the scene so he could lock it vividly in his memory. He looked at the Reverend Nathan Forrest, still ranting away. Eddie couldn't see his eyes because he was wearing sunglasses, but he knew they would be bulging and hate-filled. For the first time he noticed that the regular Klan members in white robes were springing to life; up to now they had just been holding their banners. Now they were responding to the chaos that was building in the crowd.

The reverend seemed to be going through a routine that was familiar to them. On demand they raised clenched hands above their heads and yelled.

~White Power!

Eddie scanned the crowd behind him, which had reached a new level of frenzied excitement. He turned to face them, his yells now for their benefit, and many in the front rows could hear him.

~STORM THE KLAN!
~STORM THE KLAN!
~STORM THE KLAN!

In an instant the refrain caught on. Barely a few

seconds later the crowd was chanting as one, fists raised in the air.

~STORM THE KLAN!

~STORM THE KLAN!

~STORM THE KLAN!

Eddie looked over towards the media people. Cameras clicked. He noticed a couple of them glancing at each other, as if to share the thought that everything was going better than expected.

He also saw that the police were no longer standing stony-faced. Some of them were on their radios. Most were looking at Eddie. All were waiting for instructions.

Eddie turned back to the crowd.

~STORM THE KLAN!

~STORM THE KLAN!

His own fist was clenched and punched the air in time to the chant. For a few moments he was in his element. His addiction to this kind of rush was being indulged to the point of overdose. He felt fantastic, despite the uncomfortable pain in his crotch where he was straddling the fence.

Just when Eddie felt he had had about enough, something happened that jolted him mentally as well as physically. The young man who had been running round trying to fuck everything took a running jump at the fence, making it sway back and forth. He was now in the same position Eddie had been in earlier, struggling to haul himself up. The crowd enthusiastically came to his aid. Now they knew what the drill was, so everyone within touching distance wanted to help force him upwards. But such was the momentum of the push that the young man couldn't have stopped half-way even if he had wanted to.

He landed heavily on the other side. Seemingly unhurt, he picked himself up and charged towards the stage.

It was hopeless. The first line of police engulfed him immediately. Four of them grappled him to the floor and carried him off in the blinking of an eye. He kicked and struggled, only to receive some hefty blows for his trouble. This incensed the protestors, and Eddie could see they were looking for direct action. He knew instinctively what he was expected to do: drop down the other side and try to storm the Klan, as the first martyr had done.

All of a sudden he didn't fancy it. Not one bit. He didn't fancy taking on twenty tooled-up policemen. He didn't fancy taking on the United States legal system for inciting a riot. He didn't fancy paying fines or spending time in a police cell. He certainly didn't fancy missing his flight home.

The effect on Eddie's body was like a hangover hitting home in the middle of a bender. His palms started to sweat; his breathing became quicker. In the few moments that he delayed others piled over the fence without hesitation, and came to the same fate as the first climber. When a young black woman wearing a skirt and flip-flops was helped over she landed awkwardly and twisted her ankle. She still managed to stumble pathetically towards the police lines, and screamed the loudest of all when she was whisked away.

Eddie was starting to look like a coward, and he knew it. He was still straddling the fence while others were being handcuffed in the back of a police car. A convoluted sense of pride, duty and embarrassment stopped him from dropping back into the protesters' pen. Then a plan dropped into his head. It was fairly lame, and he knew it, but with the absence of anything else he had to go with it.

~We got to go as one! We got to go together!

With that Eddie reached down and started to help those who wanted to get arrested. There was absolutely no need for him to do this, as there was more than enough assistance coming from below, but it wasn't long before he was joined by two other youths straddling the fence. When he spotted a heavily built man who was determined to get in on the action Eddie knew he had his chance. He reached down as he had done with the others. It would have broken all laws of physics if he had managed to haul the man up, as he must have weighed at least sixteen stone, and Eddie got the result he wanted. He overbalanced as the fence rocked back and forth, crashing to the ground in the protestors' pen.

It was the perfect landing. Perfect in that it looked very awkward and drew blood, but not so serious that it robbed him of his senses or caused him undue pain. He was helped up and felt he could justifiably withdraw from the front line.

Eddie realised that he had to get out as quickly as possible: he was still at risk from being arrested for being the disturbance's main instigator. He wiped the blood from his forehead with the inside of his T-shirt and decided to make his move. He put his hand over the graze and walked towards the exit as though scratching his head or ruffling his hair. It looked fairly natural. The police at the exits looked at him, but not suspiciously: their main concern was preventing people from getting in, not out. It was easier than Eddie had thought, and he breathed a sigh of relief as he strode down the block that exited Central Square.

As he reached the corner he saw a large police support vehicle, which was being used to detain those who had scaled the fence. Two policemen were leading a handcuffed man towards it. He was no longer struggling, so one of them let go and turned around to head back to the front line. This policeman was of slim build and had sandy hair and a moustache. Eddie thought he looked different from most of the other officers, who had shorter hair and were much bulkier. Eddie allowed himself to stare for a moment, which was a big mistake. The sandy-haired officer suddenly turned and looked him squarely in the face. Eddie had been recognised. The officer began to approach, but Eddie didn't hang around to find out what he had to say. He turned on his heels and ran like the wind.

The policeman was certainly not an accomplished track athlete, and after only about forty-five seconds, when Eddie rounded a corner and found himself in the entrance to a shopping mall, his pursuer was no longer in sight. He decided that the mall was an ideal place to lie low for half an hour. In desperate need of sustenance, after all the running he had done, he walked into Burger King and began to survey the menu. When he reached into his pocket for his wallet the empty lining instantly reminded him where he had left it.

--Bugger.

Eddie sat down at an empty table and held his head in his hands. He ran his fingers slowly through his hair and gently scratched the back of his neck. An onlooker might have thought this was a sign of distress, but he wasn't massively perturbed. Now he had the excuse to go back into the danger zone, and the butterflies in his stomach were already starting to flutter.

Moments later Eddie was ambling back in the direction of Central Square. At first he looked around cautiously, but when it became clear that no one was paying him any attention he grew in confidence, and his amble changed into a brisk walk when the landscaped area where he had stashed his wallet came into view. Standing no more than thirty yards away from the far side of the shrub was the police officer who had just chased him. Eddie kept up his brisk walk and focused on him as he talked expressively to his colleague.

Eddie prayed he wouldn't be seen.

He walked a little further, until he was about twenty yards away from the shrub. He realised he only had a slim chance of retrieving his wallet if he was spotted.

Eddie hoped he wouldn't be seen.

A few seconds later he was within spitting distance of the shrub. If he was spotted now he would have a decent chance of getting away, as long as he found his wallet quickly and scooped it up cleanly.

Eddie was indifferent about being seen.

Soon he was standing right next to the shrub and looking straight at the policeman, who was now sharing a joke but maintaining an authoritative posture. If he was seen now he wouldn't have a problem getting away, barring mishaps.

Eddie didn't mind if he was seen.

He got down on his hands and knees, his right hand poised to reach under the shrub and grab the McDonald's bag. The policeman wouldn't be able to see him now because he was so low down, but if he was seen when he stood up again he had a really good chance of getting away.

Eddie wanted to be seen.

He saw the brown paper bag. Before he picked it up he crawled through to the far side of the bush, and poked his head out the other side. The policeman was less than thirty yards away.

Eddie was determined to be seen.

The policeman appeared to be looking in his direction, but was still deeply in conversation and certainly wasn't taking any action. Eddie crawled right through the far side of the bush and stood upright, staring at the man who had just pursued him.

Eddie was desperate to be seen.

He bent down and picked up a large lump of soil. It was slightly crumbly, so he compacted it into a sphere the size of a tennis ball. He took one last look at his target and hurled the ball. It came down no more than three feet away from where the two policeman were standing. The soil shattered into tiny pieces, spraying dirt onto and around their shoes. The two men hopped and skipped as though they were dodging bullets.

Eddie had been seen.

In a flash he was flat on the floor again and he grabbed at the paper bag. He pulled it out, and at once he knew something was wrong. The bag had a Wendy's logo on the front. There was something inside and when he reached in it was soft and cold and disintegrated when he squeezed it. Time and the unwillingness to make an unpleasant discovery prevented him from investigating further. Before he turned to run away again something, he could never work out what, made him look at another shrub, five yards to the right. He was sure his wallet wasn't under there. Without a millisecond of debate Eddie flung himself on his front and begun fumbling around under the branches and leaves. He reached deep underneath, his fingers touching a paper bag that immediately felt much more promising. As he pulled it out and saw the familiar McDonald's logo he fully expected two policemen to come crashing down on top of him.

To his amazement they hadn't covered the ground quickly enough, so he was able to regain his feet and at the same time retrieve his wallet. He gripped it tightly and began to accelerate away just as the two policemen crashed through the bushes. They were in full flight and looked odds on to catch him. One of them laid a hand on him, but with a quick change of direction Eddie managed to shrug him off. As the policeman stumbled he opened up a gap of around fifteen feet. Eddie had no choice but to run flat out. He pumped his arms high, back and forth, as though he was back on the track again. His head was perfectly still, not looking left or right. He should have relaxed his jaw and shoulders for maximum efficiency, but in these circumstances relaxing wasn't really possible. He would have liked to have run in a straight line but other pedestrians made this impossible. Eddie dodged from side to side. It would only take one collision and everything would be over. It was obvious he was being chased by the police, and some people were actually making half-hearted grabs at him.

Eddie had put about fifty feet between himself and his pursuers. It was not enough, perhaps, and the policemen were driven on by the macho need not to be the first to give up. Their half-hearted attempts to grab Eddie were becoming stronger and stronger. He was hungry, his throat was burning and he was losing power in his legs. He was doing a lot of running today, and he was feeling the effects of his fall from the fence.

Just when he needed it least, a small, stocky man came in with a body check. Eddie saw it coming a split second before impact. He managed to change direction sufficiently to avoid making contact head on, but it was still a significant glancing blow and almost knocked him off his feet. He put one hand down to stop himself from falling over, and lost most of his momentum. When he tried to accelerate away again there was nothing left in his legs.

The policemen were within five yards of him now. It was a battle of wills. Eddie began to realise that not only did he have to avoid getting caught but he also had to pull away far enough to disappear in a crowd, or hide. His chances were slim, and as he lost hope he lost speed. His body was screaming for him to stop but his mind wouldn't allow it. He needed a break, and fast. He needed a miracle. And by a twist of fate he got it.

By now Eddie was only capable of running in a straight line. One more have-a-go hero would definitely finish him off. He was becoming slightly dizzy and tears streamed from his eyes, not from emotion but from the effort he was putting in. Had his vision been normal he would have noticed the man standing ahead and pointing a gun in his direction much sooner, but he was almost within touching distance of the scruffy black man wearing a bright red sweatshirt and grey trousers before he noticed him. He was shouting in a high-pitched voice and gesturing wildly.

But he was not gesturing at Eddie to lie down or freeze. He was gesturing him to carry on running. Eddie needed no second invitation. He found reserves of energy in the deepest stores his body had to offer and accelerated away again. It was only when Eddie ran past the gunman and smelt the bitter smell of homelessness that he realised who it was. He didn't look behind to see the frail man pointing the gun from one policeman to the other as he jabbered out threats, determined to save his friend.

Eddie rounded the next corner and entered the next block, which was lined with offices. A line of cabs waited about a hundred yards further along. He gave himself the target of running for fifteen more seconds. When he reached the first cab he collapsed into the front seat and gave the driver his address.

~Fifty dollars?

It was over double what it should have been, but it

would have been a bargain at ten times the price. He paid up front.

The next day Eddie only left his room to feed himself and use the bathroom.

RIGHT SIDE OF THE TRACKS

TV.
So much TV.
I've never watched so much.
And American TV too.
But I'm not down yet.
Need to come down. Down.
Relax to normal.
Fuck work.
Ring in sick.
Down.
Slow breaths, watch the shite.
Think.
But in my own time.

I'm riding my luck here. I've come close before but today was major league.

God knows what those pigs would have done if they'd caught me.

Fuck it, might still catch me.

Time to go, I reckon.

And that homeless guy with the gun.

Attempted murder?

Aiding and abetting a gunman?

Conspiracy to assassinate an officer of the law?

Incitement to cause a riot?

God knows what they'd have thrown at me.

These Yank cunts could have me in for a long stretch.

But I know I've got something.

Something special.

And I have to express myself.

I'll make it big.

I've never met anyone with my ideas and the bottle to see them through.

But no point in having the most bottle in the nick.

Or the graveyard.

Look at all this shite on the box. Someone's behind all this bollocks. Someone's paid to come up these crap ideas, and other people produce them.

Now imagine if people could watch my stuff, and I had a bit of cash behind me. Then I could really go big time.

But mainstream wouldn't touch my sort of stuff.

Glorifying criminal behaviour. I'd be a major villain. No one would put any cash up if coppers and teachers were the victims.

Different victims?

Like that Rat-trap show.

Now that was fucking garbage.

Filming some thieving cunt nick a bike or vandalise a shop. Some of them are set up, and the film crew just sits there and watches.

Why don't they get someone out there, for fuck's sake?

'The footage from this show will be passed on to the police.'

Big fucking deal.

Another ASBO: that means fuck all.

People want instant gratification.

You want a mob to steam in and boot the fuck out of them.

People would watch that.

I've seen them set up criminals by tempting them into the back of lorries.

Make them think they can nick some electrical goods.

Then the door slams, and the lorry drives round with the crim inside.

Big signs saying 'I'm a thief'.

But this could be the next step.

And I think I know where to start.

The paintballs in Headingley.

Since that night three years ago the copycats have got right out of hand.

Police not interested. They think it's students mucking about.

Everyone who goes out in fancy dress risks getting shot now.

I've heard there are some real nasty fuckers doing it an' all.

First it was just the geeks, disaffected dungeons and dragons types.

Then the right-wing groups started getting involved, targeting gays in drag an' that.

Then you get the sympathisers, so every cunt and his dog's wearing fancy dress.

Which means more targets.

And so it goes on.

So someone needs to stop it.

But with an angle.

And that could be me.

Back at Uni.

Sign up for that Masters.

Specialise in documentary.

Look at the risks, getting shot in the eye and all that.

Talk to former students.

Some who've been shot. Injured. Traumatised.

Make out that fancy dress is an important tradition.

Get some psychologist to talk shite about young people expressing their freedom in a non-aggressive way, or some bollocks like that.

Then use my contacts to find the shooters.

Get interviews with them.

Go undercover.

Get some footage.

Proper footage.

Set-piece down Otley Road during Freshers' Week or something.

Then sting the shooters.

Have a counter-force ready.

Shouldn't be too hard.

Recruit some rugby lads.

Film the whole thing.

Get it done properly.

Personal views from both sides.

The bigger picture.

Some inside action.

This could work.

This could definitely work.

But get home.

Had enough now.

Back to Blighty.

Regroup.

Then we go again.

PART THREE

WORLD OF WORK: STRIKEBACK MEDIA

2014
TWOC

That's the name and that's the address. What you do with it is entirely up to you. Just don't give it to the police, 'cos they'll do fuck all.

~But are you sure, Laney? How are you definite?

~'Cos they brag like fuck. My grandma knows everything what happens on that estate. They do at least three cars a week. A red Vauxhall Corsa left at the bottom of Hawksworth estate with a Bradford sticker? Fuck me. You might as well of sent 'em an invitation!

It had been three weeks since Eddie had had his car stolen and he was still pissed off. Possibly even more so, now that the novelty of getting on buses was wearing off. Someone, or more likely a gang, had stolen his car after he left it outside work to go on a night out. They had driven up the hill, probably done a few handbrake turns on the common, then set it on fire. Just for a laugh. It was their hobby.

As Eddie trudged up the hill towards the bus stop he noticed white lettering proudly scrawled across a newsagent's metal shutters.

—HAWKSWORTH TWOKKERS 2014.

When he saw this he decided that something had to be done.

Revenge taken.

Justice.

Shearer style.

TWOC SHOCK

Ryan Watts smiled and nodded in approval as his old mate pointed out the target.

~It's another Corsa. Piece of piss! Nice one, Sheldon.

Ryan surveyed the car park. It was hardly used on an evening when all the office workers had gone home. Occasionally people used it as a cut-through to steal from the scrap metal yard. It was usually deserted, but tonight there were two vehicles there. The first was a white Transit. A rental. Locked and alarmed, fitted with a steering lock. The second was a battered-looking Vauxhall Corsa. Locked but only locked. No alarm. No steering lock. No immobiliser.

Gift.

In and away in two.

It was a no-brainer.

With confidence and nonchalance Ryan threw half a brick through the driver's side window. He quickly scraped away the glass clinging to the frame, sprang the door lock, and took a seat. Within moments he was wrenching away at the steering column, in firm and assured movements, to expose the wiring underneath. He paused briefly to reach across to the passenger side, to allow his sidekick to join in the fun.

His heart began to quicken. The anticipation and excitement were building. Soon he would be motoring. His fingers were busy and his eyes were focused. Intense concentration on the wires. Soon he would be away, booting it. Handbrakes on the estate. No chance of getting caught. His confidence supreme.

Suddenly.

Bizarrely.

Something distracted him.

A figure in his peripheral vision.

~I am Big Chief Justice. Step outside the vehicle. You have ten seconds to comply. STEP OUTSIDE THE VEHICLE.

Ryan took a moment to survey the figure standing only inches away from the window he had shattered.

But only a moment.

A tall youth, a couple of years older than Ryan, was standing upright, pipe-cleaner arms folded across his pigeon chest. He stood fully six foot three in height, but his feathery head-dress took him over the seven foot mark. His brown fancy dress Indian trousers were tied as tight as they could go, but still hung loose over his slender waist. His leather brown waistcoat looked almost authentic, but his costume was badly let down by white trainers and silver-rimmed spectacles.

Middle-class pranks.

Under-class hobby.

Ryan slammed his screwdriver into the Red Indian's face.

Aiming for the eyes.

Eddie hadn't wanted Steve to wear the glasses. Not authentic. And cloth moccasins were better than trainers.

Unable to move. Unable to see. But more authentic.

The doctor said, as he was sewing twelve stitches into Steve's lower eyelid, that his glasses probably saved his eye.

Steve screamed and fell backwards. Curled up hedgehog-like. Screaming and swearing. Crying. Like a soft middle-class prat kid.

Ryan out the car.

Adrenalin overdrive.

Nicking a car.

Getting caught.

Being challenged.

Bizarre situation.

Fucking seven foot Red Indian having a pop.

Kick the cunt.

Hard.

Boot in ribs.

Boot in stomach.

Stamp on legs.

Foot on head.

Sheldon wailing.

~RYAN! RYAAAN!

Ryan looked up. His sidekick was being roughed up by someone in a Scooby-Doo costume.

Scooby-Doo had him in a headlock, and was aiming largely ineffectual punches at his stomach. Someone holding a camcorder had grabbed one of Sheldon's legs with his free hand in an attempt to up-end him.

Ryan made his way towards Scooby-Doo and the camera man with screwdriver at the ready. But before he got there he was hit hard from the side by a growling Incredible Hulk.

Ryan was stunned by the aggressive rugby tackle, and the screwdriver flew from his hand. In a flash the Hulk was on top of him. Green body paint smudged on his face and clothes.

Hulk had hold of his ears.

Hulk using ears as levers to bang his head on the ground.

Again and again.

Head bleeding.

~NOW THEN, CUNT, HOW YOU FEELING?

HOW YOU FUCKIN' FEELING NOW?

EH?

EH?

Head banging.

LIKE STEALING CARS?

LIKE THIS?

IM A FUCKIN' NUT CASE!

I'M THE FUCKIN' HULK.

AARRRGH!

AAAAARRRRRGH!

Head banging and bleeding.

REMEMBER MY FACE.

REMEMBER MY FUCKIN' FACE.

I'M GONNA KILL YAAAA.

CUUUUNT!

A few feet away Scooby-Doo was losing his grip. Sheldon was hysterical. His screaming windmill punches had gained him a little room and he had started to inflict a blow or two on the retreating cameraman.

The Hulk looked up.

The Hulk saw that the camera was in danger.

The Hulk let Ryan go.

The Hulk kept Sheldon away from the precious camera.

The Hulk helped to pin Sheldon down.

Ryan scarpered.

~THAT'S IT! RUN AWAY!

LEAVE YOUR MATE!

LEAVE YOUR MATE TO DIE!

CUNT!

FUCKIN' SOFT CUNT!

The fourth cameraman came in close to help.

The Hulk and Scooby-Doo taped up the sobbing Sheldon.

Arms together.

Legs together.

Tape over mouth.

Tape removed.

Just in case.

As the footsteps of the retreating car thief became fainter, silence descended on the car park, broken only by the sobbing of the stricken sidekick.

The skinny Red Indian lay silent on the floor. Scooby-Doo crouched over him.

~Shit, Eddie. We better get him to a hospital. Sharpish.

~OK. Take him in the van. We'll meet as normal tomorrow. I better get rid of this.

The Hulk opened the door of the Corsa and sat down. He took a single car key out of his pocket and turned the ignition to start the engine. The cameraman guided the Red Indian to the van.

The Hulk pulled out of the car park. Window smashed.

Amateurs.

The lot of them.

Including me.

Need to raise game.

Four against two and still a mess.
Need more people.
More muscle.
Make sure we only have one target.
Weak target.
Target we can control.
No swearing.
No blood.
No damage.
Clean and professional.
No one on TV will touch this.
Have to learn.
Need to invest.
Recruit.
Hidden cameras.
Mobile cameras.
Cameras with powerful zooms.
Directional mikes.
Night vision.
But mainly more muscle.
And speed.
And strength.
And restraint training.
Investment.
Risk.
Afraid of risk?
Can't live without risk.
Red Indian piss poor.
Original characters.
Strong.
Powerful.
Fast.
Original characters.
Where do I get them?

Advert in Jonny's gym?
Advert in Wharfe Valley Times?
Casting agency?
Don't know.
And cash.
Serious cash.
Hope Steve's eye's OK.
Can do without hassle.

THE GUARDIAN MEDIA SECTION

Casey Mallender rolled out the old clichés as she spoke at this year's Orange Awards: 'Each entry was highly valued. So much talent on display. Such a hard job for the judges.'

The first two I'm sure all right-thinking people would go along with. A plethora of high-quality, insightful, cutting-edge documentaries, produced by ambitious youngsters who are the first genuine thoroughbreds of the digital age.

All the films I viewed were more or less broadcast-ready technically. Their depth and variety of content proved that this year's crop had done their groundwork and their research. Yet all the while they retained the risqué exuberance of youth that makes their productions so eminently watchable.

No one minds a cliché when it's true.

Which is why, Casey, I must pick you up on your

third. Because it simply can't have been true. And there's a reason why I feel I can take leave of my usual unassuming opinions in this matter. His name is Eddie Shearer. Most of you won't have heard of this young man before, but mark my words you will.

Headingley is the social Mecca for Leeds students. The notorious Otley Run involves revellers sinking a pint in each of Headingley's fourteen pubs. What's more, a tradition has built up that the course is to be completed in fancy dress. The more outrageous the better. Two fancy dress shops in the area have built up into thriving businesses as a result. This was not much of a story until three years ago, when a group of masked men began taking pot-shots at them with paintball guns. The assailants drove at speed down Otley Road, targeting students in fancy dress. Then, in a sinister twist, they leaped from their vehicle and carried out an execution-style shooting on a man and woman dressed in Scottish tartan. Despite the whole episode appearing on YouTube days later, police were unable to track down the perpetrators.

What followed was a spate of similar shootings. The snipers were not without their sympathisers. Some of Headingley's non-student residents resent the persistent leery behaviour, and have tired of the noise, broken glass and vomit. Regular drinkers in some of the more traditional hostelries begrudge being muscled out at the bar by Fred Flintstone, or coming face to face with Borat in a mankini in the urinals.

Eddie Shearer unapologetically sides with the students. He visits specialists at Leeds General Infirmary who have had to deal with an increase in serious eye trauma. He carries out simulations to show the damage a close-range paintball attack can inflict on the throat or genitalia.

Shearer interviews students who believe the police are less than pro-active in tracking down the culprits. Perhaps after years of sorting out fights, locking up drunks and receiving abuse from cavemen and Batman, the police might be forgiven for 'prioritising resources'.

Shearer had his finger well and truly on the pulse when he managed to track down a group of hardened third year students who had had more than enough and decided to take matters into their own hands. They recruited a posse of athletes, rugby players and amateur bodybuilders, all paid-up Student Union members and all veterans and advocates of the Otley Run. They lay in wait, determined but unarmed, during key dates in the student social calendars. After three nights of waiting on tenterhooks their day came. I won't reveal everything, but I will say this. Shearer's team is there to capture it all. It makes for some quite astounding footage; it's almost as if Shearer is directing the whole thing himself.

So get yourself a copy. Download it. Borrow it. Buy it. Steal it if you have to. You won't be disappointed. It has the pace and drama of an action thriller while staying true to the documentary genre with its factual accuracy and real-life human interest.

Shearer is a driven young man, and when I asked him what he would do with the £15,000 first prize it was no surprise to see the glint in his eye accompanying his one word answer: 'Re-invest'.

If he does, and I have no reason to disbelieve him, we can expect more dynamite material from this prodigy of the small screen.

I for one will be keeping a close eye on the fortunes of Eddie Shearer as he leads a new style of documentary makers into a new era. I urge the rest of you to watch this space.

2019
ARMLEY PRISON

The other inmates ridiculed Stan for wasting his newspaper privilege.

~You won't find no tits in there, Stan. What a fucking waste!

But the *Sun* and the *Star* never did him any favours. Looking at something he had zero chance of getting hold of for the next two years just made him more frustrated.

He was there to do time, so a newspaper that ate up some time in the reading of it was essential.

He had opted for the *Star* once, but it taken him less then twenty minutes to read it from cover to cover. Including the ads and TV.

So he always chose the *Guardian*. And read it all. Every last word.

He was reading an article in the media section that particularly interested him, an interview that reviewed the meteoric rise of Eddie Shearer and his company since he had burst onto the scene five years before. It was written by the same journalist who had written a feature on him in his early days, when he was getting by on borrowed money and a significant dose of goodwill. His big break had come when a cable channel, Bravado, offered him a contract to produce his first series.

It was an instant cult hit. The money Bravado provided allowed Shearer to bring in the resources and expertise to develop his edgy, provocative reality TV. He walked a legal tightrope, but a combination of luck, good lawyers and timing kept him and his team in production.

The credit crunch of 2009 and the collapse of the banks led to the greatest depression in history. Subsequent mass unemployment saw a surge in crimes such as theft and burglary. Hard-up, hard-working, law-abiding citizens were angry, and desperate for payback. Government rhetoric about tougher sentences did little to pacify their blood lust for the thieves and vandals who blighted their daily struggle to get ahead.

And so, at first, the Rectifires were tolerated.

And then they were celebrated.

No politician dared criticise the men and women who were doing more for public morale in the fight against crime than any politician had ever done.

Soon Sky 1 had taken over the contract, and the vigilantes in fancy dress moved into the mainstream.

Eddie Shearer became a very wealthy man, to the point where money was no longer his prime motivation. In an unprecedented move he accepted a cut price contract to produce the fourth series. This was to guarantee he could bring the Rectifires into the homes of every British licence-payer. In a major coup, which some commentators said smacked of desperation, the BBC stepped in – and the show fronted their prime-time weekend viewing.

The tone of the article was glibly self-congratulatory, the journalist having correctly forecasted big things for the young Shearer, but at the same time it subtly questioned the morality of both the viewers and producers.

Like many others, Stan Simpson had been a big supporter of the Rectifires and he read the article with interest, trying to ignore the side swipes and moralising. He enjoyed watching them bring justice to the streets. Each episode brought a modicum of comfort as his life collapsed around him.

Stan admitted to himself and to others that he had been damaged by what had happened to Laura, his former partner. He had never quite managed to rid himself of the bitterness that had built up inside him since the death of his unborn child. The child he would have loved and cherished with his beloved Laura, who was everything to him.

Instead he had sought vengeance for the wrongs that had been bestowed upon them. There was no trace of the youths who had pressed a custard pie into Laura's face, and even if they had been caught he doubted if any sort of punishment would have been meted out by the toothless law courts. But Stan couldn't control his anger. Or his hatred. He walked the streets late at night, leaving Laura at home, lonely and bemused, as he looked for troublemakers, vandals and thugs.

When he caught a group of youths defacing a statue at Roberts Park in Saltaire, he chased them, and grabbed one of them by the throat. He slapped him hard round the face a few times and then hurled him down a grass bank. The youth fell awkwardly: his arm was behind his back when he landed on a tree stump. It broke badly in two places and Stan was in deep trouble. He was known to the police after a couple of less serious misdemeanours. At first they had treated him with sympathy, urging him to call them instead of taking matters into his own hands. But they had tired of his stubborn attitude, and he was issued with a caution for common assault after a child threw stones at his window.

This time he was given three years for grievous bodily harm.

Laura told him she loved him and would always love him, but she couldn't be with him and wouldn't wait for him because he couldn't let things go, and it drove her crazy. He begged and pleaded with her, but in his heart of hearts he knew he she was right. Later he heard she had moved on and settled down with someone else. She had recently fallen pregnant again, and would be a mum before he left prison. Through gritted teeth he penned a congratulatory card, but he wept as he wrote.

Stan read on about the young man who had the balls to stand up to scum. He fancied that the only difference between them was that Shearer thought and planned his actions, whereas Stan's impulsiveness cost him his liberty and his Laura.

Then Stan read a sentence that made his blood run cold.

The interviewer asked about Shearer's youth; how it all began. He replied that he was not always on 'the right side of the tracks', and that many of his earliest stunts had authority figures as their victims.

'There were one or two teachers and police constables in Leeds with egg on their faces, I can tell you.'

Slowly Stan put the pieces together.

The age of the youths. How old would Shearer have been at the time? Seventeen? Eighteen?

Shearer was from the area, and he was into filming his mates. He had seen some of their early stuff on the net. And that phrase: 'egg on their face'.

Then he thought of Laura. She would never watch any of Shearer's shows. She often left the room. During other shows she didn't like she lay on the couch and read a magazine. But never during *Rectifires*.

Never.

Did she know? She must have had suspicions.

Stan stared down at the face of the media giant on the page before him. The noise of the prison melted away as he focused on the unsmiling but contented expression. He gulped hard as he felt the old demons firing up inside. The demons he had been trying to suppress for years.

And at that moment he knew.

He knew.

2015
DAVID MARSHALL-BRIGGS

David gripped the letter from Lotsa Coffee in his hand. This was going to be the beginning. The beginning of his journey. To a time and place where his father would look at him with something other than disdain. Somehow his life had drifted off track recently. For the first twenty years of his life he had been protected by the cosy institutions around him. Woodhouse Grove School. Ilkley Tennis Club. Ilkley Rugby Club. Durham University. Bolstered by the money, influence and charisma of his father.

David had always envisaged going to Oxford University. Walking round the city he had had a sense of belonging there. The history, the architecture, but most of all the elitism. The sense of being a cut above. The chance to join forces with other high-class people.

But he simply wasn't that bright, despite the three personal tutors throughout his A level years. His projected grades were simply not good enough, and the finest personal references and trumped-up accounts of his sporting excellence didn't outweigh them. The sense of rejection and failure was crushing. In private he wept uncontrollably, but he had to pull himself together because worse followed. He fell short of his conditional offer from Durham, his back-up, and only frantic negotiations by his father, who called in favours from some old contacts, won him a place.

David never forgot the moment when he was summoned to his father's study. He stood there, softly weeping, while his dad paced around, concluding his telephone call. For once his father looked worn out. Michael Marshall-Briggs was used to tough negotiating, and turning his influence into profit. This was different, though. This time he had the emotional attachment of his first-born son. The son who had been given every opportunity and advantage. A private education, tutors, rugby trips abroad, a tennis coach.

On his seventeenth birthday David had been presented with a brand new sporty hatchback. He had tried valiantly to hide his disappointment after all the Audi TT hints he had dropped. But not much got past his sharp-witted father.

Father and son stood posing in front of the car at his birthday dinner. Aunts and grandparents cooed at their likeness as cameras clicked and flashed. Michael smiled through gritted teeth, and insisted on a handshake shot with the ungrateful twerp. David was already mentally doing the sums on a part exchange, and his hand was limp when he felt the force of his father's vice-like grip. Not a word was spoken, but David's eyes began to water as his knuckles were crushed. It was the first time David had been made aware of the extent of his father's contempt.

The physical pain he felt that day was nothing compared with the moment in the study when his father put down the phone and looked at him. Michael surveyed the snotty, snivelling teenage mess.

~Right. I've managed to get you a place at Durham. David, it's really about time you stood on your own two feet. I can't keep bailing you out for ever. You're going to have to go up there and show them what you're made of.

The relief of the news was overwhelming. He blubbed loudly, gasping for air.

~Th-thanks, Dad. I'll make it work this time. I won't let you down. I won't bloody well let you down.

David desperately wanted to hug his father, as he had when he was a child. To know that everything was going to be all right. He even took a step forward, but the look on his father's face told him this was not a good idea. David knew his demeanour was highly inappropriate in the study; the place where his father so determinedly built up his business, to give the family the luxury and privilege they were used to.

That evening David managed to pull himself together. When he met his school friends for their final drinking spree before they headed off to university he was a picture of confidence, optimism and cockiness once again.

His large circle of friends met at the Crescent wine bar in Ilkley. They had all more or less ended up where they wanted to, but feigned nonchalance about the whole process.

~Durham wanted me in the end. Did absolutely fark-all revision. Too much of the good stuff with you boys.

David raised a glass of the champagne he had bought for everyone, and a round of hearty glass-chinking and back-slapping followed.

~Think they wanted me for the rugby in the end. If you play rugby at Durham they really do kiss your arse. I hope there's some decent totty. The standard of snatch round here's gone way downhill recently. You never used to have to go into Leeds for real quality. Now there's no choice. I've set myself a target of at least two shags in freshers' week. Minimum.

~Chance to double up then, Dave?

A ripple of laughter made its way round the table. David looked up and took note of its source. It was Joseph Brookes, who had come to Woodhouse Grove School in the sixth form from a comprehensive. It irked David somewhat that he was allowed to become part of their circle. He was clearly not one of them, but his friendly laid-back nature had endeared him to the others after a frosty initiation.

The quip was in reference to last month's enquiry into the state of each other's virginity, and how far along the sexual track they were. David's problem was that he had just separated from Eva Parker after an eight-month relationship. She was top of the talent tree at Leeds Girls' Grammar, a stunning slim blonde just shy of five foot ten. Her father's riches eclipsed even David's, and in many ways they were the perfect accessory for each other.

But deep down Eva believed she was destined for greater things. She was a smart girl, and was keen not to build up too much of a history before settling down with her millionaire celebrity husband, whoever he might be. She didn't have David down as the kiss and tell type, but she told herself she couldn't be too careful. She would only appear in the Sunday newspapers for the right reasons.

So, even though she thought he was handsome, she resisted sleeping with him. And David could never say he had – or it would definitely be curtains.

Although there was one time she had agreed to it. At Craiglands Hotel's New Year ball. David's father had just purchased Craiglands, and was keen to flaunt his new investment to the great and the good.

Eva had had a little too much champagne, and David looked very dashing in his dinner suit. A lot of the older guests were saying what a fine young man he was, with so many prospects. She decided on the spur of the moment that this was the right time.

They were slow-dancing in the middle of the dance floor. He was holding her firmly, caught up in the music and the moment. She was feeling sexy, and when she whispered in his ear she could tell by the look in his eye that he was ready too. Thanks to her long legs and high heels her waist was level with his, and they were both aroused by the gentle friction. After Eva had whispered to him David pulled her even closer and their gyrating became more intense.

But something suddenly changed. She never knew what, but the atmosphere between them was different. He loosened his grip on her waist. Panic appeared in his eyes and his breathing became a little hurried. For some reason they began to dance almost at arm's length, and David was looking anywhere but at her. She was about to ask him what the matter was when he excused himself to go to the toilet. And left her in the middle of the dance floor on her own. Like a lemon. The moment was gone.

Only David knew why.

For months a Durex had been burning a hole in his wallet. He had resigned himself to the fact that he wasn't going to fourth base at the New Year ball; all her family were there, so it would be an awkward task anyway. He had spoiled many a night out by hoping that it would be the one, so tonight he had decided to relax and go with the flow. But this meant making the most of their stolen clasps on the dance floor.

With one or two adjustments he managed to arrange his todger so his bell end was poking through his boxer shorts. While he danced only the thin lining of his trousers separated him from Eva. She looked stunning and smelt heavenly. He closed his eyes. If he concentrated hard he was sure he could feel her contours. He traced the edges of her tiny silk panties very gently, and longed for the day when he would be able to slip them down. He was imagining it when she tenderly kissed him on the neck. And then again, even more softly, closer to his earlobe.

~David. David! Tonight. Up in your room. We'll sneak away before midnight. No one will miss us. I'm ready. We've waited long enough. I want you, David. I want you.

His eyes opened wide. His heart raced. His stomach turned in excitement. His thoughts were all of her. Nothing else mattered. He pulled her tighter. He looked at her face and her shimmering blonde hair. Her black designer dress revealed her slenderness but complemented her curves. She was gorgeous and she was his. He rubbed himself firmly against her once more. Tonight he was going to have her. Tonight was the night. Her silk knickers, her matching bra, soft lips all his! Eva. Oh, Eva! His Eva wrapped around . . .

Then he shot his load.

For a while he didn't know what to do. He tried to play it cool. He continued dancing, but couldn't hold her tight. He wondered if she knew. The puzzled look on her face told him she didn't, but he had to get off the dance floor.

In the toilet cubicle he discovered that there was loads of it. It was on his trousers, his boxers, and some globules of spunk were hanging from his pubes. In a blind panic he took off his shoes and pants. He scrunched his boxers up and used them to clean his cock and balls. Then he dipped them in the toilet water and used them as a cloth to scrub briskly at the inside of his trousers. He used toilet paper to dry himself and his trousers. To his dismay little white fragments stuck to his clothes, making matters worse. He cleaned up again with the makeshift cloth before dumping his boxers in the cistern.

From the cubicle David heard people shuffling about outside. He had to wait for what seemed like an age before the coast was clear. Finally he managed to get a decent blast of hot air from the hand drier onto the wet patch. In a Mr Bean moment he turned his crotch upwards, like a limbo dancer, desperate for the dryer's heat. Disturbed after about a minute of hot air, David was forced to make his way back into the ballroom. When he glanced in the mirror the wet patch was still visible, but the optimist in him thought it would be less obvious away from the stronger lighting in the toilets. Perhaps everything would be all right.

But he had been away for too long. The moment had passed. The slow and sexy music had finished. People were beginning to form circles for Auld Lang Syne. He found himself in a huddle with some old people, and craned his head, feeling that he should be with his loved ones. But his mother, his father and Eva were nowhere to be seen.

JUSTIFICATION

Michael Marshall-Briggs

Everything I have I've grafted for.
Hard.
Like this hotel.
It's mine.
I bought it.
But you can't buy balls like I've got.
Years of graft. Years of courage.
Yes, I'm smart. Yes, I have the gift of the gab.
But it's my balls that have got me where I am.
Got me my rewards.
And that's the problem, you see.

My son David will never be like that. He's enjoyed the rewards from the very beginning.

But what was I supposed to do?
Force him to have it tough?
Would he graft hard then?

He'd still most likely turn the wrong way.

It's a real Catch 22.

The best thing I can do is let him have a little reminder every now and again.

About the way of the world.

I've talked this over with Kath.

She says we should be thankful our son doesn't have to struggle. That I should see it as another reward for my hard work.

She's a kind woman, my Kath. Always sees the best in people. Probably why she's so soft with David.

We got together just before I really made it big.

It's good, because it shows she really did love me. She wanted me for me and not just for my money.

But I can't help thinking what I might have landed myself with if I'd just waited a bit longer.

Stayed a bachelor. Maybe till I was about forty.

That Lawrence Appleton over there, he seems to have got away with it.

Left his wife five years ago.

They were married for fourteen years. Two kids.

Everyone really liked his wife, but now they all accept Katrina, his Polish fiancée, as though nothing happened.

It's amazing how people forget.

Or just make out they forget.

They will if you have money.

Or power.

Could I settle down with a real stunner, maybe ten or fifteen years younger?

Kath's all done up now.

And she looks OK, especially since she had that bit of work done.

But sometimes she looks old. Especially on a morning before she's had her hair done.

And her neck. It's like a turkey. Gives her away a bit.

Now she's standing next to Katrina.

Bloody hell, don't do that. It makes things worse.

You look OK, Kath, when you stand on your own.

But don't stand and chat to her.

They look happy.

Sharing a joke.

It's been a successful year.

Appleton lost a few quid on the divorce.

And now he's coming over. I don't mind Appleton really. You get what you see.

But now he's suggesting we find out what the girls are laughing about.

Fuck off, Apple, don't rub my nose in it.

No, I really don't want to go over.

I won't be able to take my eyes off Katrina's breasts.

In that black dress.

She looks so sexy.

He knows it.

It's just on the sexy side of tasteful.

Some folk in here might say it's a little too tarty for my New Year do. Not that Appleton cares. He's just imagining those two beauties bouncing up and down in his face tonight.

Like I'm doing right now.

And having her seems to have built him up even stronger.

I was talking to him in the sauna last week. He reckons Katrina's driven him on to new things. Given his business the boost it needs.

I know exactly what he means.

But don't take the piss. He says we're going over to catch up with the girls. When really he's saying let's compare our women. I'm the one who's going to be thrashing away with this twenty-five-year-old Polish sexpot while you're unravelling that wrinkly old mare.

If you're lucky.

It makes me angry.

It's hard to be nice.

Not my idea to invite them.

But what can you do?

I can't think of nice things to say.

I'm grinding my teeth.

I can smell her perfume.

It's overpowering.

But I want it.

Kath's banging on about horse riding. It's something that she and Katrina have in common.

I ask if Katrina rode horses back in Poland.

It's a lame, lame question.

I try to look her in the eye as she answers.

I'm nodding, but I don't give a flying fuck about her father's stables.

Or the pony she had as a child.

She has some of that shimmering stuff on her chest and cleavage.

It's glistening.

I look.

I get clocked.

There's a moment's silence.

I stutter on about how much care and attention they need.

This is getting worse.

I really am talking utter bloody nonsense now.

I look again.

This time I hold it for two to three seconds.

I'm almost past caring.

Maybe if I get a good look the picture will stay in my mind and I won't have to look again.

I'm rolling my fingers.

It's because I'm imagining tweaking her nipples.

I stop.

Appleton's smirking.

He's loving this.

Sneaky bugger.

He could help me out if he wanted. He's full of useless chat when he wants to be.

He's enjoying my awkwardness.

Eventually he shows some mercy.

They politely make their excuses and wander away.

I catch one more glance of her peachy buttocks in her tight red dress.

Appleton's giving her a couple of pats.

He's showing possession.

And victory.

I know the signs.

Smug bastard.

I know how much more vigour I'd have if I was riding that every night.

I don't know what it is, but women like that seem to give me a lift.

Don't know if it's anything to do with testosterone or something, but I know it's there.

That's why I have to have my fun and games now and again.

To give me a lift.

That way business keeps moving forward and I can provide for Kath and the family.

It's about the family.

That's why I'm so discreet.

A bit of rogering every now and again.

Legitimate business trips. Overnight stays.

There's nothing planned.

I know there'll be no comebacks.

But every now and again you have to take a risk.

A calculated risk.

Because not to take risks is not to live.

And you have to weigh the risk to the reward.

Just look at my son David over there, smooching with that long-legged blonde.

What risk is that?

It's just a safe bet.

She's gorgeous too, though.

And seventeen.

I don't even think he's had his way with her yet.

Not man enough.

I can accept he's had most things handed him on a plate.

I provided most of them, for Christ's sake.

But women are a bit different.

He's got here because of me.

Because of who I've made him.

And I never got to have anything like that at his age.

Sure, I can have a bit of quality every now and again on the quiet.

But there's something special, uplifting, about walking into a formal do with a woman like that on your arm.

Maybe it's because everyone knows what you're going to do to her later.

I deserve more.

But circumstances dictate.

I know that.

But look at the pair of them.

He really is a lucky little swine.

My wife's been talking to me.

I haven't really been listening.

Something about a migraine.

And going upstairs.

She'll be upset because of the way I looked at Katrina.

But she's a fine woman. She knows the rules.

She'll be quiet for a bit, but she'll not mention it.

She's going up to our room for a lie-down. I'll nip up after midnight. She'll probably be pretending to be asleep.

So I'll wake her and wish her Happy New Year.

Then we'll be fine.

She's gone now.

I'm looking at my son.

What the bloody hell is that boy doing?

He looks so awkward with her.

Can't even dance properly.

Just sort of hugging and swaying.

And now he's at arm's length.

Not even looking at her.

I don't believe this.

He's left her, heading for the lobby.

She's just standing there, like she doesn't know what to do.

Like she's about to cry.

I'm still feeling the old fire in my loins from looking at Katrina.

So bugger it.

I'm going over.

Her eyes are watery and she seems a bit tearful.

I ask her where that good-for-nothing son of mine has gone, in a jokey, friendly sort of way.

I talk some more jolly nonsense and make her laugh.

And all of a sudden we're dancing.

But only because she's a young kid left on her own in the middle of the dance floor.

And it's the decent thing to do.

And we're dancing properly because I've bothered to learn.

She's clearly had a few lessons too.

A few people are looking over, but bugger them.

It's not like I'm being sneaky.

And this is my bloody hotel.

My wife's here and my son'll be back from the toilets soon.

We seem to move so harmoniously. Like it's instinct.

She's loving it, and looks like she wishes it would last.

Who am I kidding?

I'm loving it too.

The front of my trousers must be like a bloody great marquee!

Well, I've done it now.

I've rubbed it against her.

Old habits die hard.

But no.

Pulling me closer?

What the . . . ?

She's looking at me differently now.

I've seen that look a thousand times.

I know what it means.

You're in, Thorners, old boy.

Bloody well and truly.

But there's no way.

Is there?

Can I?

Got to be smart.

Think quick.

Be smart.

Break off.

Look like we're laughing.

Like a game.

Wag my finger a bit, like a silly old bugger telling her off and it's all just a joke.

But there's no joke here.

This is big stakes.

I'm no gambler: I've calculated the risks.

The rewards justify it.

And the risks add to the rush.

I walk off, but not before I've whispered in her ear.

And I'm away to the bar.

The last thing I need is a drink: it's her nectar I'm after.

Some silly old sod from the rugby club's talking to me. Can't even remember the bastard's name.

There's no time to be polite.

I cut him off, wish him Happy New Year and I'm away.

Through the bar and into the lobby. Then I'm straight out of the front doors into the car park.

There's nobody about as I make my way into the stone alcove where we keep the wheelie bins.

I'm not at the point of no return yet. So what? We danced a little and I arranged to meet her on the lawn.

Perhaps just to talk or give advice.

Concerned.

Concerned about my son, who might be giving the wrong signals.

But she's gorgeous.

And I want her.

Now.

I can't remember the last time I was this het up.

There's nothing else I can think of.

David and my wife flash into my mind.

I could feel remorse.

I could feel terrible.

It could ruin my reputation.

Everything.

But right now I don't give a fuck.

I've even factored in the alcohol I've drunk.

And I still have to have her.

But she isn't coming.

David's probably back now.

They'll be back in there playing silly little boyfriend and girlfriend.

I just can't get her out of my mind. Her smell, the feel of her.

Seventeen, for fuck's sake.

Perfect.

Well, if she isn't coming she's still fresh enough in my mind for me to enjoy her.

It's almost like she's still here. Dancing close.

I pull my cock out and begin to slowly wank.

I'm a respected businessman, hunched over in my own hotel.

No fuck that, concentrate.

Get this over with, then get my senses back.

Think of her . . .

And . . .

Yes . . .

Just a little longer . . .

Over soon . . .

Bloody hell, there she is.

I stop and tuck myself back into my strides.

She's standing there by the fountain, just like I said.

I don't believe it.

She looks cold and lost, rubbing her slim bare arms with her hands.

Just a kid. A poor kid.

I'm zipped up and over there.

It's not too late.

Not past the point of no return.

I've only danced with her and asked to meet her outside.

I haven't done anything inappropriate yet.

Bar rub my old man against her.

And that was accidental.

Sort of.

If we talk normally it could be like nothing's happened. Talk about David or her plans for college.

But the way she's looking at me. I know that look.

Eyes wide, unblinking.

She doesn't want to talk about crap like that.

So we talk about dancing.

Which was a mistake.

She's had private lessons since she was six years old. So she's sort of an expert.

And it's OK for her to talk about my hip movement. She puts her hands there. And tucks her thumb inside my pocket. That'll help her with her grip.

We start to sway together. Locked in dance partner pose. We're moving across the lawn, out of view of anyone who walks out of the main ballroom doors.

We stop at the little alcove where I had my old lad out.

It's cold, but sharing our body heat makes us comfortable. We're locked together and she's still mumbling on about dancing, and how it's OK to dance with passion and lust because dancers are artists and performers.

The point of no return.

We're on the border.

We're in a no man's land.

But I've had my passport stamped.

–Is it OK to do this?

And I'm over.

Kissing her tenderly on the lips.

The contact is gentle and attentive. I gently stroke the silky material of the dress that hugs her slim hips. I move my fingertips around to appreciate the firm roundness of her buttocks.

She's gentle too at first, stroking the back of my neck, pulling me closer.

Then firmer.

She kisses me harder.

She's gasping and clawing at my chest.

Then she breaks off.

And now I'm panting.

Desperate to carry on.

–No. It's not OK. You're a very, very naughty man, Mr

Marshall-Briggs. She jabs her finger into my chest and speaks rhythmically as though telling off a child. For one dreadful moment I think she's going call it off. She holds my gaze and I'm about to beg her not to stop.

But no need.

--And I can be a very naughty girl too.

Her posh schoolgirl voice seems somehow out of place, but the novelty turns me on even more.

And now she's unbuckling my belt and unzipping my flies.

She pulls the elastic of my boxers over the top of my shaft and takes me in her mouth.

As she's sucking and licking she pulls my pants down further, so she can cup my balls in her hands.

I'm groaning in ecstasy and nigh on climax before calling her off.

Because I don't want it to finish.

I stand her up and ease my fingers inside her dress, pulling her panties down.

I spin her round firmly and bend her over some beer crates.

She's lovely and flexible as she expertly arches her back, tilting her bum upwards, and exposing her holes.

I squat down, and I'm into both with my tongue, tweaking and prodding with my fingers, making her gasp and pant in frenzied high-pitched yelps.

While she's still wanting more I pull her upright and make her face me.

I pick her up and hoist her back towards the wall.

I ease myself inside her wet hole and start to slowly hump her.

She's really into this, and showing her appreciation.

Then she changes.

She gasps and becomes rigid.

But it's not the right kind of gasp.

Then I smell it.

Cigar smoke.

I realise I've been smelling it for while, but so enraptured was I that I never considered the relevance.

Out of the corner of my eye I can see someone's casting a shadow over us.

I ease myself out of her and tuck myself away before slowly turning round.

Appleton's standing there.

He has a strange look on his face, somewhere between intrigue and hilarity.

He's puffing away on his cigar, but he's not looking directly at us. He's looking at the image of us on his mobile phone.

He's still filming when Eva breaks down in tears.

She hunches her shoulders forward and folds her arms. Her hair falls across her face as she starts to sob.

Almost instantly she's transformed herself from the sexually adept young woman into a sobbing vulnerable schoolgirl.

Exploited.

This looks bad.

For a while nobody says anything.

The silence is only broken by Eva's sobbing.

–Come now, precious. Don't play the innocent little princess with me!

Appleton's voice is cruel and mocking.

–I've just seen you perform. You can watch yourself too if you like.

He offers the phone but is wary not to loosen his grip.

–Fuck off, you perv!

Appleton laughs, but he's done the trick. She's not crying any more, and there's a harder look about her again.

–There's no need to be like that. I'm not going to cause you any bother. We all have our little secrets. God knows, I have. You just run along to your nice little boyfriend and forget all about it.

She doesn't need a second invitation and says nothing more.

She gives him an evil scowl as she steps back into her knickers with as much dignity as she can muster.

She doesn't look at me as she leaves.

~So why do that? Why film us? You want to wreck my marriage and hurt my kids? Just because it happened to you?

~Happened to me? Come off it, Michael. Things don't just happen. We make things happen. You and me. We're similar. We're the driving force. Difference is, I'm honest and open about it. People can take me as they please. You have to sneak around behind some bins with a bloody schoolgirl. Your son's girlfriend no less. Top effort. Much respect to you, my friend.

He offers me his hand to shake but I don't take it.

~So why the phone footage? What's that for? Don't tell me you're not going to show it to anyone.

~Michael, Michael, Michael. What do you take me for? Would I do that to you?

See this phone? It's gone. I'm gonna throw the damn thing in the duck pond. Straight up. It's gone.

~You serious?

~I swear, hand on heart, that I'll throw this in the pond. As soon as you've finished yourself off.

~You what?

Just finish yourself off and it's over. I won't mention this to another soul. No one will know. Now let's see your handiwork.

~What's wrong with you? You must think I'm . . .

But he cuts me off.

~Don't give me any of your shite, Michael. You know a good deal when you see one. A few strokes and we're done. End of. As they say. Besides, do you have a fucking choice?

His last words are cruel, and I can see from his eyes that he's deadly serious.

My cock is becoming limper with every second that passes, so if I want this over with quickly I'd better get started.

I take matters into my own hands.

My strokes per minute must be through the roof, and my eyes are closed. I'm thinking about Eva, desperately trying to block the fact that Appleton's standing there.

To strike some sort of blow against him, I try to imagine Katrina joining in in a strange threesome, but it's too far from reality and takes me away from climax. My best bet is to replay events exactly as they happened. I think about her back in the ballroom. About dancing with her. I'm almost there. Then Appleton starts speaking.

~Good form, old boy. Keep it going.

I open my eyes for a moment. He's standing there, puffing on his cigar, arms folded, like it's the most natural thing in the world. Letting him in puts me right off. I'm further away than ever. That's probably why he opened his gob.

I up my stroke rate even further. My forearm is beginning to ache. I could do myself some damage here but I need this over with.

I get to the part where she's up against the wall. Appleton doesn't encroach this time. I'm pounding away, and if I shut my eyes very tight I can remember just how she felt. How good it felt.

~Go on, Thorners! Give it some! Go on, my son!

I try to blank him out. Wanking at top speed. But I pull too hard and I feel a sharp pain. I glance down and there are a few specks of blood on my fingers. Bastard. I was almost there. I desperately try to continue, but I lose focus. My cock's drooping badly and hurting like mad. I soldier on for a few more strokes. Fuck me. That hurt. I feel another sharp pain and I know I can't go on.

I collapse backwards, slumping breathless on the floor.

~It's no good. I just can't do it. Go on. Go back in there. Show everyone. It's over.

I'm still holding my poor sore cock between my fingers.

~Don't worry, old boy. Wouldn't think of it. You gave it

your all. I'm in a good mood. You tried your best and that's all anyone could ask. I can see how much you care about your family; you nigh on ripped your cock off for them.

He's laughing as he stands there.

He throws his cigar stub on the ground

It lands between my spread-eagled legs, and he steps forward to extinguish it.

He walks away, and I can still hear him cackling.

I don't breathe a sigh of relief until I hear the plop that tells me his phone has gone.

VISION

Eva's resolve seemed to strengthen after New Year, leaving David with only one chalk on the board. His only genuine action was a grapple on the beach in Cornwall, when he had visited his uncle's holiday home after his GCSEs. He had lived off this story for too long. To increase his tally he had fabricated an encounter at a family wedding. He thought about making up a third to make the total respectable, but thought two with plenty of prospects might be enough to pass the test.

And it almost had. No one had really batted an eyelid until Joe Brookes decided to add his twopence-worth. This common outsider sat boldly among them in their favourite wine bar. David couldn't be sure if Joe was challenging him, or if he was simply ignorant of the obvious hierarchy that existed.

--Yeah, well. Wish I'd bloody well gone to a comprehensive school where they all start shagging each other as soon as they turn twelve.

Laughter rippled around the table.

--Don't feel left out, David. You were a boarder, weren't you? Heard your tutors made sure you got a good seeing-to in the first year.

Everyone laughed now, and with greater intensity, raising the stakes.

David was genuinely angry. He tried not to lose his cool. He tried not to sound too narked, and offered an olive branch. Albeit heavily barbed.

--So you're heading to Sunderland Uni, Brooksy? I'll have to come and visit you. Bet there are some real dirt-piece girls. Don't they let people in with three Us? You'll have an awesome time, though. Deffo going to visit. First term. Stick together now we're both Geordie boys.

But David never did visit his old acquaintance. He never went anywhere near Sunderland. He even avoided it when his rugby team was due to play there. Happy in the secure confines of Durham University, his ample funds and knowledge of Rugby Union's etiquette took him to the top of the university's social circles. It was a heady haze of drinking, parties, sport and the odd lecture and seminar thrown in. Sometimes he wrote his own essays but usually he paid others, to make up for his poor performance in examinations.

At the start of the second year he was elected as chairman of the Sports Association and revelled in the prestige, organising many successful social events and fundraisers. He boosted his tally to a more than respectable total, and went some way to putting to bed his New Year demons. His frolics at Durham were punctuated with holidays abroad and occasional visits to catch up with friends around Ilkley. For the first eighteen months he was as happy as he had ever been.

It was one Thursday morning towards the end of the second year that he got a sad sinking feeling in his stomach. At first he wasn't sure why, but later he pinned it down. Someone was talking about going to a meeting with a careers advisor. She was talking CVs and work placements. The realisation hit him that they would all soon be entering their third year. All this wasn't going to last for ever, though he desperately wanted it to. His friends were talking about jobs, and he hated it.

An extra year at Durham was what David really craved. It was the most comfortable of comfort zones, where he had the status and respect he deserved. Before one summer jaunt to St Tropez he and his friends had begun work at a restaurant in Leeds city centre, owned by his friend's father. They intended to give the impression that they were paying their own way, but in truth what they earned barely paid for their pre-flight drinks.

David had expected it to be a bit of a jolly. Having a laugh with his mates, flirting with the talent, enjoying a glass of quality wine along the way. The shock of having to work for real hit him hard. Much of it was sweating away in the kitchen, and being told off by a chef who clearly had no breeding whatsoever. All it taught him was that he would put work off for as long as possible. And when he did work he would have to be in charge.

David decided to talk to his father about the possibility of doing a masters' degree, but got short shrift. His dad said they weren't really designed for people in danger of getting a third, and it was about time for him to get into the real world and start earning some respect. David wondered how his dad knew he was in danger of getting a third, and it occurred to him that he must have a man on the inside. He usually did.

There was one other way to gain the extra year: to

repeat his second year. One of his tutors had suggested this after his remarkably poor performances in the examinations when compared with his coursework. But David could not face his father with yet another failure, so this was not an option.

The sinking feeling continued. It increased until one night David just couldn't sleep. He tossed and turned and scratched and wanked, but still his thoughts raced with panic and shame: he was still pacing up and down his bedroom when the sun came up. He decided to walk to the local chemist to buy some herbal sleeping tablets, and the exercise and early morning air had a calming effect. Even so, when David got back to his room he popped three of the pills into his mouth and had a glass of hot milk. He felt exhausted, and the sedatives took him away. He knew he was at rock bottom, and perhaps when he finally admitted this to himself he was eventually able to sleep. To sleep deep and long. To hibernate.

And when David woke, early that afternoon, he had missed two lectures and an important seminar. But it didn't matter, because he woke as a different animal. He had risen with a vision. He had had his fun. He was ready to graft. Ready to show his father. During his slumber he had changed. He knew the only way was up. In his slumber he had grown some balls.

2016
MANAGER

Nigel Jenkins, the regional director of Lotsa Coffee, had his doubts about the new appointment. He always insisted on being present at interviews when management level posts were decided on. Young Marshall-Briggs gave a good interview and made all the right noises, but Jenkins was sceptical about why a Durham graduate would want to work in a coffee shop. A safer bet was someone with retail experience, and someone who was less likely to be off in six months when he found a better job. However, a word in his ear from a respected colleague had swayed his opinion, and he decided to give the youngster the benefit of the doubt.

Jenkins was glad he did. He was pleasantly surprised to find that his scepticism was unfounded. David took to the job with a tireless drive and determination. Overtime and weekend work were no problem. Despite his tender years he seemed to have natural authority, and because he wasn't afraid to get his hands dirty the staff responded to his demand for high standards. He was attentive and responsive at the training seminars, and flew through his initial appraisal.

After six months Mr Jenkins's main concern was how to keep hold of his little starlet, as there were plenty of more lucrative opportunities in the offing. His idea was to offer a fast track promotion. The new position would see David leapfrog his current manager, to take charge of two shops. His salary would be almost doubled, but Jenkins was convinced that the move was justified as it would help to keep hold of the best young talent. Of course it would mean scrutiny from national level, which usually meant anonymous observation at work followed by an interview, but he knew that a quiet word in David's ear would leave the boy thoroughly prepared for a visit during the following weeks.

It was a fresh autumn morning when Mr Jenkins called in at the beginning of the morning shift and spelled out his plans. The news, combined with a strong coffee, left David buzzing. He went about his work with an added sense of purpose. Directing staff and mucking in himself, he breezed through the morning. The Ilkley Literature Festival was in full swing, and seating at the coffee shop was at a premium. David had his staff working at a frenetic pace, keeping the tills ticking over while tables were cleared and made ready for the hordes of mums and kids waiting for Michael Morpurgo across the road.

Things went swimmingly. The shop was rammed, but everyone seemed happy as customers moved in and out at a leisurely pace. One fat woman with too many kids caused a bit of a scene when her toddler knocked over a cup of coffee. She came and asked for a cloth, but she was far too fat to be worth helping, and besides, David was far too busy delivering chocolate flakes to a MILF at the other side of the shop. After watching the fat woman fret and struggle for a while, he dispatched a crew member to make sure that at least the chair was dry. The shame-faced mother and her brats promptly left, leaving space for prettier clientele.

There was one other thing that was annoying David, something that was blighting the smooth running of the well-oiled machine he had created. In the middle of the shop sat a man who didn't quite fit in. He looked different from the other customers. The women wore skinny jeans, long leather boots and fitted designer jumpers, while the men wore woollen scarves and spoke loudly in posh accents. This character looked drawn and hung over, and seemed oblivious to his surroundings. He wore tracksuit bottoms with a loose cotton shirt tucked into them. His laptop had been plugged into a power point without permission. All morning he had been sitting there, day-dreaming and staring at his computer, taking up valuable seating space that could have been occupied by a high-spending and more deserving young family. To make matters worse, all he had purchased was a medium-sized Americano.

When the man got up to use the toilet, David noted the title of the book he was reading and had left face down. It was *Porno* by Irvine Welsh: an open-mouthed blow-up doll stared out from the front cover. This confirmed to David that he had to take action.

As the man slowly made his way back to his seat two attractive well-dressed women were standing at the entrance, surveying the shop for seats. David blocked the man's path and looked straight at him.

~Look, you're going to have to buy another coffee, otherwise it's time to leave I'm afraid.

~OK then. I'll have another Americano.

~It's not table service, you know. You'll have to go to order it.

The man looked at him. David half-expected him to lash out, or at least say something abusive. But he just stood there, his eyes suggesting that thoughts were ticking over. Then he shuffled over to the counter.

David had won the first battle of wills.

Not long afterwards the man left, but not before taking a snap of David on his camera phone. David had been unnerved at first, but laughed about it later with his colleagues. He was pleased that he had got rid of the scruffer, keeping the class inside his shop at a desirable level. It was not long before he had completely forgotten the incident.

Unfortunately for David, this man was not the type to forget about him.

APPRAISAL

David looked carefully at his calendar. Mr Jenkins had more or less guaranteed that today would be his appraisal, although the visit was supposed to be unscheduled. He had been assured that he would have nothing to worry about as long as he performed to his usual high standards. The interview that followed would be a breeze, once he had been primed with the likely questions.

David had arrived especially early, and made sure he was thoroughly prepared. Taking no chances, he had rung all his staff that morning to give them a little pep talk. As he unlocked the front door and turned the closed sign to open he felt confident and ready. Not complacently confident, but a confidence based on hard work and preparation.

He walked behind the counter, ready to welcome early customers. David normally hoped for some talent to flirt with, but for today he was happy to settle for hassle-free and smartly dressed.

He momentarily crouched down to switch on the sound system. As he did so he heard the door open and footsteps slowly make their way inside. He adjusted the volume and stood up smiling, but his smile didn't last for long.

Standing there was the most despicable-looking creature that David had ever seen. The man was in his fifties, but looked at least twenty years older. His creased yellow skin hung loosely round his hollow features. He had greasy tousled hair and a grey matted beard. His lips were pale and cracked and an occasional tooth jutted out from rotten gums. He wore a long tattered overcoat and string-tied jeans.

--One small latte, please.

The words were slow and deliberate. Almost rehearsed.

--The thing is, sir, we're not actually open yet. There's a nice little café a bit further down the high street.

David laughed nervously.

--Actually, a little more reasonably priced than us if truth be told.

The homeless looking man looked back at David, not registering if he understood or not.

--One small latte, please.

--Look, you're not going to get served, so please leave. If I don't give you permission to be in here you're technically trespassing.

The old tramp was beginning to look a little bewildered, but didn't move a muscle.

--One small latte, please.

David realised his bullshit was having no effect, but he carried on all the same. He picked up the phone and pretended to press some buttons.

--Yes, it's David Marshall-Briggs here, manager of

Lotsa Coffee on the High Street. Just having a spot of bother with a trespasser. Would you be so good as to send someone over? How long? About five minutes? Right, look forward to seeing them. Bye. Thank you.

David looked over at the tramp and held his gaze.

~One small latte, please.

David was beginning to get flustered. Clearly his bullshitting hadn't worked. Time for plan B. He leaned forward over the desk and lowered his voice as he opened the cash register.

~Right. That's a five pound note. Please take it and leave. That's enough money to buy three cups of coffee down the road. That's my final offer.

The old man paused for much longer. His sad eyes translated the currency into cans of White Lightning.

~One small latte, please.

And he dropped a plastic money bag filled with copper and silver on the counter.

David counted the money. Something was definitely wrong. The grubby shrapnel came to exactly the right amount.

SITUATION

David could not quite believe what was happening. One hour after the tramp arrived the coffee shop was full. When regular, respectable Ilkley customers walked in they surveyed the scene, raised eyebrows and sheepishly headed back out. Because that tramp was the first in a long line of delinquents. Those who didn't look homeless, David reckoned, had never before set foot outside the grimy flea-ridden council estate where they were spawned. Others looked like common criminals. Dark hollow eyes that were too close together peered out from under baseball caps.

They all sat by themselves, and not one of them was moving. This meant that a genuine Ilkley customer would have to share a table. And this was clearly not happening.

To make matters worse each of them had ordered a small latte and nothing else. The café wasn't even making any money.

AS IT WAS FOR DAVID

Homeless undesirables. On today of all days. A defining moment in his life. And now a sinking feeling of panic. All these wretched individuals taking up the tables of his beloved, clean, smart, professional, white, respectable, caring, knowing, beautiful, wise, wholesome, polite Ilkley people.

One looked familiar.

Vaguely.

But no idea where from.

It was a thinly disguised Eddie Shearer, the man whom David had kicked out. And forgotten about.

Now he was heading for the empty lavatory, which David had insisted was cleaned twice. Spotless, disinfected, heavenly smelling.

For now.

Eddie was in the loo.

Eddie had not forgotten how he had felt.

Now David would feel it.

Only much worse, he hoped.

Eddie, half-disguised in a sort of chav/homeless combo, locked himself in the clean lavatory. His shell suit bottoms tucked into his white sports socks. His New York Yankees baseball cap cock-eyed on his head.

All morning Eddie had been stoving up a massive shit.

Down came his pants. But he sat on the basin.

Outside, a smart man in a suit had breezed in.

He moved with authority. And David's heart was in his mouth.

But the man seemed pleased. He sat down and conversed with the customers. He seemed not to notice their despicable nature. Smiling, laughing. Happily ticking the boxes on his clipboard.

Very good. Very good.

Questions to David. But not challenging.

Meanwhile Eddie squatted.

Curling out his smelly turd.

Then back to his seat. Back to his book.

Cue the customers.

Complaining.

Why hadn't anything been done?

Not in front of the inspector. Please no.

But we've been asking to get it cleaned up all morning.

Not what we expect.

We have standards.

We spend a lot of money in here.

Yes.

On our lattes. And Americanos. Espressos. Mochas with extra cream and chocolate twirls. We expect things to be done.

But this man refused. Looked down on us.

A barrage of voices.

Out of order.

Treating good customers like scum.

All we want is a decent clean place to get a coffee.

Inspector concerned about the new protégé. Questions asked. A harsher tone.

But the toilets are clean. Spotless. Smelling fresh. Because David had insisted on it. No stone left unturned. And no one had used them since he last checked.

Had they?

So they look.

There's a turd in the basin. Some smeared on the tap.

David gulped. Felt tears in his eyes. Anger? Fear? Disbelief?

He's not sure. But there's no time to work it out.

The inspector was in a rage. He seemed bigger now, and threatening. Nasty words. About letting down these good people.

But David knew these weren't good people. He could tell by the way they looked. And they didn't even spend much money. So why would he say something like that?

Inspector not for turning.

Pointing at David.

Accusing.

Making demands.

Almost physically forcing him into the toilet. Not fat and jolly any more.

Big.

Big and threatening.

~Clean that up!

David could have a word with his staff to . . .

~Get that cleaned up right away.

Voice soft, but full of authority.

~I'll just have a word with . . .

~No. You. Do it. Now.

Inspector in his personal space now. Hands on hips.

~Get it sorted right away.

~OK. Just need some gloves, a bucket and some . . .

~Get it sorted. NOW. These good people have waited long enough.

Tramps, thieves and chavs looking on. All attention on him. Because they deserve to drink coffee in a nice place without the smell of shit. They pay good money.

To escape, David would have had to push past the inspector, who held the keys to his promotion. Perhaps this was all just a test, to see how far he would go.

Toilet paper in a roll round his hand. And he scooped it up. And wiped. With everyone looking on. He dropped pieces of turd down the pan and felt he was going to gip. But still he continued, as quickly as he could. To get it over. Then some got through the paper and down his fingernails.

The basin was looking cleaner.

And then they all started to leave. One by one. Leaving their empty coffee cups. Without saying a word they filed out like ghosts.

The actor too. His job done. Unusual role, but good money.

Soon the shop was empty. Bar Eddie, who was going to say something to the person who kicked him out and now has shit on his hands. He had thought a lot about what he might say at his moment of triumph.

But a look is enough.

More than enough.

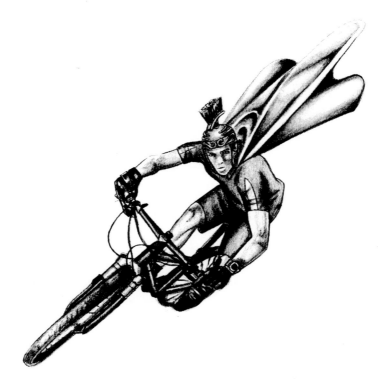

WHEELZ

2018
WHEELZ

Too much of an all-rounder. That's your problem. Jack of all trades, master of none.

These words echoed around Connor Green's head as he sat in the back of the Transit as it crawled round the car park of Bradford Interchange.

They were the kind of comment that had been made over and over again, casually or in jest, around the locker rooms or in the club-house. At first they never bothered him in the slightest. He had supreme self-confidence in his own ability. He just loved cycling, of any kind, and never met anyone who could match his ability. From speed around the track on a racing bike or doing tricks on a BMX he had it all.

But others improved. They concentrated on what they were best at. They trained and improved. Picked up sponsorship. Lottery funding came. The chance arose to go full time as a racer, but the selection process wasn't kind to him. They chose people he had beaten. Regularly. But they were riders who were committed. Who were punctual, professional and polite. Who didn't miss training because they had a BMX meet. Or got themselves injured by trying some over-ambitious trick.

He thought about the British cycling team, and what they would be doing at the Olympic village. Maybe they would be training at the velodrome, maybe receiving a pre-race massage or briefing. Or just getting kitted out in their smart, tight-fitting British uniform. That's what he thought about most. What they would be wearing.

He thought about what they would be wearing because in the reflection of the blacked-out windows he could see himself quite clearly.

And he looked like a dick.

He thought about the streamlined helmet and skin-tight shorts they wore. He looked at his own helmet, with a camera on the front and the two foot tall bright green mohican protruding from it. His red top and shorts were skin-tight lycra, but his bright green cape made a mockery of aerodynamic design.

The adrenalin was kicking in. It was more than a race. More than any competition he had been in. In competitions he always felt in control. He was utterly at home on a bike. This was different. He was way out of his comfort zone. And he had no idea how things might turn out.

A man in the front wearing headphones and studying a monitor suddenly spoke.

--OK, Wheelz. Get yourself ready. We're good to go.

Connor mounted his bike for the third time that afternoon. The first two had been false alarms. With the tension eating away at him, he really wanted this one to be the real thing. He crouched low over his handlebars, partly to gain power on the start and partly to avoid scraping his mohican on the roof.

The man in the front seat monitored the picture on his screen. A track-suited youth was lurking by the bait bike. He had moved away once but returned, and now had both hands on it. Suddenly he yanked it hard, springing it free from an ineffective chain. In a flash he was on it and pedalling away, down the hill and towards the town centre. Seconds later the doors of the van sprang open.

As instructed, Connor surged out of the van, using the exit ramp to propel himself into the air. He was used to generating power over short distances and used this to create maximum lift. The result was spectacular. An air raid-style siren sounded as fireworks cracked. Connor lifted his front wheel skyward, his cape flying behind him. He landed and spun round in one movement.

He paused for a couple of seconds, looking straight at camera one, smiling and nodding with what he hoped was a determined and confident gaze. Then he turned his head, focusing his eyes on the target that was gathering speed while weaving in and out of pedestrians.

To his right a small tent designed to cover manholes began to spark and crackle with pyrotechnics. A muscular man adorned in silver body paint burst out of it. His only clothing was an all-in-one silver leotard. He charged out as if he was competing in the hundred metres final at the Olympics. Head down, slowly rising from a crouched start position, he pumped his arms and knees high, keeping his torso still and eyes forward. The Silver Bullet was well ahead of Connor and closing on the target.

From the multi-storey car park adjoining the interchange the sound of a motorbike loudly over-revving could be heard above the commotion.

Connor glanced over to see the familiar sight of

Bladze, the final competitor, straddled behind the driver of the trail-bike, his roller blades almost touching the tarmac as they sped the short distance from the car park to the pedestrian precinct.

Bladze's entry into the race was the most spectacular of all. Dressed in a white vest and raggy denim shorts, he contrasted starkly with the other two pursuers. His lean, toned body was adorned with black body paint, which formed shapes similar to cave paintings. His wild, spiky hair completed the urban neanderthal image that the stylists were looking for. Connor thought he looked like a dancer in a pop band, and the sexy image irked him slightly: he was sure everyone else was made to look as ridiculous as possible.

As the motorbike swung its back wheel round to come to a sudden halt, Bladze dismounted leap-frog style and landed smoothly, maintaining the speed built up by the bike. He crouched low in the style of a speed skater, eating up the ground between himself and the target.

The race was well and truly on. Startled pedestrians looked on in amazement, bewilderment or sheer panic as not one but four men madly dashed through town.

Those who were agile enough dived for cover. Those who weren't stood rooted to the spot, some crouching, some with arms covering their heads in the hope this would offer some protection.

After a promising initial early burst the Silver Bullet was flagging. He kept his lead for a hundred and fifty yards, but after having to sidestep a double buggy he struggled to find the stamina to run down the thief.

Bladze cruised past him. It looked effortless but he moved at breathtaking speed. He arced in and out of pedestrians with a nonchalance that defied the risks he was taking. Connor, from his position about sixty feet behind, could not believe the path the rollerblader was taking. He seemed to select the riskiest path possible through the stricken crowds of shoppers. Connor was sure that every change in direction would bring the inevitable collision, but Bladze continued to ghost through the pedestrians, a faint brush with a shopping bag the only contact. He was the true superstar of this game.

Connor, meanwhile, was still in contention but happy to bide his time. He pedalled along at a slightly safer speed, unwilling to match Bladze's audacious risks, taking safer routes round pedestrians while Bladze was happy to slice through the small gaps between them.

It was not long before the rollerblader was within striking distance of the bicycle thief. Connor looked on, expecting his colleague and rival to take the target down. But Bladze was in the mood for showboating. When there was no longer any room on the pavement he skated along low walls or benches. At one point he sprang over a rubbish bin with legs flailing on either side, quickly following this up with a low, long jump-style leap to clear a street vendor who was sitting on the pavement.

The stricken thief was now all too aware of the commotion behind him and was pedalling frantically to try and put some distance between himself and his pursuers. What had seemed like an easy steal was turning into a surreal nightmare way beyond his limited imagination.

Bladze, satisfied that he had put on enough of a show, was poised to strike. He hit maximum speed and prepared to put the thief out of his misery. Just as he was about to pounce a group of three teenage girls rounded a corner with their arms linked together, inadvertently forming a wall.

The bike thief swerved towards the centre of the

precinct. Bladze took the riskier route, which saw him veer briefly into the entrance of a sandwich shop. As he did so he clipped the shoulder of an old lady, who dropped her bag, stumbled a few steps and collapsed in a confused heap.

Bladze had lost some serious momentum. He spun round and came to a complete standstill, putting one hand on the ground. For a split second his eyes met those of the confused old lady. One side of her glasses was dislodged and her mouth remained wide open as she gasped for air with high-pitched wheezing noises. Bladze could see that was badly shaken but her injuries were in no way life-threatening. As a result he picked himself up and pressed on, determined to continue the chase. As he picked up speed an unwelcome green cape and red lycra flashed past him.

Jolted and less confident, Bladze was no longer picking the risky lines of attack. He stuttered along, his movements lacking fluidity, unable to gather enough momentum to overhaul the two figures on bikes.

Connor saw his chance. He rose over his handlebars and forced all available power through his pedals, closing in on his target. The two cyclists were side by side as they passed the window of an electrical retailer. Connor veered in front of him, their wheels locking together and the thief colliding head-first with the window. The thick glass held firm, and he crashed to the ground. Dazed, he tried to stand up, but the man with the green cape and mohican thrust a forearm into his face.

In what seemed like seconds another two men had arrived. The first, covered in funny drawing on his arms and legs, began to tie his limbs together with flexes. A silver man in a thong, who was more out of breath than the other two but seemed more angry, manipulated him into a sitting position with angry grunts and gestures.

After only a couple of minutes all three left the tracksuited youth, who was breathless, aching and disorientated. A crowd of onlookers began to gather, some in scorn, some in amusement and a good few in sympathy. After ten minutes uniforms forced their way through. They dispersed those who remained, spoke into their radios and began to lead him away.

THE SILVER BULLET

THE SANDWICH SHOP

Imran wants to help.
  She was a customer in his shop.
  And he likes to help.
  The smart man in the suit.
  With the ID tag on his belt.
  And glasses and shiny shoes.
  Important man.
  Shiny shoes.
  Tie with a big wide knot.
  Firm but friendly.
  Organising things.
  Looking after the old lady.
  He sits her down and speaks softly to her.
  He speaks more firmly to the others in the shop.
  To go and get tea.
  Hot and sweet.
  For the shock.
  And a glass of water.

Call her love,

Tell her it's OK.

And go over the details of the crash.

Of what happened.

She got run into and knocked over.

And she cut her head and got confused.

Imran moves forward.

Close enough to hear.

Hear him be nice to her.

Hold her hand.

Stroke it.

Call her love.

Give her space.

Don't crowd her.

Go over what happened.

Details important.

~I got knocked over. They were going ever so fast.

Smart man nods.

Sympathetic.

~That must have been when I cut my head. It was rollerskates . . .

Stops nodding.

~That's right. The man on roller skates who checked if you were OK. *After* you were hit by the bike. Then I came along. This nice man and lady saw it too. The man on the bike hit you. He was stealing it. But he's been caught now. Thanks to the man on the rollerskates. You've been really brave. The man on the bike. The one in the tracksuit. He knocked you over. But you're going to be fine.

Imran comes closer.

Imran tells what he saw.

~It's OK. Thanks very much. We've got three witnesses now.

The man puts his hand on Imran's shoulder.

~But I saw what really happened. It was that guy on the roller blades. That dude with the vest and spiky hair . . .

Smart man puts both hands on Imran's shoulders.

Smiling.

Hands squeezing tight.

Too tight.

~We've established what happened. It'll be dealt with. Thank you, Imran.

Imran turns away and fingered his name tag.

Confused.

The police arrive.

Smart man not so involved now. Moving away. Sitting down.

Watching.

From a distance.

Policeman checks old lady.

Speaks to two people who saw the thief in the tracksuit knock the old lady over.

Old lady says the same.

She thinks.

Imran shakes his head.

Confused.

He served the old lady.

Saw her leave.

Get hit by spiky guy on rollerskates.

Imran steps forward.

Smart man stands.

Stares at Imran.

Shakes his head.

And stares.

Imran goes back to his till.

And checks his float.

2021
AGENT

Eddie looked down at the name in his diary and tapped it thoughtfully.

Terry Proctor (sports and showbiz agent) 10.30am.

He wondered why the name was so familiar, and why it gave him a bad feeling. He felt he was just about to place it when the intercom buzzed.

~Yes, Judy?

~Sorry to disturb you, Mr Shearer. I have a gentleman here. Tel Procter. Says he has an appointment and you know about it.

Eddie sucked through his teeth.

~OK, Judy. Show him in.

No sooner had he finished speaking than the door burst open. In walked a short fat man dressed in a smart pinstripe suit. He sported an orange tan and an oversized gold Rolex. He had rings on all but one of his fingers.

~Now then, Edward, me old mucker.

I've only met you twice.

~It's been a while. What was it? The launch party? Week before you went live? Yeah, I remember. Nice little party you put on there, Ed.

I don't even think you were invited.

~Nice little bit of business I put your way there, eh, Ed?

Don't touch me. Cocky southern . . . You make my skin crawl. Hate the way you say that word. Bizniss.

~Anyways. Might be able to help you out again. You got a blinder off me, eh? The big man? Old LV. Those punters can't get enough of 'im. And made more than a few quid for yourself, you lucky boy.

I make money because I'm unique, thorough and hard-working. Not because of your muscle-bound, overpaid, egotistical ape.

~Well, a little birdy tells me that you're on the lookout for a nice bit of slice to up your ratings. You're a clever boy. Not much gets past you, Edward! A man after me own 'eart!

Don't point at me, prick. My office. My company. My time. And you haven't allowed me to speak yet. Rude bastard.

~Well, Eddie, just you wait and see what I got in store for you. This bird's right up your alley. And you might be right up hers if you play yer cards right!

Rude, vulgar, sexist, presumptuous, gobshite, Cockney cunt.

Feast your mince pies on these. These are the girl's early days. British athletics team. Heptathlon. You know, Ed, where they compete in eight different events.

Six. Prick.

~But she weren't focused enough. Had other distractions. She could earn better dough in the modelling game. That's when she got the old bangers done. Put free seconds on 'er four 'undred metre time. Not that we'll be complaining, eh, Ed? I mean – look at this pic 'ere! Looks like she got Right Said Fred fighting to get art of 'er Lycra top, but she'll still easily 'ave the Gary to catch those scum that you get your boys after.

So she looks the part. Got the credentials. But what are you going to be charging, you robbing bastard?

--Now they told me you could be a man of few words, Eduardo my friend. And I can see from your face that you like the look of this girl. But I ain't gonna waste your time with any more of me bullshit. The pics and 'her records speak for themselves. So let's get down to the numbers. I can ave 'er fully contracted to you. Three years, let's say, when she's still in 'er prime, for a hundred and fifty a year. Throw in fifteen k for my expenses and I'll ave her tied up, all the small legal stuff. She'll be in your team. This is just what you need, Ed. She's gonna make you a facking fortune.

Eddie sat back in his leather chair. He stretched his arms behind his head. He gazed beyond the agent. He thought back to his youth. To the grass banks at school. He thought of the athletic girls that ran round Keighley running track. He thought of the gymnasts at Bradford's Richard Dunn Centre. Beautiful, athletic, sexy. With potential for greatness. Before they jacked it all in to be with chavvy lads in shit council estates. And earn peanuts in sports shops. Or sandwich bars. And piss their fitness against the wall at the nightclubs. Their sporting prowess a crumbling memory, held only in the boxes of plastic trophies and certificates that rotted in the lofts of their parents' houses next to scratched chopping boards and old cutlery, still too shiny to throw away.

Now he could make something of one of these girls. Turn her into a heroine. A crime-fighting heroine. He had the means and the imagination. Pay her three times as much as she would earn in a shop. And a fifth of what this dickhead was asking.

He leaned over and pressed the intercom button on his desk.

~Judy. Judy.

~Yes, Mr Shearer?

~Would you mind coming in here and showing this idiot out of my office.

KEELEY

KEELEY

Keeley breezed through the front door of her parents' Keighley council house. Her young twin brothers paid her no attention, transfixed by the wrestling on the thirty-six inch television. She hung up her gym bag and took a sip from her water bottle. She felt toned and refreshed from the body pump session she had just enjoyed. Her strength and stamina had embarrassed some of the male members, who had loaded too much weight on their bars in order to outdo her.

She had pretended not to notice, concentrating on her breathing and the speed of her reps. But inside she was smiling. Smiling and aware of the attention. She speculated whether the attention was based on her prowess, or whether her slim hips and toned legs, hugged by three-quarter-length Adidas lycra pants, were drawing the glances and winks. Not long ago she would have been repulsed by any such suggestion, but more recently she had allowed the notion to occupy her mind more and more, ground down by her peers as she was constantly exposed to casual conversation with sexual undertones, as well as a stream of pictures in her favourite magazines of what was thought desirable.

This was why she had eventually had her belly button pierced. Just before she entered her gym class she had caught sight of herself in the mirror. The small silver dolphin glinted in the centre of her flat, slightly bronzed stomach. Its body was arched, as though it had leapt out of the water and was preparing to dive. Dive into the hidden mysterious depths that the hairy-arsed men in the back row who ogled her could only dream about. She liked what she saw and smiled confidently, her white teeth complementing her pretty face and contrasting with her dark shiny hair.

Keeley went upstairs and switched on her mobile phone. Moments later she heard the familiar sound of a text message alert. She checked the screen and to her dismay it was her athletics coach again.

~Missed you at track. Don't forget Yorkshire champs nxt mnth. Need 2 b on top form to regain title.

Her coach had taken to harassing her by text in response to her apathetic approach towards training. He had seen this before in many of his promising female athletes. In Keeley he sensed real potential. Her personal best was already under fifty-three seconds, and he felt that if she had the opportunity to train full time she had the potential to go all the way. He sensed a steel and courage that he had not experienced for a long time. Her commitment and attitude had been second to none. His plan was to introduce her to the hurdles. Her flat speed was there for all to see, and with some dedicated time put into her technique international honours were not out of the question.

The guilt began to set in, almost physically poisoning the feeling of well being that Keeley had walked into the house with. Once she had been hungry. Dedicated to the point of obsession. She had lapped up the praise and admiration, but after years of awards and titles it was becoming old hat. At one time she had craved the admiration of her peers at school and college, but now she had lowered her sights, and it was merely acceptance she sought. She noticed how easily accessible this was once she changed one or two things about her appearance. First a little lip gloss. Skinny jeans instead of tracky bottoms. Hair straighteners and the silver dolphin. Cigarettes and alcohol were next on the list, but she had resisted up to now: she still valued her health and fitness incredibly highly. But knocking half a second off her personal best wasn't motivating her the way it used to. She was seeking something new. Something different to channel her energy into. She had half-decided that she wanted to be a gym instructor, taking classes and advising on fitness. She saw how popular and happy gym instructors were. Keeley had even talked it over with her coach, who urged her to fulfil her potential on the track.

~You can't go back. There's no use waking up one morning when you're thirty-five and deciding you want to be an international athlete. Now's the time. You won't get a second chance. Seize the moment.

His words hit home, but soon she felt her hunger waning. She tried to deny it at first but it became unavoidable. She felt so refreshed and alive when she was chatting and meeting new faces at the gym and doing regular workouts like everyone else, instead of pounding the track night after night.

She lay back on her bed and let out a long sorrowful sigh. She fiddled with her phone, contemplating a reply to the text message. By the side of her bed lay the latest copy of *Track and Field* magazine. At one time she had eagerly digested every page as soon is it dropped through the letter box, but now it lay rolled up, still in its cellophane wrapper, delivered by her stepdad from the waste paper pile.

She tore off the covering and began to thumb through the race results and advertisements for trainers. No longer interested in the latest training phenomenon or the form of her closest rivals, she was soon at the back pages and the classified ads. She blankly gazed at them until an oversized box in the bottom left-hand corner of the page caught her eye.

UNIQUE OPPORTUNITY

A position in our organisation has arisen for a (female) talented athlete/sportsperson. Dedication and ambition are essential qualities. The successful applicant will also possess speed, agility, strength and endurance in abundance. Experience of TV work/ modelling would be an advantage.

Text your name, house number and postcode to 07800 543432 for an application form, or apply online at www.strikebackmedia/recruitment.co.uk.

StrikeBack Media

She read it once. Then a second time. And a third. She tried to find a reason why it might exclude her.

She sent two texts in the next three minutes, her nimble fingers typing text on her phone almost as quickly as most people write with a pen. One was a mumbling excuse-ridden apology to her coach. It mentioned minor injuries, college work and the need for a gym session.

Its recipient pondered it with frustration and regret.

The other text changed her life.

2022
R FACTOR

Eddie Shearer was watching the recruitment procedure from a distance. He sat in the passenger seat of his Land-Rover, surveying the faces and profiles neatly arranged in the file on his lap. His people had already vetted the hundreds of applicants and made a short-list of sixteen. Group and individual interviews had been going on for most of the morning, with athletic ability to be put to the test in the afternoon.

His team had been briefed thoroughly. They knew what they were looking for. Grace, sexiness and beauty, but with a hard edge. They had to find someone with all these attributes who also had the ability to chase down, wrestle and grapple with criminals.

As Eddie mused, Vera Scott came up to his window. She was Eddie's most trusted employee – reliable, efficient and perhaps the one person who understood him since the original gang disbanded. Well into her fifties, she had a wealth of experience and business acumen. She almost fulfilled the role of a loyal mother, defending or excusing her son's crazier jaunts. Vera viewed things slightly differently. She was well maintained and confident that ten years before she could easily have charmed him into the sack. Eddie was not oblivious to this, and used his instincts to get the very best out of his employee.

~Good morning, Eddie.

~Good morning, Vera. Some impressive girls on show out there. Any who can really cut the mustard?

~There's one very strong contender. Very strong.

Vera reached for the file on his lap and thumbed through the pages until she reached the profile of a tall smiling blonde in a swimsuit.

~Amanda Davies. Six feet tall. Former Bradford Girls' Grammar and Loughborough University, no less. Graduated with a first in sports science. She was an age group national champion in the butterfly and has been working as a personal trainer since leaving university. And she came second in the Aireborough triathlon only last year. She's confident and charming and she's done a cover shoot for *Runner's World*.

~What about gas, though? She got the speed? It's that explosive power over the first thirty to forty that'll make the difference.

~She came third in the agility testing. She's not the quickest but she's no mug. But just look at her. She's beautiful. Strong and aggressive too. And she can switch it on and off instantly. During the drills she was knocking hell out of a girl with those foam clubs one minute but once the whistle went she was nice as pie. I checked them out for that. Made a point of chatting to them straight after their bouts.

~Now why doesn't that surprise me?

~You'd be amazed, Eddie. Some of them were still panting and cursing. You could see the rage. Too flustered to talk. We can't have that on a live feed.

Eddie was loath to admit that the finished package seemed to have dropped into his lap. Pygmalion-like, he had rather liked the idea of spotting potential and dragging it up from the gutter. He scratched around for excuses.

~Don't you think she looks a bit too plastic-perfect? We're a ground-breaking organisation. Shouldn't that be reflected in our first female Rectifire? She's going to look like an extra from *Baywatch*.

Vera spoke with suppressed laughter, but there was an authoritative tone to her words.

~Eddie! We've got wardrobe people. Stylists. Hairdressers. You can shape this girl into whatever you want. What matters is that we find you the finest quality lump of clay.

Eddie ground his teeth and forced a thin smile, uncomfortable that his motives were so transparent to Vera.

~Honestly, Edward, Some days I wonder how you got where you are.

She lunged at him gently and playful with her forearm. Her hand lingered in his for a second or two. This made him feel fractionally better.

~Well, what about this one?

Eddie had turned the page to a young-looking dark-haired girl.

~Last year's Yorkshire under eighteen four hundred metre champion. And look at her times this year. I know a bit about athletics, and that time she ran at Barnsley must be pushing national open age standards. Must be.

~But she's just a kid, Eddie. Not nineteen till

October. And she seems quite shy. Struggled to string a sentence together.

~We've got people who sort that. We can train her up. Educate her. What was she like strength and aggression-wise?

A sheepish smile came over Vera's face.

~If I'm being honest she was a really feisty mare. Fought well above her weight. Wouldn't take a backward step. For anybody.

~And that's exactly what we want! A little battler. A foxy little grafter. From Keighley! It's the girl next door. The girl in the street who's going to stand up and be counted. Someone the public's going to really identify with. Not some made-up poncy failed blonde model.

~I don't know, Eddie. You're not letting your emotions rule your business brain again, are you? And isn't that what you employ me for? To keep you in check?

Eddie laughed, knowing how right she was. And how her interventions, prudence and bottle had probably saved him the best part of a million quid.

~OK, OK. Let's look at this objectively. From a business point of view. What event have we got next?

~The six hundred metres.

~Right, V. You get over there and make sure our two contenders are in the same heat. We'll be at the end of the home straight. Imagine we're the massed ranks of the British television audience watching on Boxing Day. Let's picture a scum bag running away from them, then we'll decide who looks best. Who they'll want. Then we'll know who's our girl.

She turned to face him with a mock-stern expression, and jabbed his chest with her finger, like a stern teacher telling off a naughty child.

~But we'll have it recorded. From different angles.

274

I'm not having you . . . bullshitting me, imagining things that aren't there.

~Vera Scott! Language!

~Well, you drive me to it. And it's the only word that fits.

She was laughing, but he knew she had a serious point. Eddie's perception was enhanced or distorted when he felt strongly about something. Vera had the unique ability to point this out without rubbing him up the wrong way. She could use video footage to destroy his illusions: he was amazed at how frequently this happened. She was methodical and brutal in her analysis. Unlike Eddie, she knew what the viewing public wanted and expected. And for that she always enjoyed his grudging respect and gratitude.

~It's a deal. Now go and set it up.

~Yes, sir!

She saluted and winked before turning to walk away.

Eddie raised her hand to give her a slap on the bottom. At the last second he thought better of it.

She strode purposefully towards the track-suited group of young hopefuls. Slightly disappointed that her buttock felt no smart.

SHOWDOWN

Eddie and Vera positioned themselves on canvas chairs, looking down the length of the running track. They were a short distance away from the finishing line with a perfect view of the home straight. Four cameras were positioned at different places around the track. They heard a crack in the near distance and a group of eight young women accelerated away from the starting line. Amanda Davies headed straight for the front. She had led the way throughout the whole process in stature, charisma and athleticism. All the time maintaining her composure and a friendly smile as she consoled beaten opponents, deceitfully hugging and delivering Iscariot kisses as she eliminated rivals.

The only thorn in her side was the little dark-haired chav girl. Who refused to lie down. Who caused her to be flustered. Who took her into a third and deciding bout in the sumo. Who belied her slender stature and tender years. Who was now cruising along behind her in second place. Putting doubts in her mind. And why was this little chav cow breathing so easily? Surely she must smoke forty a day and live on a diet of crispy pancakes?

Sitting in second place, Keeley started to have her doubts. Six hundred metres was bread and butter to her. She did this in her sleep. Her coach made her do eight with two minute rests, to build up endurance. But she had never done this distance in a competitive race. The blonde girl in front had surely gone out too fast. To run at this pace and to be able to keep it up she surely had to be an athlete of national standard. But Keeley had never heard of her. Never seen her at any of her meetings, or read about her in *Track and Field*. She would surely have noticed her before now.

Keeley decided to sit behind her, a comfortable distance away. She had made the mistake before of going out too hard and blowing up. If the girl really was this fast there was no point in running out of gas and finishing well down the field. She had to show what she could do. And after all the grappling and wrestling in the morning session, this had to be her best event.

In the lead, Amanda passed the finishing line for the first time. She had four hundred metres to go. Her peripheral vision as she rounded the bend told her she was defending a ten to fifteen metres lead. She noticed two figures watching her from the edge of lane eight.

From a distance she looked good. A tall running action, long strides and her blonde ponytail bobbing up and down behind her. Her ample bosom was well strapped in, but gently heaving up and down as though complementing her natural momentum.

Inside her bosom Amanda's chest was starting to hurt. She had run many races but her distances were usually five kilometres and above. She wasn't entirely sure how to pace herself, so she resorted to her usual approach of looking to destroy the competition early. She had run the first two hundred metres at more or less maximum speed. Her legs started to burn ever so slightly, and the thought of keeping this pace up for another four hundred induced a sick, panicky feeling in the pit of her stomach.

But she was in the lead. By a good distance.

And she was mentally tough. She thought about the discomfort she was feeling and told herself her weaker opponents would be feeling it more. She pressed on, driving herself even harder, trying to force the pain out of her mind and body.

In second place, Keeley got a shock when the girl in third suddenly appeared on her shoulder, attempting to pass as they rounded the bend. Keeley moved through the gears and her opponent was left floundering, dropping back in behind and deflated at the wasted effort of running the longer distance round the outside with no reward.

By increasing her speed slightly to see off her challenger, Keeley inadvertently moved closer to the leader. It was then she heard a sound that was music to her ears.

The girl was struggling.

Badly.

She heard the blonde dragging the air violently into her lungs and throwing it back out again. Her running style was exaggerated and ragged. Keeley became aware of her own controlled breaths. Her legs felt supple and springy, injected with the adrenalin of the race; they thrust her onwards without complaining. And yet they had not been asked to work at maximum effort. They were coiled springs, itching to be released and deliver a devastating burst of speed.

At four hundred metres Amanda still held her lead. She was hurting badly, but still believed. Her legs were threatening to turn to jelly. Her chest burning, she already tasted battery acid in the back of her throat. She couldn't hear much around her: the sound of her panting filling her ears and mind.

But she was aware of a presence not far behind. Somehow she knew it was the chav girl. Like an irritating stone in her shoe. But she *must* be almost done. Surely her challenge would die soon.

In second place, with two hundred to go, Keeley was ready to strike. She considered attacking round the bend but something held her back. She was confident she had enough left to leave it to the straight. The field was closing up behind her as the leader slowed, but almost out of respect for the blonde goddess no one took up the challenge and passed.

Around the final bend Keeley was cruising. Her whole body was twitching with impatience to use the speed she had built up and harnessed. Just before the end of the bend she let it go.

Her burst of acceleration was devastating. In a matter of seconds she was ten metres clear. Amanda had nothing in response. Not believing what she was seeing, Amanda fought desperately to stay in contention.

But she was gone.

She lost all form as her head bobbed up and down like a nodding dog. Her arms began to flail sideways, and her breasts cannoned into one another as her whole body clumsily stuttered. Her flushed face was sprinkled in small flecks of snot and saliva.

Keeley was feeling fantastic. She gracefully lengthened her strides. Her face was determined but her head remained still and composed. She ran faster and faster, the sound of plodding and panting behind her becoming more distant. Her arm action was unusually low for a sprinter, something her coach had tried to alter, but it made her speed seem effortless and graceful. For this exercise it was perfect.

As she crossed the line her beaming white-toothed smile gave away her joy and satisfaction. Two figures sitting near the finish line stood up and applauded. The lady she recognised from the morning sessions: she had been organising and directing the girls as though she was someone important. She thought she had seen the man before, but couldn't quite place him. The lady beckoned her over and began to ask questions.

Keeley felt invigorated and more confident than she had done in the morning. The endorphins suddenly handed her pleasantries for her hosts. For a few moments she could have been chatting with her friends on a night out after a couple of bottles of Smirnoff Ice. In that slender window when she was confident and relaxed but not slurring.

She answered questions about her background and interests. She said the right things about the race. She was modest about herself and complimentary to the other runners. And she wanted to carry on talking. All of a sudden she had plenty to say. A story to tell. She was mildly disappointed when she was thanked for her time and ushered to the side as the tall blonde girl was brought in to replace her. She hadn't felt this good in a long time.

Keeley walked off the track towards the changing area with a slight swagger. She noticed that a man with one of the cameras positioned around the track was pointing it at her and following her as she walked. She released the bobble that held back her dark shiny locks and shook her head, so they fell loosely onto her shoulders. She ran her fingers through her hair, tipping her head backwards and arching her back. Then she winked at the camera and blew a kiss. Not quite knowing why she did it or where it came from.

DECISION

Vera Scott sat at her desk and logged into her email account. She had eight messages. One was untitled and from her boss. She opened the attachment that came with it, a video clip. At first it was completely blank, with background music gradually increasing in volume. She recognised it instantly as the theme tune to *Steptoe and Son*.

As the image came into focus she saw it was Amanda Davies, struggling with the latter stages of the previous day's race. It was a cruel but clever piece of editing, the music subliminally suggesting a slow pace and clumsiness. Her ragged, graceless movements seemed choreographed to the soundtrack. Her face was contorted with effort, expelling all traces of the beauty she clearly possessed.

The music faded, and was replaced by the actual sounds picked up by the camera's microphone. Amanda was hurried into an interview, clearly bewildered. She had pushed herself so far out of her comfort zone that she could no longer see properly, the two figures in front of her just a haze of yellow and blue specks. She wailed incoherent replies to the questions, and her hands kept touching her face and covering her eyes. She kept looking down towards her feet, and at one point her head almost collided with the camera lens. Vera smirked for a moment, and would have felt sorry for the girl had she not had her emotions hardened by years of viewing video clips of people coming a cropper.

The images and sound gradually faded away, only to be replaced by a second soundtrack. Again she recognised it quickly: the introduction to *The Final Countdown*. She was being primed to expect greatness and achievement. And that is exactly what was delivered.

Keeley's assault down the home straight was played at full speed. It showed just how devastating her acceleration was. It took a matter of seconds for her to open up a ten metre lead, and then the film speed slowed down. Keeley was clearly in focus, her head still, her face relaxed, her athletic body moving in harmony to maximise straight line speed. She personified power and grace. Over her shoulder the pack battled to keep the winning distance down to a respectable margin.

The music faded so she could be heard as she spoke to the camera. She spoke clearly and confidently, belying her recent exertions. The footage slowed right down again and the music returned to its former volume. Keeley ran her fingers through her hair and winked at the camera. The picture froze. Crude yellow writing flashed over her image.

~YOU'RE HIRED.

VIXEN

2023
SET UP

I ain't happy about this, Wheelz. It ain't right. We never got no leg-ups like this. We got there ourselves. We had to bust our asses at the gym or round the track to achieve what we got. Now I'm not saying no woman should never be on the team. But if she is she has to be capable of doing it herself.

Connor Green sat sipping a coffee out of a plastic cup. He analysed what his colleague was saying to him. Various questions came into his head.

My name's Connor. Why are you using that stupid stage name?

Why are you slipping in words, phrases and double negatives to make you sound a bit American? You're from Baildon.

Why is this such a big issue? Do you really want to see this girl get whacked?

As usual he only expressed a small amount of what he

was thinking.

~Don't you think we should just make sure this kid's OK on her first run?

Alex Brown, aka Lord Vengeance, slammed down his bottle of protein shake on the table. The whites of his eyes were bulging and contrasted with his black skin. His oversized muscles seemed to twitch in anger. It was as though they were an extension of his personality, which is perhaps why he always wore so little.

~Wheelz, my brother, you gotta wise up to the way of the world! Think about it. With this exposure think about the coin she's gonna make. And it's mainly our work. And do you think they're gonna give us a cut? No way, José.

~I had a chat with her before, though. She's an OK kid. She told me she was only pulling thirty grand. And she was well happy with that. Thought it was top dollar. Give the kid a break, eh?

~Thirty grand! That's just the start. Think about the extras. Endorsements. Sponsorships. Public appearances. Chicks always get loads more of that shit. She'll be modelling underwear, doing perfume, *FHM*, the lot. And it's all on the back of our leg-up.

It occurred to Connor that Alex totally believed his hype. The tabloids and chat shows had labelled him as the crime-fighting hero who gave Britain hope. Alex never really stepped out of this role. Connor felt sad for him.

The reality was that Alex didn't really want to step back to who he really was. He was easily recognisable as the only black guy in Baildon. He worked on the door in a bar in the village centre and coached the rugby team. He was a major under-achiever considering his size and speed, and often lied that he had turned down various offers to turn pro because he wanted sport as his hobby. His great passion was body-building. To the untrained eye he was quite simply huge, with well-defined muscles. He had won a couple of amateur competitions for the north of England, but he was always too fond of junk food to achieve the perfectly cut figure that would catapult him into the big time.

Around Baildon everyone was friendly and paid Alex the necessary respect that local muscle/rugby team captain could come to expect. But he often felt that people were ridiculing him and laughing at him behind his back. His closest friends reassured him that this was not the case when he confided in them under the influence of drink.

In reality, though, his paranoia considerably underestimated the snide comments and mocking laughter that were aimed in his direction.

Eddie Shearer and the Rectifires team changed all that. The right combination of drugs, nutrition and heavy gym work pumped his body up to comic book proportions. He stood proud and tall at his rebirth. He was Lord Vengeance. Feared by scum but admired by millions, who tuned in every week religiously to watch him perform. His agent told him that it was the ultimate fantasy for thousands of British women to be rescued by him and taken somewhere plush to be made love to. He thought about this often, and particularly when the lack of someone really close to him left a void in his life. These thoughts always seemed to fill the void, albeit temporarily, but left him shallow, sexist and bristling with arrogance. This state of mind prevented him developing any meaningful and lasting relationships, and so the cycle continued.

~Listen, Al. Let's just do it for her this once. She might not even be able to hack it. And what you gonna do anyway? Refuse to go on? Go on strike? I know the company makes us do some ridiculous stuff but they pay our wages. And if you look at your contract I bet they've tied it up so we could get our pay docked. They might just get rid of us. I know we're popular, but do you think we're really gonna be that hard to replace?

The thought of losing everything and the mention of contracts beyond his understanding silenced Alex for a while. He sat there brooding, nostrils flared, thinking about his next move.

–OK, I'll do it. This time. But tonight, after we've done, I'm getting straight on the dog to my agent. Let's see what he says about it. He'll sort that Shearer out and get us our dough. But I ain't happy, my friend. Not happy at all.

DEBUT

Kyle thought his arm would break. It hurt so much he didn't care about the filthy floor that his face was being forced into. He stole shallow gasps of dusty air and tried to keep his body at an angle where the pain was bearable. The three men who had grabbed him were pinning him down in a disused elevator on the ground floor of the Arndale shopping centre. They held him down firmly; he was totally dominated and offered no resistance. He was braced for blows to start raining down on his head and body, as they had the last time he was in this position. He hoped he would lose consciousness quickly and wake somewhere where he was going to be looked after.

But the blows never came.

He clenched his buttocks together tightly for fear of something worse, but his assailants didn't seem interested in that either.

Whatever was about to happen he wanted it over fast,

because the anticipation was killing him.

Out of the corner of his eye he saw the face of the huge black man who was kneeling on top of him. He was sure he recognised the face but couldn't place it. For a fleeting moment he was convinced it was a famous boxer he had seen on television, but his brain couldn't work out why such a person would be doing this to him.

Effortlessly the black man pulled away the plastic bag Kyle was still clutching in his free hand. It contained all the CDs he had stolen and had hoped to sell to pay for a couple of bottles of vodka.

A voice above and behind him calmly gave instructions.

~We're going to take these off you. But we want you to go back and steal some more. Do exactly what you just did. And you can run when you get out of the store. As fast as you like. But don't hurt anybody. Do you hear? Nobody. If you do we'll be watching and we'll come and hurt YOU.

He was released and told to stand up. He looked at the three men who had appeared from nowhere and bundled him into this place as he walked casually out of HMV. For the first time Kyle began to hope that he might be allowed to leave without a serious kicking. He realised he had wet himself. He considered turning and fleeing, not enthusiastic about the instruction to return to the scene of his crime. He decided to walk away a good distance before hotfooting it.

The black one seemed to read his mind. In a dynamic and sudden movement he stepped forward and jabbed Kyle straight and hard in the stomach. Doubled over, his victim was hardly able to believe how much power had been generated in such a short movement. His breath was sucked out of his guts again, and he crossed both arms across his stomach in agony. The punch had more than done its job, and any thoughts of pulling a fast one began to evaporate.

~That's just for starters. If you try any funny business you can expect the main course and dessert all in one go.

Full of pain and fear, Kyle decided to play along with the whims of his captors.

September *TV HOT.*

HOT NEW BABE WOWS 'FIRES FANS

Rectifires fans were not disappointed when they tuned into the opener in series two. Speculation has been rife about the identity of the latest recruit to the 'fires team. Rumours had been flying around the sports and showbiz world that a Premier League soccer star was on the verge of being recruited. On the back of the huge success of series one, and the sale of the franchise to Sweden, StrikeBack Media were expected to flex their new financial muscles by tempting a national hero into their ranks.

A StrikeBack spokesman today revealed that it was never their intention to raid the Premier League of its finest talent, although he did admit that speculation had done their viewing figures no harm at all.

In stark contrast a young unknown by the name of ViXen became the latest star of this cult crime-fighting show. Little is known about the identity of this new starlet, but *TV Hot* can reveal that she comes from an athletics background with no previous TV experience. Well she certainly lived up to all the hype, beating the guys to claim her first 'kill' and managing to look stunning all the way through!

She's a natural in front of the camera, and our money says that Rectifires might just enjoy a new influx of male fans desperate to get an eyeful!

The blokes who were out shopping with their wives certainly got a treat they weren't expecting.

Stewart from Holmewood contacted us by email:

I was out with the missus and kids shopping for school shoes when this hot chick in lycra comes tearing past! We're all massive fans of the Rectifires, so we couldn't believe it when we got to see the new girl in action right in front of us! She was gorgeous and couldn't half move. The thieving scally had no chance. She even let me shake her hand and posed for a picture with the kids. She was so down to earth. But the wife isn't too chuffed that I haven't washed my hand for a week!

You can rest assured that your favourite TV mag will be right on the case to gather all the latest gossip and feedback about this little hottie! Make sure you order your copy now. It'll be dynamite.

TEL'S REVENGE

Eddie knew Vera didn't mess about. When she said she needed to meet him urgently he knew she meant it. It wasn't going to be because she needed time off because her dog had died. It was bound to be serious business. He wasn't wrong.

~Eddie, you're about to get a call from Tel Procter. He's the guy who provided us with Lord Vengeance. He's also the guy you kicked out of your office without speaking to.

Eddie smiled.

~I don't think you'll be laughing when you hear what he has to say. By all accounts Alex has been stirring up trouble. He's been speaking to a few of the other Rectifires. About Keeley, mainly. He thinks he's being short-changed. I don't think he likes someone else taking the limelight. Especially when he has to do all the dirty work.

~Come on! That's why I pay him a hundred and fifty grand. He gets five times what she does.

~Yes but think about what she's making from endorsements, TV ads and interviews. She's all the rage.

~That's not my fault. I pay what I pay. Why doesn't he go moaning to them? It's nothing to do with me. I've got no control over magazines and beauty products. This is ridiculous.

~That's just it, though. He's laying the blame firmly with you. He's been getting less air time, and because the pursuits involving Keeley are fixed he reckons his marketability's suffering. He wants compensation.

~Get him in here. I'll give that idiot what for. He was a bloody nobody when I took him on. I made him into what he is. I remember that snivelling oaf begging me for chance. Some knucklehead working on the door of a tinpot Baildon bar! I put him on a hundred and fifty k, and this is how he thanks me! Get him in here. Where's his number? I'm gonna ring that prick right now.

Eddie was on his feet and scrolling through the address book on his phone. Vera took it from him firmly.

~He has others, Eddie. Tel Proctor's claiming he looks after five of your Rectifires.

~What!

~There are other media chancers, just like you were. Some of them with money. They'd be happy to set up a copycat show, making it bigger and better in some way. And taking five of your key men away would give them just the start they need.

~It wouldn't work. People always go for the original.

~Maybe. But only when shows are long established. If you take out the Sweden stuff, we've only been going for a year. TV's littered with companies nicking programmes and improving them.

~It can't happen. I won't let it.

~It gets worse, Eddie. I've been working with a few

focus groups. I asked loads of questions to disguise what I was really interested in. But it seems what makes us so popular is that people believe in us. They value our integrity. They need us to be authentic. They like the fact that crims sometimes escape or our lot get hurt. I gave them a list of choices asking what single event would make them turn off, and eighty-five per cent opted for the revelation that shows were fixed. Eighty-five per cent! Think what it would do to our viewing figures if it got out what we were doing with Keeley. Combine that with a mass exodus of our top stars and we'd be finished.

~But that'll never happen. How could it get out?

~Think about it. Perhaps we were naïve when we set up their contracts, but the confidentiality clause only applies while they're employed by us. You can imagine a potential rival setting up an interview with Vengeance and his mates to reveal all. And clever editing of our footage would leave no doubt.

~We could always sack him first and release something that would really discredit him.

~It's a possibility but a major risk. I've seen the projects we have in line for this series, and they're dynamite. I think you've done a great job. They're bigger, edgier, better researched. The extra effects will really capture the public's imagination. But we don't have the time and resources to recruit and train new Rectifires. Especially with some of the more extreme stuff we've got planned. We're going to need experience.

Eddie knew she was right and wasn't afraid to admit it.

~OK. So I suppose the question is what do we do about it.

~I think it's best we appease them right away. Maybe we can offer something that'll buy us time until we can deal with them properly.

Eddie squirmed in his chair. He could see Vera's logic, but hated the idea of handing over large sums of cash because of one petulant greedy oaf.

--And what do you think I should say to Proctor?

--Play it cool. Get as much information out of him as you can. Be polite. But not too polite. We don't want him thinking he's got you by the balls. Don't commit yourself to anything.

--OK. Thanks for your support, V. I need to speak to this guy. I'm going to try to catch him on the hop. I'll ring him now and find out what's what.

DEAL OR NO DEAL

Terry Proctor almost swallowed his cigar when he looked at the caller ID on his phone. Eddie Shearer was ringing him – for the first time. Terry had been planning to speak to him later that day, after he had practised his lines and gone through all the possible scenarios that the exchange might bring. There was the possibility of a big pay day in it, and a chance to put one over on the northern monkey who had thrown him out of his office and made him feel like a proper muppet.

He took a deep breath and picked up the phone.

TEXT

Vera Scott was in her office when the familiar sound of a text alert sounded on her mobile phone. She was just starting to look forward to a meal and a long soak in the bath after another exhausting day.

—Just spoken to Proctor. Think I can sort this. Get up to my office now.

Although she was about to pack up and head for home, her boss clearly had other ideas. She sighed in the knowledge that their conversation could easily run into an hour or more, putting paid to her plans for a relaxing evening.

She decided against texting back, and headed straight for the elevator that would take her to Eddie's office apartment on the top floor.

Inside his office Eddie was pacing round his desk. He was starting to get slightly irked that two minutes had passed without her replying to his text. He was used to instant responses from her.

Perhaps she's having a crap, he thought, trying to calm himself.

~But she should always take her phone to the shitter!

His voice increased in volume and his fist slammed onto his desk as he barked out the last word.

The idea in his head was so good it had to come out fast, and it had to be relayed to someone he could trust. Many of his ideas had been blown out of the water by Vera, because they were uneconomic, too illegal or just plain ridiculous, and although at first he resented her for it on reflection he could always see the common sense behind her intervention. If it was do-able, Vera was the woman to make it work. There were too many moments when an arse licking yes-man would have caused serious damage. Vera was definitely not a yes-man.

Eddie had not felt as much excitement about an idea for a long time. He could think of nothing else. It was as though the idea had built up an energy of its own, and like an out of control beast was charging around and bouncing off the walls in his head. It needed to be killed or tethered and tamed. That was Vera's job.

Three minutes had passed and Eddie was getting really angry. He was about to ring her or perhaps, for dramatic effect, charge down the steps to her office, arriving breathless and flustered and demanding her instant attention, when she confidently breezed in, forgoing the knock that lesser mortals were compelled to give. She looked him up and down and straight away knew why she was there. His eyes were sparkling and his fingers were twitching. The adrenalin made it impossible for him to stay still. He had what he liked to call a 'one stoner'. An idea that would slay two problems simultaneously.

~You called, Mr Shearer?

She spoke calmly and used his formal title, almost

mocking the agitated state that she knew and controlled so well.

~I got an idea. I got a fucking idea.

He put both hands on her shoulders and looked her right in the eye.

She smiled ever so slightly. For a moment the words 'You don't say' crossed her mind, but experience told her it was best not to rile him unnecessarily.

~Go on.

~I got thinking after I spoke to Proctor. I did like you said. Played it cool. I got as much information out of him as I could. He loves to talk, that guy. I was polite-ish but professional.

Vera couldn't help a slight smirk this time. She reminded him of a schoolboy trying to convince his mum that he had been good at school. Luckily he was in full flow, his eyes glazed, and he didn't notice.

~That Proctor's given too much away. He just can't help himself. He's lost himself a fortune in just one phone call. I've been thinking about this Vengeance prick. You know, V: with him it isn't even about the money. I mean, we can sort out some extra income streams for the greedy ape but we won't have to pay. Endorsements and sponsors will. We just have to make him the main man again.

~But Keeley's your main man now, Eddie. That's why our viewing figures have almost doubled. That's why we're in all the trashy magazines. That's why America's starting to show an interest. You'd have to get rid of your favourite little Keighley gladiator to keep him happy.

~Oh, but do I, Vera? Do I really have to?

Eddie paused, his eyes twinkling.

Vera knew she was supposed to beg him to reveal all, but it was the end of the day, she was tired, and she should have been at home. An hour ago.

Eddie threw a couple of cardboard files down on the desk.

~Take a look at these two.

Vera opened the file to reveal mugshots of two Asian youths in their early twenties.

~Our research team's been tracking these two since *Keighley News* covered their court case. They had sex with two white girls in a car, one fifteen, one twelve, after plying them with vodka. They were cleared by a jury of rape. They managed to convince them it was consensual. The girls had stolen some booze and lied to their parents about where they going. But there's still a hell of a lot of bad feeling among the white community in Keighley. Apparently there's a lot of this stuff that goes on but never gets to court. Channel Four had a documentary ready to go a couple of years back, but it got pulled. Too inflammatory. Or so they say.

~So are you saying that these two are still at it? This kind of thing?

~Not quite.

Eddie held up the first of the pictures.

~Iqbal. This one seems to have got the hard word from his family. They married him off pronto. Had his nose clean since the court case. Doesn't associate with his partner in crime any more.

Eddie returned the picture to its file and picked up a second one.

~But this fella. Usmaan. Now he's a different proposition altogether. He seems to think he's untouchable. You wouldn't believe some of the stuff our researchers reckon he's been getting away with. I'd really take a lot of pleasure in sorting him out. He's a genuine sleaze. As well as that he associates with drug dealers, and my sources suggest he's been working for a couple of them.

~And how does this relate to our little problem?

~We set something up. With Keeley and Vengeance. But we let him take the glory. Then we give him some special award at a ceremony, or some such shite. And get it sponsored. We won't have to pay him a penny more. We just make him feel like the big daddy again.

~I see.

~Now the idea I've got is risky. Very risky. For starters we need to get Keeley disguised somehow. She's well known, especially round Keighley. We need to get hold of some top make-up people. I mean film standard. But most of all I need you on board. I want to try and think of how you can make this happen. You can do it, V. We gotta be well planned and cover up some legal stuff. But if we pull this off it'll be immense. And it'll solve all our problems.

~Go on.

~OK. This is what we do . . .

KNOWLEDGE

Eddie. She doesn't know.

~What? Doesn't know what? Who?

~Keeley. She doesn't fucking know!

Eddie tried but failed to keep from his face the look of shock provoked by Vera using the f-word. She had burst into his office, her face flushed, her eyes watery behind her large round glasses. She stared at him, unblinking, showing concern to the point of distress.

~You're going to send her into a situation like that and you haven't even told her!

~She knows she's going in to sort out a sleazy bloke.

~You more or less one forced me to agree to this, Eddie. And I did it on two very strict conditions. First that she *knows* and second that she *acts*. Now I hear that you're going to . . .

~Authenticity, Vera! Authen-fuckin'-ticity. Your words, not mine. We need to get our integrity back. How will it look if she just puts it on? This way she'll be a genuine reality TV star.

~But she won't, will she? Victims are never stars. You know that full well.

She's just the bait. No woman in their right mind would agree to this. It's sick. That's why you kept it from her.

~We don't know he's definitely going to use it. We might just send Vengeance into the club to give him the brush-off.

~Come off it, Eddie. Hello! This is me you're talking to! That's not going to make great viewing, is it? That's not going to make our figures rocket and appease Vengeance. You chose this creep because you know what he does to girls like Keeley. That's what his file says and that's what you're hoping will happen. What if something goes wrong? Have you thought of that? This is a girl's life you're playing with.

~She'll be miked up. She'll have a micro-camera round her neck. There'll be spotters in the club. We'll pull the stops out. Do a maximum security job. We'll even make sure all the taxi drivers are our people.

~You think you can control everything, don't you? This is all just a big game and you're the fucking puppet-master. But you're going too far this time. There are words for men like you. You've changed. You're well out of control. Or maybe you've always been out of control and I've been too stupid to see it. You just pull the plug on this right now or I'll walk. And I won't be coming back.

~Bloody hell, Vera, so you've decided to climb onto your moral high horse. Isn't it a bit late for that? How many dodgy situations have we got ourselves out of before because of your lies and cover-ups? And all of a sudden you've grown a conscience. What – is it because we're dealing with a girl now? A girl who'd be a nobody but who's now earning thousands because of where I put her.

You were quite happy putting all the other muppets in danger. That shoplifter you sent Vengeance after. You knew he carried a blade! But that's OK. What, because he's a bloke? Because he's black?

~Don't you even dare suggest that! How could you! That's different and you know it. I'm don't even know why I'm standing here arguing. You're a fucking psycho. You belong in an institution. I'm leaving.

~Well fuck off then! There's plenty more where you came from. And next time I'll get somebody with a bit more loyalty and a lot more bottle.

Those words hurt Vera more than any others. To have her guts and loyalty questioned after everything she had been through with him pierced her soul like a dagger. Her face flushed and tears filled her eyes.

But Eddie was in no mood for sentimentality. He grabbed her firmly by the wrist and led her outside the sanctity of his office. The other staff, who had been peering over their computers towards the raised voices, cowered behind their screens again.

Eddie surprised himself at how calm he sounded as he addressed everyone.

~This is Vera Scott. She used to work here. She used to be in charge of you lot.

But now, all of a sudden, she thinks I'm a psychopath. She thinks I belong in an institution. The things we do here are too crazy. Does anyone else think I'm a nutcase? Anybody else want to walk out on what we've all worked so hard for? Well? No? Just as I thought. Everyone else wants to be part of the most exciting TV show in history. Everyone else believes in firing a shot for the victim. Everyone else realises that to be successful, to stay ahead of the game, we've got to keep pushing boundaries. We're StrikeBack Media! We aren't producing fucking *Countdown* here. So Vera will be leaving us. Her choice, not mine. And maybe things will start to run smoother round here. Without someone putting a spanner in the works. Without someone stabbing me in the back.

Eddie was seething as he spoke. But even the intense anger he felt couldn't mask the sadness that tore at his soul. He knew that what he prophesised in his parting shot was highly unlikely, and nigh on impossible.

Still holding Vera's wrist, he led her into the lift that would take them down to the lobby. Now, without an audience, there was silence. The sadness inside Eddie fought a battle with his anger. But with all the aggression he had worked up there was only going to be one winner. He looked her squarely in the face. She was wearing the silver earrings he had bought her the previous Christmas. He recalled the gushing card he had written her. At the time he had worried that he had gone a little over the top with his praise. She had framed it, and kept it safe in a drawer of precious things. Now he looked at those earrings and felt ridiculous.

~And I'll have those back an' all.

In one swift move he yanked both earrings clean out of her lobes.

There was more blood than he expected.

She didn't cry or scream. She couldn't speak. She held her ears to stem the bleeding.

For the first time he saw genuine fear in her eyes, and he felt powerful but shallow at once.

As soon as the lift doors opened she was running for the car park. Eddie opened his mouth to call her back. He knew he had gone too far. But what could he possibly say? So he said nothing. Instead he headed for the Gents', where he threw the jewellery in the bin and washed the blood from his hands. He checked no one was in any of the cubicles and sat on a toilet seat. He pulled out his phone and scrolled through the names until he came to the one he needed.

It was a name he never spoke but a name he knew he could trust.

—I have a job for you. It's simple. Vera Scott. She's just left the office. She should be easy to find. Take her somewhere. No, I don't want you to hurt her, but she doesn't leave. Take her phone off her too. She doesn't leave. Under any circumstances. Until my say-so. Just keep her there. No, you don't need to threaten her. Feed her. Make her comfortable. Look, if you must know she's probably going to blab about some filming. And I can't have it. You just make sure she's contained. I know it won't come cheap. Yes, I can pay. Just make sure it's done. No comebacks.

TRANSFORMERS

Keeley felt strange as she looked in the mirror. There was definitely extra intensity in her excitement as she prepared for the show this time. The image looking back at her from the mirror was not her own. The make-up artists had been busy for almost two hours, subtly changing her skin tone, eyebrows, lips. Tape and small amounts of putty had exaggerated some of her features and negated others. On her head sat the most lifelike blonde wig she had ever seen, and a pair of contact lenses turned her eyes from deep brown to bright blue.

The make-up artist was pleased with the result. Most of all, the girl looked believable. She had resisted the temptation to really go to town. Keeley's basic look was the same: she was just a little tartier and more docile-looking. She had also lost the trademark dark sunglasses that she wore as ViXen, opening the windows to her soul. When she hung her mouth open slightly the transformation was complete. The small production team that gathered round all agreed that you wouldn't have recognised ViXen, but you could believe it was her once you were told.

Most of the other Rectifires felt foolish in the outfits they were made to wear, but Keeley always felt empowered by the aura she felt it created. It commanded respect, and made her instantly recognisable as the superstar she was. Now all that had been stripped away, and she felt a little vulnerable.

She told herself she should still feel confident. She still had the speed and the strength, no matter what she was wearing. She knew she could expect the very best back-up from the rest of the team. But for some reason she didn't feel confident. All the right words were being said by the production team and the other Rectifires, but somehow the words didn't seem to carry the same sincerity they had done before. She couldn't put her finger on the reason. Perhaps it was just that Vera wasn't there. Keeley had never liked Vera all that much, but her busy efficiency had always reassured her that everything was in hand.

One other factor that played on Keeley's mind was the lack of detail in the briefing. On all the other shows she had been involved with planning had been meticulous. The intended end result was always clear. Risk assessments and back-up plans were always in place. She was always given a clear exit strategy in case anything went wrong.

For the latest operation all the rules seemed to have changed. She was shown photographs of an Asian guy who was the target. She was told that he had been guilty of a lot of 'sleazy behaviour' and she was going to be a kind of honey-trap. The details were sketchy. Phrases such as 'go with the flow' and 'see what develops' were bandied about. This was not what she was used to. StrikeBack Media never just saw what developed. They didn't react to situations; they created situations and manipulated them for their own ends.

Wardrobe did their job in kitting her out. The look they gave her was perfect.

Daft.

Tarty.

Easy prey.

The fitted T-shirt had small tassels hanging from its short sleeves. Its low neckline exposed slightly more cleavage than was tasteful. Printed across the chest was the cartoon character Little Miss Scatterbrain. A masterstroke of subliminal entrapment.

They had a short debate about whether or not to leave the silver X in her pierced belly button. They decided it was the one piece of authentic ViXen that should remain: a symbol of her true power, as well as gratifying their most observant viewers.

~X marks the spot!

Her short pink skirt was considered a little too much, so it was replaced with a black one of equal length.

Keeley was happy with the outfit, apart from the shoes. She could run in a skimpy T-shirt. She could run in a skirt. No problem. What worried her was the red high heels. She would have a lot of trouble escaping in those. But she was told it wasn't that sort of gig, and trainers would have given the game away.

So she put the heels on, as her contract specified. She tried walking in them. She could move OK but it was a series of tottering steps compared with the confident strides she was used to taking.

Finally she was sprayed all over with Vanilla Impulse, which made her sneeze violently – and part of her nose fell off. The wardrobe staff quickly fussed around, smoothing and repairing her. In no time at all she was ready for action.

TIZER

As soon as Keeley stepped out of the taxi she was in role. She knew exactly how to behave; she had witnessed it a thousand times. The company had hired an extra to be her friend. They linked arms, chatting and laughing, appearing to rely on each other to keep themselves upright. Their high heels made a loud clicking as they struck the pavement. Keeley hadn't had a drop of alcohol but her unsteadiness in heels helped with the illusion of being slightly drunk. They took their place in the line at K2 with Keighley's other revellers.

Keeley heard some static, then a voice in her ear.

--Move your fingers.

--What?

--Keeley, don't look like you're talking to yourself. Face your friend. Your fingers are obscuring the lens of the camera in your bag.

Keeley had forgotten all about the hidden camera lens disguised as the buckle of her clutch bag. She adjusted her grip.

~When you get inside locate your target and turn your bag towards him. Then just leave it alone. Don't worry, we've got plenty of other cameras, but it would be nice to get your perspective.

She paid her money and made her way inside. It was still quite early so they had no problems finding a table. The extra went to the bar and bought a couple of bottles of a red alcopop. She sat on the high stool, her shoulders moving to the dance music coming from the large speakers at the side of the dance floor.

~Keeley.

The voice in her earpiece was back. This time she didn't say anything, but moved her head to show that she was listening.

~Send your friend back to the bar. Get two more of the same drinks. But get her to ask for a glass. A pint glass would be better. Yes. Ask for a pint glass. All your drinks must be in pint glasses. Repeat. All drinks in pint glasses.

Keeley didn't question her instruction; she just passed it on to the extra. But she was confused. It didn't seem right. A girl like the one she was playing wouldn't want a pint glass. It didn't look right. She couldn't dance without it sloshing about. It felt awkward and big in her hand. And surely it couldn't be safe.

After about half an hour of swaying, drinking and pretending to chat, Keeley realised that she had inadvertently almost finished her drink. It didn't taste at all like alcohol, and she must have been taking big gulps.

~Go and get two more bottles each. And don't drink so fast. Try to keep your glass at least half full at all times. Go for a top-up when you need, but make sure you're always half-full.

The club was beginning to fill up. Bodies began to occupy the dance floor. Tentatively at first, but then in greater numbers and with more vigour.

Despite beginning to feel the effect of the alcohol, Keeley was becoming more and more uneasy. She wanted to get this over with. She wanted it finished. And most of all she wanted to know what 'it' was.

After what seemed like an age the voice in her ear spoke once more.

~OK, Keeley. Time to move in. We have a positive sighting of your target. Remember. Let him make the running. Encourage him, but not too much.

Keeley nodded her head. She tapped the extra on the shoulder and indicated it was time for a walk.

~Right, Keeley. You need to go upstairs. Wait until a seat becomes available at the back of the upstairs dance floor. You should recognise him.

When Keeley got upstairs she couldn't see the seats because of the number of people dancing. She had to negotiate a route across the dance floor. It was awkward carrying her pint glass as she was bumped and groped.

Eventually she reached the other side, and immediately spotted him. Usmaan was bigger in real life than Keeley had imagined from studying his pictures. He sat with a group of four others. They all looked very similar. Spiky dark hair, with patterns and motifs shaved into the side. Adorned in labels and gold. None of them could sit still. They shook hands and patted each others' backs. Their laughter seemed forced and aggressive. And they couldn't leave their phones alone. Flipping them. Clicking them. Talking. Texting. In and out of their pockets.

~There's a table free, Keeley. Grab it. Quick.

Keeley spotted the place where she was being asked to

sit and positioned herself a few feet away from him. Her extra sat with her back to the group.

It didn't take long to make eye contact.

He looked her up and down and, against her normal judgement, she held his gaze. He nudged his friend and made a comment. His friend momentarily stopped texting to check her out. He seemed to nod in approval and said something back, which led to more laughter and another strange handshake.

The next time Usmaan looked over, Keeley gave him a wink and ran the fingers of both hands through her hair, arching her back at the same time.

Usmaan and his friend burst into hysterical excited laughter. His friend slapped him firmly on the leg and briefly grabbed his crotch.

~Good work, Keeley. Keep it going. Nice and subtle. Soon we're going to need you to go over and talk to him. We're going to try and help things along a bit. Just sit tight for now.

A group of girls was dancing provocatively near Usmaan and his gang. One of them broke away from the main circle, and beckoned Usmaan's right-hand man towards her. Not believing his luck, the young man obliged. She began to dance with him, gyrating and rubbing up against him, but working him gradually away from Usmaan.

In almost identical fashion the process was repeated three times, until Usmaan found himself sitting alone and bewildered.

On her table with Keeley the extra began to fulfil the final part of her role. A handsome young man came over to chat her up, and in no time at all their lips were locked together.

Keeley turned to look at Usmaan, and rolled her eyes

and shrugged her shoulders. Usmaan turned his palms upwards and did the same. But then an idea clearly crossed his mind. He patted the empty leather seat next to him, and gestured for her to come and sit down.

—OK, this is it, Keeley. I want you to try and keep him chatting for about ten minutes. Then, when I tell you, make your excuses and go to the loo.

SUPPORT

After three and a half minutes Keeley was struggling. She couldn't seem to engage him in any kind of conversation. He was simply propositioning her in different ways and to varying degrees. It was all based around finding somewhere more private. Back at his place, in his car, a quiet corner of the club. He didn't want to talk about work or music or even sport. She found it difficult to talk without telling him to fuck off. She understood now why he had been selected as a target. Her clutch bag was on the table, the buckle pointing upwards and towards him. He never considered it.

But she soldiered on. Giggling, deflecting, smiling. He had commandeered her personal space and had long since slid a long arm around her, engulfing her slim frame. He smelt of strong aftershave, but it still failed to mask the stench of stale sweat that wafted from his pores.

Out of the blue Usmaan took a firm grip on the nape of her neck and pulled her towards him. The kiss was aggressive and wet and it took all her strength to force him off. He kept his face just a few inches away from hers, and glared at her. His leering eyes looked wide and wild, and his mouth hung open as though hungry with lust.

Just before she thought she was going to gip, Keeley heard the voice in her ear. Much quieter this time, but clear enough.

~You're doing great, Keeley. We're going to get you out soon. But first you need to nip to the loo. Leave your bag and drink and reassure him that you're coming back.

Keeley began to make her excuses. She looked Usmaan in the eye when she told him she was coming back, but it was not until she forced herself to kiss him swiftly on the cheek that he relented, and released his hold on her hair.

As instructed, Keeley left her bag and drink behind, promising to return. Usmaan's expression changed as he noticed the two items. The glazed look on his face was replaced by one resembling a light bulb moment.

Keeley was worried.

More so than she had ever been on a Rectifires' mission.

Something wasn't right. She couldn't say exactly what, but she had an intense feeling of discomfort. It wasn't just the repulsive physical nature of the man. There was something else, and she began to speculate.

Keeley worried that perhaps he suspected the presence of the camera, or was going to make off with the bag – although by now that seemed to be a desirable outcome compared with spending another moment in his presence.

She also worried that her disguise might have been compromised. There had been speculation in the tabloid press and in some internet chat rooms about a planned sting on the Rectifires by a company signed to a rival channel.

But there were no other production companies in K2 that particular night. Just a handful of StrikeBack Media employees, who watched Usmaan pour a dangerous quantity of Rohypnol into Keeley's drink.

TARGET

Usmaan

Fuckin' real in 'ere man.
Every week.
It's every fuckin' week. Wall to wall.
All fuckin' gaggin' forrit am telling yer right now man.
Fuckin' short skirts. Tits out. They fuckin' love it.
It's fuckin' unreal.
It's just take yer pick time innit.
I don't take no shit from these white bitches.
No messin' about.
They wan' it they're gonna gerrit man.
No fuckin' problem.
Iss all they want. Iss all they know.
They want ma fuckin' black cock am tellin' yer innit.
Even righ' now there's one bitch looking over.
I'm no' even bothered righ' now know wa'a mean.
Jus' happy chillin' wi' ma crew for a while innit.

Fuckin' 'ell bitch chill out will ya.

Me jus' wanna talk business an' cars an' that wi' me boise innit.

Plenny o time for shaggin' later on innit.

Fuck me.

Bit o' class an' success an' that these fuckin' lot can't 'elp 'emselves am tellin' yer.

'Cos they're not used to it.

White lads pissin' all the money away on beer.

Can't even buy 'emselves decent cars.

Yer see 'em all drivin' round in secondhand Corsas or Saxos and that.

What a fuckin' joke.

No wonder they don't know how to get laid man.

See yer take care o' yerself an' buy nice things an' that.

Get respect innit.

An' respect gets yer sex.

Same every time.

I've lost count o' how many white bitches just come up to me an' tell me they wannit.

No fuckin' bullshit man.

Fo' real.

An I used to be right nice an' that. When a first started.

But now a don' even bother.

Fuckin' waste o' time.

Honestly man.

Just fuckin' give 'em it innit.

No messin'.

Fuck me darlin' you really is gaggin' for it.

Fuckin' swarmin' round us, nah mean.

Bein' picked off one by one.

Look at the way that bitch is going for it wi' Ackie on the dance floor.

Fuckin' 'ell.

An' that little slag is looking over again!

Wos that?

Little Muss?

Little Miss? Scatterbox?

Little Miss Scatterbrain?

Fuckin' 'ell!

I'll be scatterin' somethin' o' me own on that fuckin' neck tonight!

Fuckin' come 'ere then bitch.

Come on then you know you wannit.

A seen yer looking over.

A seen yer baby.

Don't mek me gerrup and come over.

Am fuckin' comfortable 'ere innit.

Thass it, come to Daddy.

Come sit right down nex' me.

An' you can talk all yer want.

Think I care about who you are or where yer come from?

When them titties comin' out tha's all am bothered about innit.

We can go righ' upstairs where iss nice an' quiet.

Or there's some kitchens downstairs tha' they 'ardly ever use.

A know one o' the bouncers.

Let us in there no problem.

Or straight back to my place.

Go for a little ride an' that.

Go for a cruise.

Put some tunes on.

You like PURE?

Got loads o' their shit man, authentic records innit.

Well make yer mind up, fuckin' ell.

Don't start playin' hard to get now bitch.

Don't even think about fuckin' off now.

Go to the toilet?

You better fuckin' come back an' all.

Waste my fuckin' time comin' over an' that.

Got better things to do.

You don't wanna be tied up wi' bitches like that wastin' yer time.

Leave yer bag?

You are comin back.

An yer drink?

Big fuckin' mistake.

We're definitely fuckin' on for it now.

Might as well get the car started up.

Get my fuckin' loopy love potion in there man.

Fuckin' stir it round.

Good as gold innit.

Fuckin' pulled by half ten innit.

Not even getting value fo' money by payin' to get it.

Might even ask fo' ma money back.

I hope that shit kicks in pretty soon. Won't have to talk to the daft bitch any more.

Does my fuckin' ead in.

Tell you what luv.

There'll be no more fuckin' about soon.

An' everyone saw yer comin over.

Fuckin' pissed as it is anyway.

Don't even know the difference half o' these bitches.

Come on then, sit back down.

Drink yer drink.

Fuckin' 'ell that wo' quick.

Fuckin' thirsty bitch.

Or alky more like.

Motherfucker down in one.

Near the exit an' all.

Fuckin' genius man.

You wanna rest yer 'ead on ma shoulder.

Down in one like that gonna make yer dizzy innit.

Yer just need to relax for a minute.

Tek it easy.

Or a bit o' fresh air might do yer good.

Probably what yer need.

These fire exits jus' over here.

Yer just need a bit o' help walkin' an' that.

You'll be fine. Just need a bit of air.

Noisy as fuck in there.

Woow!

Come on luv. Stand up.

You gonna bang yer 'ead if yer do that again.

Come on. Concentrate. You're not that bad.

Yer can come back to mine to chill.

If yer really want to.

A mean am not forcin' yer, don't get me wrong.

But if thas what yer thinks best I can drive yer.

Fuckin' nice Merc with leather seats an' that.

You've probably never been in one before.

Fuckin' two litre. Alloy wheels. V8 turbo.

Fuckin' boots it up Bradford Road.

Don't fuckin' puke, though, or al fuckin' knock yer
out.

Serious.

DAMAGE

Usmaan Hussain pulled his modified Mercedes onto the single parking space in front of the small terraced house he rented. The thumping sound of the bass suddenly clicked into silence as he pulled his keys out of the ignition and made his way to the passenger side.

Usmaan loved driving his car at night. The neon strips came into their own, as did the huge shining exhaust and alloy wheels. Less obvious, in the dim lighting were the signs of rust and age that he sought to cover up with tinted windows and rear spoiler. Sitting on the red leather seat sat Keeley, the girl he had drugged, and intended to rape.

Keeley was still conscious and aware of her surroundings. She felt very confused, yet strangely relaxed at the same time. She was sure she was walking because she was in an upright position and moving, but she could barely feel her feet touching the floor. She was aware of somebody with her, a presence on her left side. But she wasn't sure if she was being carried or guided.

Usmaan was pleased that Keeley could walk of her own accord. He preferred it when the girls showed some signs of life. He would happily hump away at a limp body, but always enjoyed the added authenticity of the odd moan, movement or whimper from beneath him.

Keeley's next memory was of climbing some stairs, her progress slow and languid. When she reached the top there was no pain, but she recognised the sensation of carpet brushing against the skin on her face as her assailant hauled her onwards.

When Usmaan finally got Keeley into his bedroom he hurriedly removed her T-shirt, hauling it in short tugs over her head. He was delighted she was still able to stand, and allowed himself a few moments to savour what he was about to devour. He looked at her standing there, her pert breasts sitting invitingly in her bra. He noted the strange necklace that sat high above them. It stood out now, against her bare skin, and something about it, he didn't know quite what, deeply concerned him.

With an added sense of urgency he began to claw at her breasts and greedily kiss, lick and bite her neck. As he became more frenzied his victim stood, rocking slightly but totally passive. He scraped the hair away from her ear, and took her lobe in his mouth.

Then he spotted something that made him break off.

—What the . . . You some sort of fuckin' deaf bitch?

He began to pull at the small mechanism inside and around the back of her ear.

Usmaan's initial concerns started to grow. He started to piece things together. Then he was sure he heard a voice, faintly but clearly, coming from the earpiece in his hand.

~Keeley? Keeley? Are you there? No response. Send them in. It's time. Send them in.

Usmaan was in shock. His mind began to race. He was trying to work this out. He looked again at the girl's face. He thought he'd seen her somewhere before. TV? Magazine or something?

Then Lord Vengeance crashed through his bedroom window. The entrance was by no means a clean one, but went as well as the stunt coordinators had hoped for. The operations team had done all they could, disguised as council employees, and had weakened the window frame. But it still took a couple of ferocious kicks from Lord Vengeance's weighted boots to smash the window. The abseil harness that he had used was still attached, and his legs and face were bleeding from glass lacerations.

The finer details of the staged entrance were completely lost on Usmaan. He had never experienced anything as shocking. He felt his throat close up and his blood run cold.

In a heightened state of frenzy, fuelled by adrenalin and pain, Lord Vengeance began his rehearsed tirade of righteousness. It was lucky for both parties that his abseil harness restrained him from moving further into the room, as the punishment he would have meted out might have been fatal. Instead he just stood there, ranting, accusing, condemning, flecks of spit shooting from his foaming mouth.

Usmaan was suddenly aware of the presence of two others, much calmer, and busy and purposeful. One seemed to have entered the window by means of a ladder and was crouching on the floor working away at the harness. The other was a cameraman.

Those few seconds when the man was fiddling with the harness allowed Lord Vengeance to gain some

337

semblance of self-control. When he was finally released he slammed Usmaan against all four walls of the bedroom, sending CDs and ashtrays tumbling noisily to the ground. The young man was knocked unceremoniously to the floor and hauled down the stairs feet first, banging his head on each and every uncarpeted step along the way. Vengeance left Usmaan outside the front door, where a medical team restrained him. A crowd had already begun to gather, and more and more came as news of the commotion spread.

By the time Lord Vengeance emerged for a second time almost a hundred people were in attendance.

This time he emerged slowly and carefully. In his arms he carried a semi-conscious ViXen. The punters' princess. He looked down at her, his tough, bloodied face showing concern for his brave friend and colleague. A ripple of applause greeted them, as cameras flashed and a medical team fussed around them.

The applause turned into cheers as a doctor confirmed that both Rectifires had only suffered superficial injuries. Lord Vengeance enjoyed the accolades for a few moments more before being ushered away and swept into the blacked-out people carrier for that all important de-brief.

2024
'AVE IT!

There were questions raised. People talked about morality. People talked about placing people in danger. People talked about copy-cat vigilante groups getting it badly wrong. People talked about the real motives behind screening the Rectifires. But these people were the minority. They were the sort who read posh, poncy newspapers and had no idea about the real world. What the ordinary man in the street thought.

But the *Sun* did.

On its front page it ran the headline "AVE IT'.

Beneath was the photo of the moment when Lord Vengeance crashed through the bedroom window of the house in Keighley, where his dearest friend and comrade was about to raped.

The picture had been slightly enhanced, so that the red, white and blue flag on his swimming trunks was sharper. The *Sun* had captured the mood of a nation.

'Ave it' became the rallying cry before acts of aggression up and down the country, especially when the violence was carried out on the side of the good and the righteous.

Britons were empowered once again. The *Sun* commented that Britain hadn't seen unity against a common enemy since the Second World War. After years of pandering to paedophiles, and hugging hoodies, criminals were getting a real taste of justice from the great British public, inspired by Eddie Shearer and his Rectifires.

The offices of StrikeBack Media were well and truly buzzing. Everyone wanted a piece. The staff felt as if they were at the centre of the world. There was talk of unlimited budgets, franchising, merchandising, expansion, awards, a Hollywood film.

Eddie himself struggled to keep his feet on the ground. Deep down he knew it. He was wasting time and energy on an idea that he couldn't get out of his head. And his staff were doing nothing to dissuade him. He had built up an organisation of too many yes men.

His plan was to replace the Queen with a special Christmas screening, following his own message to the nation. When he told his production team they backed him. He was more in touch with the people than the Queen. He had saved the BBC, and was justified in making scheduling demands. He wanted full editorial control and no censorship. The people around him made him believe it was possible, but what he really needed was Vera to tell him it was bollocks.

He left meeting after meeting with BBC bosses feeling defeated and frustrated. He realised there were some things even he couldn't change. He just needed someone to tell him. It made him reflect. Eddie thought about what had made him successful. Yes, he had had plenty of crazy ideas, but they were always in perspective and their achievable goals were clearly set out. All around him people were running out of control. He had a vision of things getting out of hand and everything blowing up in his face. He knew what he had to do.

He had to get Vera back.

He was in no doubt about this, but how could he possibly approach her?

He knew it was for selfish reasons. He shuddered when he thought about the way they had parted. How he had held her against her will. He doubted that she would even take his call, let alone agree to return. He couldn't begin to think what on earth he was going to say. Apologising wasn't really his style, but this was going to have to be an exception. He would have to swallow his pride and get on with it. He wasn't looking forward to making that phone call.

That's why Eddie was so surprised when Vera came to see him.

RECONCILED

Eddie was amazed at how well the conversation went. Perhaps, looking back, his mind's eye had exaggerated the look of hurt and anger in Vera's face. Maybe much of what she had said was heat-of-the-moment stuff.

She seemed re-motivated, looking younger and with a new sense of purpose. She hadn't exactly apologised but played down what might have been said or done in the heat of the moment between two close professionals under extreme pressure. She said everything he wanted to hear. It was almost as though Eddie himself had written the script. They shared jokes about certain employees, and Eddie revealed his fears about the way things had been going since the spectacular date rape episode.

Vera conceded that although she still disagreed with his methods the episode had been a huge success, and on reflection the ends justified the means. Keeley had escaped relatively unharmed and another sick criminal had been brought to justice. Strangely, it was precisely the fact that everything went so well that bothered Eddie slightly. He somehow felt that their relationship had a depth that would demand a longer and more intense period of healing. Everything back to normal after a couple of drinks and an hour's chat didn't ring true somehow.

Anyway, he had the outcome he wanted, and he had way too much on his plate to think about these minor concerns.

CEMA

I t was a surreal moment.

Eddie sat alone and anonymous as he often liked to do when he needed to think and reflect. He was tucked away in a the corner of Cellar V, a dimly lit and trendy bar in the centre of Leeds. He was enjoying a bottle of red, people-watching and pondering.

He was thinking how it was everywhere. So suddenly. As though it had always been so.

The CEMAs.

He had recently found out that the acronym stood for Cutting Edge Media Awards. They were prizes that celebrated innovative production on radio, film and TV. There was an article about last year's award night in a magazine that was lying around the office. There were snippets on the entertainment news about tips for future winners. And increasingly the title was cropping up in the media sections of broadsheet newspapers.

Two smartly dressed attractive women sat down at the

vacant table nearby. From what he could hear of their conversation, he deduced that they were media professionals or in public relations. They spoke about work and gossiped about romance before their conversation turned to the CEMA awards. They chatted enthusiastically, mixing name drops with complimentary adjectives. The more they talked the more animated they became, gesturing and laughing as the acronym kept cropping up.

CEMA.

They seemed not to notice as he turned to look at them squarely. Eddie took a moment to analyse their features and digest the conversation. When their discussion moved on he turned away, sitting back in his comfortable leather chair. He took another sip of wine and smiled. He was confident he knew exactly what kind of women they were. He made predictions about the cars they drove, the character of their husbands and the décor of their sitting rooms.

Eddie tuned out and thought about himself again. He felt contented and had a surge of self-worth, partly induced by the alcohol. He was pleased.

BUSINESS AS USUAL

There were raised eyebrows around the offices when Vera returned, but Eddie made a point of stating publicly that he regretted the circumstances that had caused her to leave, and that she was going to be an integral part of the future success of the organisation.

Vera threw herself back into her work, and before long it was almost as if she had never left.

Eddie was delighted. The buzz and excitement were still there, and he felt they were pulling in the same direction. Vera, her old assertive self, organised and prompted, but most importantly of all cut out the time-wasting and nonsense that happens as people fall in love with themselves.

By far her most important role, though, was to listen to Eddie late at night after everyone else had gone home. He ran ideas past her, non-starters being killed on the spot while those with potential were explored and assessed. Most importantly she knew what made him tick. A great success was never enough; there had to be another big thing. Eddie knew it was in there; he just needed some help getting it out.

The Christmas Day idea was born from a need to galvanise the nation and go mainstream with the Rectifires' ideology. Vera pointed out how bad an idea it was, how it could look as if he was trying to be king. Eddie blushed, because that was how he sometimes fantasised about himself. She said he would lose his popularity among ordinary people if he started to act as if he was above them or better than them.

Vera suggested that he might go in completely the other direction. Become as much like an ordinary member of the public as possible and still pull the strings. She suggested that people who try to take over eventually fall. Someone always tries to discredit them or knock them off their perch.

Eddie couldn't remember who brought it up, but they began reminiscing about *Secret Millionaire*, the TV show from 2008. They both agreed it was a fascinating format.

~You could disappear into society. When you find an area in dire need you send in the Rectifires. You'd be an urban legend: never seen, but always heard. Take Bin Laden, for instance. He never made a habit of public appearances, but look what he inspired people to do. You could do the same but on the side of good. People would say they've spotted you. There'd be unconfirmed sightings, which we'd encourage. You'd be the voice of hope. Then we'd give you small cameo roles on each show. A long shot of you disappearing down a subway, a shaky shot of you blending into the crowd, or speeding down a canal on a jet-ski to escape the paparazzi. Always unconfirmed, of course, to heighten the interest and keep things fresh. Just think about it.

Eddie didn't need to answer. The look in his eyes told Vera everything she needed to know. He was already imagining it. It made perfect sense. What a move to bring Vera back. It was just what was needed to keep StrikeBack Media one step ahead.

~OK. OK. I like it. It could work. But what about a launch? How are we going to get this thing off the ground with a real big bang? I mean, with all due respect, V, that last episode is going to take some topping.

~I know, Eddie. There's no way we can outdo Lord Vengeance abseiling into a rapist's bedroom to rescue Keeley. We'd be wrong to try. But we can think about our methods, and how real everything is.

~What do you mean, real? This is the ultimate in reality television. There were people out there on the street watching, for Christ's sake! We had a live crowd!

~Sure you had a live crowd, but it wasn't live TV. We had music and effects added. There are rumours that the exit scene was re-shot. And the footage coming down the stairs, it was obvious that was added later.

~Yes, but do people really care? They want great footage and a great story, and that's what we gave them.

~A lot of people don't care. But a growing number are looking to put the boot in. It won't be long before they become the majority. Or someone else comes up with something fresher. Something edgier.

~So what are you suggesting, V? Is it what I think?

~You remember that documentary, three years ago, *Inside Rectifires*.

~Of course.

~We thought that would be the making of us. And in a way it was the break we needed. Gave us a lot of publicity. But people keep banging on about it. Misquoting figures, making assumptions. How many times have I heard that only thirty per cent of Rectifires projects actually make it to air, because something goes wrong or the criminal escapes. People say it's a set-up. The criminals know or are paid off. Scenes are added or deleted or staged.

~Well, we both know that's all true, in a way.

~Yes, Eddie. But we can control it. We can make it lies.

~How?

Vera smiled and paused for dramatic effect.

~By going live. Think about it. We launch Eddie Shearer as the urban crime-fighting legend, with our first ever showing of *Rectifires Live*.

~But that goes against everything you stood for. About us controlling the TV and not the other way round. I mean, think about everything that could go wrong. Everything that *has* gone wrong. And on live TV.

~Yes, but we do control it. People will forgive us being less spectacular because we're live. It's not written. No one's sure we'll be successful. People will be tuning in to see if we make a mess of it.

~But what if we do?

~We won't. Not if we control things. For a start we choose easy targets. Stick with the sex crime theme, but target someone who's going to be easy to take down. In plenty of open space with loads of back-up. We basically make it nice and easy for ourselves. We do our research. I know you can pull it off.

~So what exactly do you have in mind for me?

~That's the beauty of it. You can basically do as much or as little as you like. I mean, as you know, we've got people who can do the research for you. Or if you feel like it you can 'guise up and get your hands dirty. All we'll need is something like an audio recording of you giving information about a criminal who needs targeting, or a crime hotspot that needs cleaning up. You talk about how you've lived anonymously among the people and discovered a need. From your hideaway you call the Rectifires and give them their instructions. We start with the live launch. We can go back to normal after that.

Eddie loved the idea. It put him back in the firing line, and the element of risk well and truly captured his imagination. The thought of snooping round dodgy areas and rooting out scum fired his adrenalin. But most of all he was in love with the urban legend tag.

~I like it. I must admit I like it. It's not like you to come up with something quite so risky, but I do admire your audacity. So what's our next step? Where do we start? Who's our target and what do we need?

~I've got a couple of leads already.

~I thought you might, Vera. I bloody well thought you might.

~There are just a couple of loose ends I need to go and tie up, and I'll be right back to you with the details.

They shared a moment together, holding each other's gaze. Eddie felt that trust had been restored. Vera looked as though she was waiting for him to say something else. He wondered about asking her a favour.

~On something else, V. Have you ever heard of CEMA?

~Of course. We've been linked a few times, but everyone always assumed that it wasn't the sort of thing you went in for. All that back-slapping when there's work to be done.

~How come I've never heard about it?

Vera laughed.

~Because sometimes you walk around encased in that bubble of yours. Oblivious! Apart from when it's something you actually want to hear.

~I was just thinking it would be nice for us to get some official recognition.

Vera smiled, tilting her head and raising her eyebrows knowingly. Eddie swallowed, embarrassed at his own vanity.

~I mean, not for me. I couldn't give a shit. But it's the sort of thing that the team would get off on, isn't it? Day out at an awards ceremony and that?

~And I'm sure that, being a team player, you could cope with the indignity of receiving it on their behalf.

She knew him too well, and Eddie blushed deeply, unable to think of a witty response. Vera put him out of his misery.

~I know some people connected with CEMA. I can have a word in their ears. From what I gather they don't make awards on the productions alone. If we want the top award they'll want to know about the person behind everything. They'll come and spend a day talking to staff. Then they'll have half a day or so with you at some posh hotel, getting to know you, your philosophy, your vision, that sort of thing. They take a lot of trouble, which is why the CEMAs are so highly regarded. They're like media knighthoods.

PREPARATION

Eddie sat in his office, listening as Vera updated him on the progress and preparations for the live show. He fired questions and concerns at her, but everything was in hand. She spoke clearly and efficiently. Not wasting words, not wasting time. She assured him that the rest of the team were focused on their assigned tasks. He believed her too. He sensed drive and efficiency returning, and it felt good.

~There's just a couple of things I need you to do before you disappear into the criminal wilderness.

~Oh yes?

~Just run your eye over this press release. It's basically preparing them for the next series and revealing how you'll be disappearing from public view for a while, to track down criminals who're blighting the lives of ordinary people.

Eddie briefly scanned the document, trusting Vera's judgement on the wording, and signed it.

~And we need to do a few trials on your voice.

~My voice?

~Yes. When you've located a target or a crime hotspot you'll release an audio tape explaining why you're sending in the 'fires. They're going to do some audience research into what will inspire and intrigue people the most. You have a few cards to read as though you're in different parts of the country. It'll take twenty minutes. Half an hour tops. I've hired an agency. Easiest way. They're waiting for you in reception now.

~OK. Better get down there. Don't want to keep them waiting . . .

Pleased he was different and enigmatic. Pleased no one would ever be able to make predictions and assumptions about him.

CRAIGLANDS

Eddie was pleased with the way things had gone. The representatives from the CEMA awards had been for a look round. They had spoken to staff and held a forum about him in the conference room. He wasn't supposed to be present, but had arranged for listening devices to be strategically placed. The chance to have so many people gathered around saying nice things about him was too good an opportunity to miss. It had resembled a wake, with employees queuing up to say what a great boss he was and how wonderful it was to work for such a groundbreaking and exciting organisation.

Of course Vera had briefed everybody as he knew she would.

He was sitting in the back of a limo, making small-talk with the two judges. They had both told him briefly about their backgrounds. He hadn't paid much attention, but he picked up that the bloke was a TV documentary maker and the woman was some sort of half-blind radio executive who gave production opportunities to underprivileged and minority groups.

He had never heard of either of them, but Vera had prepared him with a folder of the key points about their work, so he could feign knowledge and interest with well-placed questions during the journey.

They were heading to the Craiglands Hotel in Ilkley for an informal lunch and then a panel interview.

Eddie strode in through the large double doors, feeling confident and relishing the challenge of the interview that was about to come. Lunch was an unwelcome distraction. Adrenalin always quelled his hunger somewhat, and he couldn't really relax and enjoy his meal knowing that he was being constantly evaluated. He was eager to get on with the real business.

At last he was invited to take the lift to the interview room on the top floor.

THE ELEVATOR

Three men in a lift.
And a half-blind woman.
Tension.
From me?
Yes, tension, but more than that.
Greater tension. I can sense it.
Nervous laughs and coughs. Silences that need to be filled.
Why are they so tense?
It's only some shite interview for a poxy award.
Feels like a sting. In the old days.
That sort of nervousness and hyper-adrenalin.
And that guy. The hotel manager who came in to operate the lift.
Know his face.
Swear I know.
Couldn't be that . . .
Surely not.
Could it?

Elevator doors open now.

At last.

We're out of the doors. The penthouse suite?

Now climbing more stairs. Higher.

Like we're going to a top secret hideaway.

No hotel rooms here. Through two sets of heavy double doors.

~No chance of being disturbed up here!

I try to laugh.

~That's what we had in mind, Mr Shearer, that's what we had in mind.

It's that blind bitch.

She sounds like she's trying to be clever, but it comes out sinister.

Well sinister.

They seem to have closed in around me now.

We're heading towards another door.

I know this body language.

Like guards and a prisoner.

They want me in that door for some reason.

I need to find an excuse here.

A way out.

Am I being paranoid?

Hope so, but this is weird.

Make out I've got a message. Need to get back in touch with the office.

Feel for my phone in my jacket pocket.

Not there. Not there. Not fucking there.

Lifted?

During lunch, maybe.

Must have been. It's always fucking there.

Well and truly lost my bottle now. I'm fucking out of here, CEMA award or not.

I turn to my right. Talk to the manager cunt.

~Listen, I just remembered, I'm ever so sorry, I'm just going to have to nip downstairs and . . .

Then I clock him.

I know who he is.

He knows that I know.

I know that he knows that I know.

I can see the hate in his eyes. He starts to speak.

It's like it's something he's wanted to say for a long time.

But it sounds like it's over-rehearsed. He's fucked it up.

I'm not waiting around for him to get it right.

The cunt from Lotsa Coffee who cleaned up my shite.

I stick my nut on him.

Hard.

In that moment I want to knock his nose back inside his face.

His head snaps back and he goes down.

There's blood, and he's squirming on the floor.

But the other bloke's onto me.

Frenzied.

He's shouting and bawling. Loud and high pitched.

We grapple.

Both our heads bang against the wall. The banister. The carpet.

The blind bitch is standing there. Tall and straight. Her eyes rolling round way too fast. Not focusing.

I hang in there.

Maybe I could really do this guy. But I just want to get away.

Need to get away.

I get my elbow free and hammer it a couple of times in his mouth.

He starts to bleed and spit blood, so I ram the heel of my hand into the weakened area.

This guy is on a mission, though, and he keeps coming. He's hanging onto my waist and I'm dragging him along the carpet.

Then suddenly a shrill voice pierces the mayhem.

~Let him go.

He's still on me but the voice I recognise repeats itself.

~Let him go. NOW!

This time the psycho obliges.

I don't waste time saying my goodbyes, and I'm off round the corner and down the stairs towards the lift.

I knew I recognised that voice. I've never been so pleased to see anyone.

It's Vera. Come to sort things out. She'd obviously smelt a rat and followed us. Make sure things went OK.

Fucking genius, that woman, but that's her job.

She's come prepared.

She's got a canister. Looks like that CS gas or pepper spray or something.

But there's a look on her face.

She's never looked at me like that before.

Well apart from that one time . . .

And now she's lifting the canister up.

Pointing it at me?

She fucking is!

What the fuck?

And it's onto me.

I feel three splashes on my face.

Nothing for a couple of seconds.

Then it sets in.

Every fucker starts coughing and sneezing.

But not as bad as me.

I'm drowning.

I'm fucking drowning here.

I'm trying to sneeze and breathe at the same time.

Can't get any fucking air in.

My lungs are burning.

Every time I grab a breath I take in more of this shite.

And my eyes are fucked.

I try to open them but it's agony.

I've never felt itching like it.

So I press my face on the dusty carpet.

And I rub it.

Hard.

Try to breathe through the carpet. Like it's some sort of filter.

And lie still.

Helpless.

Totally fucking helpless.

They can do what they want to me now.

I don't give a shit.

Just make it stop.

PENTHOUSE

Long before Eddie had scraped the mucus from his eyes he had blindly become accustomed to the room that was to be his soundproof prison. It was roughly twelve feet by ten. The source of water he discovered in the corner that he used to soothe his eyes was a toilet, minus its seat. Above it was a small basin, which contained a number of basic toiletry items. There was a laptop computer plugged into the wall and high above was a skylight. The door that he had been bundled through was locked, sealed and had had its handle removed. There was a single mattress with a blanket and pillow on top. Along the other wall was a large chest crammed full of dried food, cans and bottled water.

In the centre of the room was a large, sealed envelope with his name on it. Once he regained his vision he opened it and began to read:

Eddie,

Welcome to your new home. It isn't pretty, but it's not meant to be.

First things first: don't consider trying to escape. It'll be a waste of time. It's not possible. You know me, Eddie, I'm thorough. This is an extremely meticulous and well-planned operation, even for me.

I'm sure you've worked out by now that the CEMA awards don't exist. I made them up. I designed them so that you'd want one and come looking for one. I've spent a lot of your money hiring people to talk about the CEMA awards and write articles about them. Quite ironic that you came to me to try and win one.

And you aren't going to be missed either. Just remember the statement in your press release. That you're going to disappear for some time in your quest to repair the fabric of Britain.

We can use your voice and make broadcasts that sound as though they're live or recent. You remember the sound tests. With a bit of clever editing we can make it sound like you're commenting or reflecting on recent events.

If only you had a family, Eddie. They'd miss you. But you can't love anyone, can you?

Rich, successful, reasonable looking, not unattractive.

You have issues. So many relationships, but always called off after two or three months. Eighty-one days, to be precise. Always eighty-one. No one ever noticed that, but I did. When I started checking up on old diaries. I never worked that one out and you never told me. But you will, Eddie, just as you're going to tell us everything.

You see, the way I feel about you isn't unique.

There are others. You'd be amazed how far back they go. Some from your school days. The partially sighted lady who posed as the CEMA judge. That was Rachel Cassells. Or Wringing Wet Rachel as you might remember her. Suffering all through her school years while you carried on with your stupid pranks. Perhaps it wouldn't have been so bad if it had just been a daft schoolboy thing. But to carry on? To make a living out of it? Become a millionaire out of it?

You remember sticking that custard pie in the policewoman's face? That was you wasn't it? Well, she had a miscarriage. And her partner ended up in prison. Because he couldn't cope. Couldn't cope with you getting away with it.

And the hotel manager. I think you recognise him now. He owns the hotel, since his father died a year ago.

We all met via the internet, you see. A forum, discussing you. You were held up as some sort of hero, but a few of us knew what you were really like.

If you think this is harsh, Eddie, you should be grateful that I got my way. I'm not going to scare you with the details of what the others wanted to do to you, because I need to keep you calm. Calm enough to think. And write.

Because we want you to write everything down. Right from the very beginning.

When did you turn into the person you are today?

I must admit, and I've told the others, I thought I saw some good in you. I liked your approach to Keeley at first. You looked out for her and gave her a break. But perhaps she was just a cheaper option. When it suited you, you sent her out to be drugged and raped to boost your ratings.

We also want you to think.

Think hard about the consequences of your actions. Every single one of your scams. Did they have victims? How did they feel? What might have happened to them? What's the worst that could happen? Ask yourself that.

Was there anything you could walk away from? Or was everything just too damn exciting to turn down?

After you sacked, humiliated, assaulted and imprisoned me, did you really think you were so wonderful that I would just stroll back in, all forgiven, as if nothing had happened?

We want to know, Eddie.

So you're going to stay here and write. You have everything you need to write your memoirs and exist in reasonable comfort. Feel free to use your imagination, to speculate about the consequences of your actions. But we want detail and we want it to be good.

We'll come back and we may release you.

But that depends on you.

We want eighty thousand words and we want it from the beginning.

High-quality stuff.

This was my idea. I don't see what good beating the crap out of you will do. This way you'll have to think. Now that might be worse, Eddie, but we think it'll help you.

Allow yourself a moment or two to become acquainted with your new surroundings, and then I suggest you get writing.

Best wishes,

Vera.

ROBERTS PARK

Lord Vengeance

This is what it's all about.
THIS IS WHAT IT'S ALL ABOUT!
The Vengeance ready to strike.
The Lord about to go to work.
And you better show, Percy.
You better show now, motherfucker.
I'm relying on you now.
The people wanna see me now.
Going out live to millions.
Bringing peace and justice. Through strength.
'Cos that's what's needed now.
Strength and power.
This ain't no job for no woman, or some punk on rollerskates.
This is the real deal.
When you got a situation like this you need the

Vengeance man.

And I am ready. Am I ready.

Ready to rock!

I'm looking fucking huge!

I'm looking fucking good!

Ain't no man gonna get in my way tonight!

This is my night, bro!

This is my night, cuz!

That Shearer can stay away too.

Stay in the shadows, old man.

Don't you even think about no cameo role.

'Cos you just might feel the strength of the Vengeance Man too.

An' now we're rolling.

Now we're cooking.

We got eyeball.

We got eyeball on the filthy motherfucker.

We starting to move now.

Slowly does it now.

I see you.

You see her.

But you don't see me.

We in position now.

Don't even think now.

You do your stuff, Percy.

I'm sure as hell ready to do mine.

That's it, Percy.

Nice and close.

Stay quiet all.

Stay fucking quiet.

We're nearly there now.

Don't nobody spoil this.

We're all too close.

Worked too fucking hard.

Don't talk to the bitch, Percy.

Do your fucking stuff!
That's it.
Hands on your coat, you dirty bastard.
Open the fucker.
Show your fucking cock, you little prick.
Get on with it.
Can't stand this no more.
Gonna have to move in soon.
Regardless.
Ready to erupt.
Just a few more seconds . . .
He's gonna . . .
Yes . . .
No . . .
Yes . . .
GO, GO, GO!
AAAAAARRRRGH!
Grab the dirty bastard.
By the throat.
Squeezing.
Hard.
Harder.
No sympathy for you.
Scum.
I can lift you.
Scrawny fucker.
Pick your scrawny sixty kilograms right up.
And now I'm talking.
I'm gonna tell you like it's guttertrash!
–Percy the Pervert!

You have exposed yourself to the good women of Ravensbridge for the last time.

Women will now be able to walk the streets without fear of meeting scum like you!

TRAPPED

Eddie
No one is coming.
No one is coming.
Do I really deserve all this?
Maybe I do.
My face is still burning.
My eyes are streaming.
Being forced to look at this.
Forced to re-live.
And write all this down.
And then everyone will know.
And I am alone.

Percival
No one is coming.
To this hospital bed.
Do I really deserve all this?
Maybe I do.

My throat is burning.
My chest is hurting.
Being forced to look at this police statement.
Forced to re-live.
And everyone will know.
I just want to be alone.
With Gladys.

Gladys

No one is coming.
And I've fallen.
Do I really deserve this?
Maybe I do.
My neck is twisted.
I can't turn away.
Forced to watch.
And everyone will know.
I want it to end.
Please make it end.

EPILOGUE

I feel calm today.
So very, very calm.
I'm ready to leave my prison.
And everything will be right again.
My feelings are balanced now.
Vera knew, you see.
Knew all along.
That all I needed was time to think.
Alone.
By myself.
With no intrusions.
Just me.
And my thoughts.
She said to me once that I'm a self-healer.
And she was right.
I've healed myself.
Sure it was tough, thinking about all those people that I hurt.
Thinking about my motivations.
What drove me.
But making me write it down got it all out.
It's left me now.
One hell of a journey, but it's gone.
And Vera knew that.
Because she loves me.
If she can see me now she'll know anyway.
If she can't she'll read my work.
Just like she said.
Seventy-five thousand words.
Considered. In depth.
My mind and soul opened up and scoured.
Clean.
She might come for me soon, but if she doesn't that's fine.
I can wait now.
I'm keeping the room clean now and looking after myself.

Clean on the outside as well as the inside.

There's plenty of time to think.

Meditate.

Plan for the future.

Seeing things so clearly now.

So calm.

People will see me in a different light.

Even read my work if they want.

I'm heading in a different direction now.

Serenity.

That's what I seek.

No adrenalin needed.

I've done the cold turkey.

So pure.

So clean.

So clear.

So calm.

And to think about all those people that Vera made me write about.

It used to make me angry.

But not now.

I see who the real victims are.

Vera, and all those people I hurt.

And I want to meet them again.

I'll see them and put things right.

They can read what I've put.

Nobody can change the past, I know that.

But we can put things in place to make a better future.

I have skills that can be put to good use.

Not for the greater glory of Eddie Shearer.

Not for TV ratings, or column inches.

For them, but also for me.

To finish off my healing as well as theirs.

But most of all I need to get to know people.

Time to get to understand others properly.
And then I'll be revenged.
On the whole fucking pack of them.